FREECURRENT
DESCENDANTS

DEANNA J. COMPTON

Published by IGH Publishing

 IN GOD'S HANDS
PUBLISHING

ACKNOWLEDGEMENTS

I would like to dedicate this book to my mom and dad who inspired in me a tendency to look at life with a sense of humor. When mom was diagnosed with brain cancer in 2006, she faced the end of her life with grace and composure with the love for her family being always her top priority. Dad succumbed to the effects of Alzheimer's disease in 2012. He was a hard worker all of his life and could tell a good story with a gleam in his eye as he subtly made his point or waited for his listener to understand his dry wit. We also lost my mother-in-law in 2012 to a heart attack. The last time I saw her she hugged me and said, "I love you, Deanna." They are all missed and I appreciate the love and support they always gave me. Thank you for letting me share my story with you. I hope you enjoy it. Please post your reviews on-line. It is greatly appreciated and important to a new author.

Imagination lets our minds take flight.

e-mail Deanna Compton at: freecurrent@comcast.net
Visit my website: freecurrent.net

PRELUDE

"Stop your whining," the bad man said out loud as he pushed a sharp instrument between the dragon's scales and injected another potion. The dragon did not understand what the man said. She did not understand human language at all. Dragons communicated using mental telepathy, but this human was not accessible mentally. The man was hurting her again and she cried out in pain. Pulling against the chains that held her captive did no good but she did so anyway. Her wings had been bound to her body and they ached ever-increasingly as time dragged on. Dragon bane permeated the air and she had difficulty breathing. It was horrible and the pain never ended. How long she had been held captive by the bad man, the she-dragon did not know.

Over the course of her captivity the man had used many potions on her. He had injected her painfully between her scales countless times. The food she had been fed had been poisoned and the water she was forced to drink had been infused with different chemicals. Although the many concoctions had little effect on her, she was beginning to weaken physically. She was sick and she knew it wouldn't be long before she died from the captivity. The question of why this man was hurting her was left unanswered. Her crying actual dragon tears did not move him to release her. The man seemed to gain some type of pleasure from torturing her.

Even though she was a young dragon, death would be a relief. It wouldn't be long now.

Chapter 1

ELYSIA

The atmosphere burned hot as lightning sizzled the air with dazzling brightness that left Jesse blind for seconds after. She felt her skin prickle from the released free-current energy and could smell the charge of electricity as she took in breath after excited breath. The gold pendant at the end of the chain that hung ever-present around her neck seared uncomfortably with its own energy against her skin. She didn't pause to consider the implications of having lightning strike at the precise moment she and Felcore had entered the gate, even though she could no longer see the stars shaping the constellation of the Condor with her incapacitated eyes. The adventure had begun and her heart provided a steady rhythm keeping time with her exhilaration.

She jumped involuntarily as a warm soft head pushed up on her dangling right hand. Amused by her own intensity, she responded by scratching her golden retriever's head while they continued to walk forward into the unknown. Her moccasin clad feet noted with sensitivity that the ground had changed from rock to softer dirt. Looking back, Jesse could see the lightning bolt shaped gate was once again visible with stars shining in arrangements varying for each constellation as they rotated sequentially at regular five minute intervals. She knew the gateway back to Earth would feature the Big Dipper constellation, and although she was tempted to test it to make sure, she would have to wait more than an hour for it to make itself visible through the jagged opening. As she gazed with interest at the different star patterns, she considered lingering to satisfy her curiosity.

Felcore gave a slight bark making Jesse turn around. Her eyes adjusted and came to rest on the cave entrance which was not too far from where they stood. Soft moonlight radiated through the passage illuminating the large cavern in silver silkiness. The cavern walls shimmered as her eyes moved over them, the composition of them embedded with material that sparkled in the faint light. A sweet aroma that reminded her of lilacs danced enticingly on the gentle breeze that drifted in from the outside world. She breathed in deeply, enjoying the scent.

The excited golden retriever barked once again and started toward the cave entrance. Jesse began to follow her furry companion when a loud humming sound advancing toward them stopped her short. She cocked her head sideways and listened. Her dog mimicked her action with comical precision. The humming vibration of wings stirred the air that filled the cave. It sounded like a group of hummingbirds, massive and very excited. She had once watched a documentary about the infiltration of the killer bees from the south. They were a mean breed with aggressive tendencies and Jesse would just as soon avoid any confrontation with their likeness. She stood rigidly waiting with apprehension.

Before she could react, the air around her seemed to turn into a whirlwind. Felcore began a chorus of barking that echoed loudly off the cave walls as he circled around, jumping and prancing into the air as he twirled. Jesse could feel rather than see the presence of creatures flying around her. The humming of their wings was a steady drone in her ears adding to the racket that Felcore was making. A small hand reached out of the whirlwind and touched her hair, her face, her arms, her legs and then another hand and another until she was unable to locate an inch of her body that had not been physically scrutinized by the miniature fingers. Whispers and murmurs filled her head. "*Jessica. . . the one . . . Jesse . . . healer . . . Jesse . . . she's come . . . the one . . .* "

"Enough, please! Felcore, quiet!" she ordered. Jesse had to wait only a second for things to calm down. She took a deep breath to steady herself before looking down by her feet where the creatures had landed and remained staring at her with curiosity. The deflected moonlight glistened on their translucent wings as they fluttered slightly with motion as negligible as a breath. As everyone stood staring at each other for multiple moments, the freshly rising sun sent morning rays of light cascading through the cave opening turning the silver of the moonlight into gold. It was magical as it reflected off the cave walls that sparkled in a marvelous display of radiance.

Six sets of bright blue eyes, shining with intelligence, looked up at Jesse. Subtle differences individualized each wisp, but they commonly had curly blond hair, gold furry tufts on the tips of their pointed ears, four long delicate wings crisscrossing their backs, a height of about one and a half feet, tanned skin, bare all the way to the tips of their toes, and they were obviously all male.

A wisp with a narrow chin and a bit of gray frosting the tufts of his ears stepped forward, smiling at Felcore as the dog came to stand protectively beside Jesse. "Would you like to break fast with us, my lady?" he asked.

Before Jesse could respond to the invitation, another wisp, somewhat rotund compared to the others, stepped forward and grasped her by the hand eagerly. "You must be hungry, my lady. It is already past sunrise and breakfast will be on the table by the time we return. Please, do come," he said persuasively.

All six started shaking their heads and murmuring affirmatively that breakfast was waiting and that they should go.

Jesse held her ground as the wisps turned toward the cave entrance. "Wait. I have a few questions I would like answered like where am I?" she asked. They all turned back around at the sound of her voice and looked at her with what seemed to be exasperation.

The pudgy wisp holding her hand let go and looked back and forth from Jesse to the cave entrance indecisively. "But, breakfast is waiting!" he affirmed.

All the other wisps concurred, "Yes, yes. Breakfast is waiting."

The wisp with the narrow chin reflected the other wisps' anxiety as he said, "Questions and answers can wait until after breakfast, my lady. It is breakfast time now."

Felcore gave a short bark of agreement and wagged his tail enthusiastically.

Again the pudgy wisp took Jesse's hand. "My mate makes the best blueberry waffles this side of the gate. She uses freshly picked blueberries and a batter better than any batter ever blended," he bragged.

Involuntarily, Jesse's stomach growled at the thought of blueberry waffles, her favorite breakfast food. "I love blueberry waffles." Jesse caught and held the wisp's gaze squarely. "How did you know?" she asked.

The thin-chinned wisp sighed heavily. "Questions . . . questions . . . questions . . . Can't this wait?"

From the others, "Yes, I'm hungry . . . I'm starving . . . It's time for breakfast, not for discussion. . . Let's go! Please!"

Unanimously, "Yeah, let's go!"

Jesse remembered the way Gabriel described Rew as having a bottomless pit for a stomach in her diary and couldn't help but smile before she gave in, "All right. But, at least tell me your names so I know who to ask to pass the syrup."

"Of course my lady. How foolish of me. Pardon my forgetfulness." The wisp with the bony chin stepped forward and bowed extravagantly. "My name is King Lew. The wisp holding your hand is Wes. He will act as your guide during your stay with us. From left to right is Moa, Tam, Frey, Yim and Tes, Wes' brother. Welcome to Elysia, Jessica Gates," he said.

Felcore barked arrogantly.

"Oh, and of course, you are most welcome as well, Felcore. Will you join us now, my lady?" he asked again.

"I would be happy to as long as you promise to answer my questions after breakfast," Jesse paused and waited for a response.

"All of your questions will be answered, my lady . . . after breakfast," Lew replied.

"Please, call me Jesse."

Wes squeezed Jesse's hand and pulled her toward the cave entrance. "Come on, Jesse. I'm starving." He chatted on and on about what was on the breakfast menu, articulating with heightening excitement about the delicacies that awaited them.

Warm rays of sunshine touched Jesse's face as she passed through the wide threshold that led out of the cave. She stopped for a moment to drink in the beautiful landscape that met her eyes on the other side. Standing upon a ledge that overlooked a valley extending as far as the eye could see, Jesse drew in deep breaths of fresh air and savored the veritable patchwork of colors. The land offered a wide diversity of terrain, from mountainous forests to sandy beaches. Jesse thought she could even see an area of desert far off on the distant horizon. A lake shaped abstractly like a four leaf clover was centrally located in the colorful valley, junctured on the left from where Jesse stood by a sparkling clear river. On the right side of the lake a cascading waterfall dropped from a rocky shelf sending mist into the air creating rainbows as the sunshine enhanced the water droplets. The morning sunrise painted the sky the color of rainbow sherbet. White fluffy clouds sailed by lazily.

The fragrance of lilacs she had noticed earlier came from a tree that grew beside the cave entrance. The shape of the tree reminded Jesse of a bonsai, although much larger in size, with a twisting trunk and dense shapely clusters of leaves. For some reason she felt a sense of sadness as she gazed up at the splendid branches. Reflexively diverting her gaze, Jesse made eye contact with Felcore who stood beside her whimpering slightly. She brought her hand down and stroked the top of his head reassuringly. "It's okay, boy," she said. Her eyes were drawn back up to the canopy of the tree as a smothering feeling of dread tightened her chest. She didn't understand the effect this sickly tree had upon her; couldn't identify the source of the darkness that seemed to draw a shadow across her soul. It was fleeting, but certainly palpable and memorable in its impact. Sadness permeated it and radiated out.

"Come on, Jesse. If you don't hurry the food will be cold," Wes pleaded with her again as he looked down the hill where the others stood looking up at them, waiting.

Jesse shook off the blanket of fear that seemed to have wrapped itself around her heart and smiled at Wes as she set out after him. Felcore plodded merrily at her side, his recent discomfort quickly forgotten.

They picked an easy trail through a sparse forest of birch and an occasional pine. A soft breeze tickled the tiny leaves on the tall white birches, leaving them fluttering reflectively in the early morning sunshine. The ground was soft and sandy underneath Jesse's moccasins as she followed almost inaudibly behind Wes, who flew a short distance off the ground and often had to turn back and wait for his slower companions.

As Jesse neared where the others stood waiting, the aroma of cooking food mingling with the scents of the forest became more pronounced. Her belly rumbled audibly as she inhaled the wonderful smells. The anticipation of a hearty breakfast made Jesse unconsciously hasten her footsteps as did Felcore beside her. The sharp sound of instruments tuning up touched Jesse's ears along with the steady murmur of many voices speaking simultaneously in breezy conversation. The bleakness she had felt just moments ago was completely dispelled by the joyous atmosphere.

Wes almost spun in circles with excitement. He chimed, "They are about ready to start breakfast. We must hurry or we'll be late. Quick! Follow me!" The rotund wisp flew much faster than Jesse could walk, but she kept an eye on him as he sped away in front of her as she tried to keep pace with Felcore, who walked in his own state of excitement with his head and tail held high.

Upon entering a large sunny clearing, Jesse paused in her march and absorbed the scene. Long wooden tables paralleled each other in double rows of ten, each accommodating approximately fifty wisps, who sat upon simple wooden stools; or a more appropriate term would be "danced" because every wisp in the congregation was in constant motion. Food was being served on enormous platters and in vast bowls, each carried by four or more wisps who hovered over the tables, depositing their steaming deliciousness squarely and surely in the center of each table. More wisps arrived with baskets brimming with colorful fruit, which they distributed, five baskets to each table and then took the first available empty seat.

Wes motioned for Jesse to follow him as he started toward one of the nearby tables. Her feet obeyed, propelling her forward into the center of activity. Felcore loped along beside her, happy and enthusiastic. Wes was indicating for Jesse to take one of the two empty stools near the end of the table when the sound of stillness hit Jesse like a silent thunder clap. She touched Felcore's nose for reassurance and looked to Wes for assistance. He seemed oblivious to the change in atmosphere until he caught Jesse's anxious glance and looked around as he noticed that all eyes were on them.

Slowly, Wes climbed upon an empty stool and cleared his throat. He said, "Friends and fellows, it is my distinct and sincere delight to introduce to you Lady Jessica Gates, Elysia's hope and grandest prospect for a fulfilling future for us all." He bowed to his audience and waved his hand formally in Jesse's direction.

Jesse felt her cheeks heat with pumping blood as she again felt all eyes rest upon her. It wasn't that Jesse was shy, because she was far from that. She just didn't enjoy being the center of attention, especially in a crowd of strangers. It made her feel particularly vulnerable and she didn't like being vulnerable. She picked up her hand awkwardly in a feeble gesture of greeting. "Hi," she said quietly. The polite smile that touched her lips was vanquished when the community began cheering, clapping and otherwise expressing a boisterous welcome.

Felcore started barking and jumping around, adding his voice to the tumult. Jesse tried to make herself as small as she could as she again looked to Wes for help. Wes, misinterpreting her distress, solicited the crowd for silence. "Excuse my forgetfulness, this of course is Jesse's guardian dog, Felcore, golden retriever . . . and . . . *a really good dog*," Wes finished in a rush of words, having lost appropriate expression to describe Jesse's dog.

Again the cheering became deafening and Felcore wagged his tail in delight. Wes stepped off from his pedestal and turned to Jesse before taking her hand and leading her to one of the empty stools, which she gladly sunk down onto. Wes looked about in embarrassment with funny little noises coming from his throat, "Uh, uh, oh, uh." He leaned up close and whispered in Jesse's ear, "My lady, you must say something. They expect to hear you speak." His eyes were wide and eyebrows expressive as they danced up and down, as if he could pick Jesse up and place her on her feet with his facial muscles.

Jesse felt a twinge of fear, remnant from anxiety she used to feel in Language Arts class just before having to give a speech. She remembered her father had advised her to envision her audience all sitting in their underwear to make them seem less intimidating. Jesse felt her face redden as she realized this audience was completely nude with few exceptions, male, female, young and old. Her fingers touched her own soft old blue jeans with a sense of relief as she shook the butterflies off with a little effort and got to her feet. The crowd quieted in a wave from those closest to Jesse to the tables furthest back until silence prevailed. Jesse smiled and reached down to pat Felcore's head where he again stood beside her. "Thank you for your kind welcome to Elysia. I don't know what you expect of me, but I assure you I am just a simple traveler who got lost," she said feebly. A ripple of chatter ran through the gathering before Jesse continued. "I'm sure that after breakfast everything will be cleared up. Thank you again for your generous hospitality. Please, go ahead with your meal." Jesse sat down immediately and attempted to avoid everyone's eyes, including Wes's.

Reserved clapping was terminated by King Lew's request that the servers continue bringing breakfast to the tables. The band started to play a bouncy tune that reminded Jesse of down home New Orleans' jazz, with singing horns and a heavy drum rhythm. Pitchers were brought out and placed on the tables by wisps in sprinting flight. The young wisp who placed three pitchers before Wes and Jesse stole glances with bold overtness at the human and the dog. He returned Jesse's friendly smile shyly before flitting away. More servers deposited platter after platter of food before them until they were fully involved in eating. Jesse fed Felcore from her own plate portions of sausage and biscuit and various other items she thought he might enjoy. Wes declined to speak even one word as he engulfed mouthfuls and drank tankards full until long after Jesse had finished her own meal.

The female seated across from Jesse scowled at Wes with playfulness in her eyes. To Jesse, she said, "You have to forgive my mate, my lady. Wes's stomach takes priority over everything, including rudimentary politeness. My name is Lodi." The female wisp's appearance was similar in kind to her husband's, with curly blond hair atop her head, gold tufts of fur on the tips of her pointed ears and bright blue eyes. However, Lodi had a narrower face with highly defined cheekbones and small firm breasts that completed her feminine form.

Felcore placed his head in Jesse's lap and she began messaging it lightly while she smiled at Lodi. "Please, call me Jesse," she said.

"Very well, Jesse. Have you had enough to eat?" Lodi asked.

"Oh, yes. Thank you. It was delicious, especially the blueberry waffles," she replied. Jesse patted her stomach with her free hand in a gesture to demonstrate her satiated appetite. Wes chose the exact moment to belch loudly and Lodi was completely unsuccessful at restraining her amused giggles.

He uttered between a bite of sausage and a bite of sweet roll, "S'cuse me."

Lodi moved aside slightly to let another wisp gather her dirty plate and utensils as the cleanup crew made its way between tables up and down isles. She said to her mate, "Wes, you are always the last wisp finished and the first one here for each and every meal. Your passion for eating surprises even me sometimes."

Wes swallowed and took a long pull from his tankard of milk before letting his eyes come to rest lovingly on Lodi's animated smile. "I have to keep up my strength in order to keep up with you, my love," he said. Wes snatched the remains of the sweet roll from his plate and shoved it into his mouth as someone began clearing that side of the table from behind him. Other wisps began excusing themselves from their tables and making their way out of the clearing, the majority passing by Jesse and Felcore with curious glances and quick greetings. The band continued to play an odd assortment of jazz and a type of music that Jesse couldn't relate to, consisting of long horn notes that in Jesse's opinion seemed misarranged and ill-suited to the ears.

Soon after the table was cleared of dirty dishes, Jesse, Felcore, Lodi and Wes were left alone at their end of the table. King Lew joined them, sitting next to Lodi, who kissed him casually on the cheek in greeting. Lew looked at Jesse and his eyes clouded over with seriousness. "Did Wes and Lodi answer all of your questions, my lady . . . uh, Jesse?" he asked.

Jesse replied, "No, I have several questions, if you wouldn't mind providing some answers before I go. You have already told me I am at a place called Elysia, but how did I get here? I should have ended up . . . somewhere else."

Lew responded with a straight forward answer that surprised Jesse after all of the evasion to her questions, "We intercepted you while you were still in the gate between Earth and Risen. It was important to us that you visit Elysia first, Jesse. You did nothing wrong. You read the constellations correctly and would have ended up there had we not interceded."

"But, why did you intercede?" Jesse asked folding her hands in her lap as Felcore eased into a laying position at her feet and sighed heavily.

Jesse saw sadness in Lew's eyes as he gazed back at her. He said, "We need your help. You are the one."

Fear interpreted as frustration gripped Jesse's chest as she asked, "What do you mean? The one that what? I'm afraid you have mistaken me for somebody else. I am just me, Jessica Gates, typical American teenager . . . " As Jesse said the words, she knew she didn't really believe it. "But, how can I help . . . ? I would if I could, but . . . What do you expect me to do?"

Lodi spoke to Jesse with a gleam of excitement in her bright blue eyes and an undertone of compassion in her voice, "We want to instill in you our way, Jesse. Wisps are guardians of the gate. It is our purpose to help those in need when the balance of the universe is jeopardized. We travel from world to world and lend assistance to any and all who are in danger of becoming overwhelmed by forces greater than their own. Although we have been granted enormous awareness of power, we are sworn to use our magic in only subtle ways to persuade others to use their own strengths to overcome adversity. It is our mandate to not interfere directly, but to take a passive role while we try help without magical intervention."

Jesse interrupted with a comment, "It all sounds pretty ineffective. I mean it sounds like you help without helping."

Lodi smiled, "Sometimes it seems that we are less important than a single rain drop is to a lake of water. But, if you stand back and watch, you can see the ripples that result from that single drop of rain."

"Don't you get frustrated?" Jesse asked as she shuffled her feet to a more comfortable position causing an audible grunt from Felcore.

The serious expression Lodi suddenly wore made Jesse involuntarily hold her breath. She replied, "Yes, especially now. A powerful corruptive force never before encountered has recently been prevalent. The decay is now strong enough to touch Elysia. Even as we speak, it leaks through the gate a little at a time into our world. We cannot break the rules as written in the "App Endix" by interfering directly however critical the situation may be at the time or promises to become in the future. It is our hope that you will be less constrained by the inaction that burdens us, and therefore, in a better position to set things right. Jesse, you are our greatest hope for a stabile future." Wes reached across the table and took Lodi's hand as her voice broke with emotion.

Jesse had so many questions in her head after Lodi's answer that she didn't know where to begin. "I don't understand. If you can't act, how could you interfere and bring me here? And why me? What about Rew? I read about him 'acting' on his own. Is he not one of you? How long will it take to teach me wisp magic? Are you sure I am your girl?" she finished with the last question in a string.

Lew smiled tolerantly and answered. "We didn't really interfere with you in the gate, we simply asked Felcore to bring you here. As far as Rew is concerned, well, Rew is Rew. Let's see, was that everything? Oh, yes. Why you? Because you are the one; we are sure," he said.

Under his breath, Jesse thought she heard Wes mumble, "Relatively sure, anyway."

Neither Lodi nor Lew seemed to hear him or they both ignored him. Lodi played with her own delicate fingers on the surface of the table while she spoke, "The amount of time it will take you to ascertain wisp magic is less than the span it takes for a leaf to fall to the ground from the top of a tree on your own world. Do not fear, Jesse."

A shiver ran up Jesse's spine. For some reason, she thought of the beautiful tree that she and Felcore had felt in pain upon exiting the cave on Elysia. She had been afraid. Whatever hurt it seemed to have wanted to possess her soul. She wanted to ask about the tree, but couldn't find the courage. Instead she asked, "What about Rew?"

Lew sighed and then smiled. "Rew is my son, prince of the wisps. He was assigned to oversee things on Risen many years ago just after he had reached maturity. Always a passionate boy, he became personally involved and let his emotions rule his actions instead of his intellect. I'm afraid he bent a few rules in his youth and still pushes the boundaries at times. But, he is a fine boy and will make a good king when I am gone."

"Where is he now?" Jesse asked. She figured that if he had just reached maturity when he first was assigned to Risen, which was before Gabriel's arrival in 1983, he had to be at least forty or fifty years old by now in human terms.

Lew sighed again and ran a hand through his curly blond, slightly gray hair. "On Risen of course. He does visit Elysia from time to time. Rew loves to come home and spend time with his mate, Dolli, his seven sons, and ten daughters. But, he always returns to Risen. Rew is very fond of the creatures who live there. How do you know him?"

Jesse unzipped her backpack and removed Gabriel's diary, running her fingers momentarily over the soft leather binding before handing it to Lew. "My Grandmother Gabriel speaks of

Rew in her diary. It was over thirty years ago when she knew him," she said.

Lew flipped quickly through the pages before handing the book back to Jesse. "Yes, Rew has told me stories about your grandmother. He was always especially devoted to Gabriel," he told her.

"Do you know about her? Is she still alive? Is she on Risen?" she asked. Jesse sat forward in her seat anticipating news that she was surprised to find she cared so much about.

"I am afraid I do not have the answers you seek," Lew stated simply. Jesse held his gaze with her coppery brown eyes for several moments before letting the matter drop.

She paused, frowning, deep in thought. The wisps watched her with concern etched on their small brows. After a moment, Jesse looked up at them and smiled. She said, "I think you are all crazy for putting your faith in me. I am not anybody special . . . just Jesse. But, if it doesn't take too long, I will stay and learn what I can about your magic and I will do what I can to help you."

Lew clapped his hands together and bounced up from his chair. "Excellent!" he said.

Felcore jumped up from his nap and barked, confused from being awakened. Jesse ruffled him behind the ears. She caught Lew's eye and held him in her gaze and said, "Don't expect too much . . . I don't want you to be disappointed in me if I fail."

Lodi looked shocked. "Certainly not! I will endure no more of that kind of talk, my lady," she reprimanded.

Lew grasped Jesse warmly by the hand and looked into her eyes. "As long as you try you will not disappoint me. I will leave you in the hands of Lodi and Wes for now. Farewell," he said, kissed her on the cheek and then turned and kissed Lodi on the cheek as well before taking flight and disappearing out of sight.

Wes spoke to Lodi as if Jesse wasn't there. "Perhaps Jesse would like a bath before lunch."

Lodi smiled at her husband and then turned to Jesse and said, "We have wonderful hot springs in our desert region. I think a bath and a nap would be ideal. What do you think?"

Jesse shrugged her shoulders and chimed, "Sure."

Lodi flapped her wings and began ascending. Wes looked back and forth from Jesse to his mate. "Uh, uh, Lodi, uh, Lodi . . . they can't fly."

Lodi stopped flapping her wings in midair and dropped like an apple from a tree, landing with a thud upon her stool. "Oh, my. I didn't realize. You poor girl," she said.

Jesse felt like laughing, but she maintained her decorum. She assured her, "No, really, it's all right. Where I come from we use machines to fly. It really isn't too much of an inconvenience."

Wes looked at Jesse incredulously. "Can you tell me how. . ."

Lodi interrupted, "Somehow we need to get Jesse and Felcore to where we want to go."

Wes began, "Well, I think . . . "

Interrupted once again by his mate, Wes's face scowled as Lodi's lit up. She said, "I know. We could give Jesse and Felcore wings."

"That's ridiculous. It would be against the rules, not to mention . . . " Wes fluttered his own wings in exasperation as Lodi cut him off a third time.

"I'm sure it's not completely against the rules. It would just be temporary, Wes . . . just while they are on Elysia. Come on. Let's do it," she said clapping her hands together with excitement.

"But . . . " Wes began.

"Come on, Wes," Interrupting again, Lodi smiled sweetly and took Wes's hand.

"Oh. All right," he said. They both looked at Jesse, who suddenly felt like a white mouse in a laboratory cage. Felcore sat watching the two wisps as he cocked his head curiously to the left.

Wes grabbed Jesse by hand and propelled her off the stool. "Let's go over there where we have more room. Come on, Lodi. We've got to get going before we are too late for lunch."

Felcore and Lodi followed Wes and Jesse to a small grassy patch, where they all stood in a circle. Felcore wagged his tail happily unaware of what was about to happen to him. Jesse dropped her backpack on the ground in front of her and waited.

Lodi spoke quietly, "You will have to take off your shirt, Jesse."

Jesse realized the logic of having to have a bare back in order to sprout wings, but she didn't feel comfortable enough to disregard her modesty just yet. She bent down and opened her pack, drawing from it a simple bikini top that would keep her covered and still offer plenty of room for wings. She peeled off her cotton tee shirt and folded it neatly before stuffing it into her pack and tied on the bikini. "Okay, I think I'm ready."

Lodi looked at Felcore who barked once in response.

Jesse watched in awe as a crumpled set of four wings began unfolding between Felcore's shoulder blades. She could feel her own doing the same with a ticklish feeling in the unreachable part of her back. As the wings straightened, they seemed to harden in the warm sunshine until they were fine planes of stiff iridescent tissue. Jesse could see the wings on her back out of the corner of her eye. She flapped them experimentally once, twice. Glee built up inside her. She couldn't help but laugh as she watched Felcore try his wings out, flying up and down, tail straight, betraying his utter confusion.

Lodi and Wes stepped forward and took Jesse's hands. Lodi shouldered Jesse's backpack and Wes held onto Felcore's collar. Lodi said, "Follow our lead."

Before Jesse realized what was happening they were far above the ground. She could feel her wings fluttering on her back in an involuntary motion. A sudden panic caused her to stop in midflight. The ultimate drop brought her wings automatically into motion again as she held onto Wes and Lodi with a death grip. Jesse noticed that Felcore seemed to have accepted his new aerial ability with little trauma. She decided just to relax and enjoy the sensation. As soon as she did, she was surprised at how easy it was and soon was soaring without the assistance of Lodi and Wes. Felcore too, was soon flying independent of any aid and began wagging his tail in delight causing him to sway back and forth like a pendulum. He was a comical sight and Jesse laughed out loud. Flying was so much fun!

The ground was a blur beneath them and it seemed that they had been in flight for only minutes when Wes motioned them down. She could feel the dry heat as they descended to the warm desert sand. Jesse, being a desert rat from the southwest, felt very much at home in such a climate. This desert had very little foliage, but a large expanse of fine golden sand dunes. It smelled and felt wonderful. Laughter and cheerful conversation met Jesse's ears as they crested a dune. Looking down she thought she was looking at a scene from an old beach movie she used to see on television, the kind with Gidget, Moon Doggie and their friends. Spread out, playing in the water, basking in the sun and in the shade of palm trees, or playing at some care-free game such as beach blanket bingo, were perhaps twenty or more wisps. Some of them took a moment to wave a greeting at the new arrivals.

Skimming over the sand as their wings fluttered with ease. Jesse and Felcore hesitated and then followed their guides as they landed on the beautiful warm beach. They were met with a hearty welcome from all and provided a large blanket next to the water in the inviting sunshine. The clear lake sparkled before them enticingly.

Lodi and Wes immediately took to the water and dove in and out of the massive oasis hot spring with carefree abandon. Felcore pushed his nose into Jesse's forearm, urging her to hurry up so they could join in on the fun. Jesse realized she was the only one on the beach with clothes on, but she wasn't quite sure that she was ready to forego her years of social conditioning. After only a moment of indecision, she stripped off her jeans and bikini top, removed her moccasins and set them aside and took a running dive into the water. Felcore beat her by at least five steps and together they let the hot spring water rinse off the dust and grime they had collected along the trail. It was marvelous and they luxuriated in the clean and relaxing warmth.

They spent the next couple of weeks at the desert oasis, swimming, playing and resting. For food they fished and gathered fruit and nuts or made trips to nearby villages to join in common meals. During that time Jesse's bruises healed completely and so did her spirit. Most of the time they spent alone on the beach secluded temporarily from the world in their little corner of paradise. Occasionally they were joined by different groups of wisps who soon became friends as they shared time together. Jesse was disappointed to see their vacation end when it inevitably did. It was a time she would never forget and would forever treasure.

She was lying on her stomach, drawing pictures in the sand with her finger and flapping her wings in time to the tune playing on her MP3 player, a song by a group named "Pearl Jam", when Lodi tapped her on the shoulder to get her attention.

Lodi scowled at the noise coming from the ear buds. Jesse had let her listen once, but Lodi didn't understand the words and thought the music was "undomesticated". Wes, on the other hand, thought it was exceptional and had some ideas that he wanted to present to their musicians when they went to dinner that evening. She addressed Jesse again, "Can you hear me?" Mouthing the words, instead of actually saying them aloud, her lips accentuated each syllable dramatically.

Jesse rolled over and pulled the ear buds out of her ears. "I'm sorry, Lodi, did you say something?" she asked.

"Is that the only kind of music you have on Earth?" Lodi asked, making a face as if she had just eaten a sour pickle.

She replied, "Oh no. We have all kinds. I enjoy a variety including pop, country, but mostly rock. What is on my MP3 player is what I like the most. My brother Jake likes country and my dad usually listens to classical." Jesse looked woeful as she thought of her father and fourteen year old brother, Jacob. She missed them very much.

Jesse had felt it necessary to leave home in order to keep Felcore from being taken from her and possibly put to death. She had run away from home after an incident in which she was assaulted by a boy named Mat. Felcore had defended her by attacking Mat, which resulted in the boy's death. She had fled New Mexico with her dog, leaving behind her father and her brother, Jacob. She felt a twinge of guilt as she thought of the pain she had caused her family. It was hard for her to think about what she was putting her family through with her disappearance, even though she had tried to dispel her father's concern with her last phone call. Surely, it wasn't enough and in her heart she knew it. It was for Felcore's safety that she had fled, but there was a part of Jesse that wanted to follow in her grandmother's footsteps and discover her own providence. Most of her guilt was rooted in that desire. Even though the brutal assault on her by Mat had put what followed into motion, she felt that this course in her life was inevitable.

"It is time for us to go, Jesse. The sun will be in the right position tomorrow and we must travel to Mount Galaxia. Tonight we'll stay in the village," Lodi said, looking sad even though she smiled.

"Yes, let's go. It's nearly dinner time and I'm hungry," Wes pleaded impatiently.

Jesse was drawn thankfully away from her ruminations. "What? . . . Oh. Of course. Lead the way," she commanded.

Lodi and Wes took immediately to the sky. Jesse on the other hand, stayed behind for a moment to absorb as much of the oasis as she could before having to vacate their little haven. She felt so safe there and regretted having to leave. Felcore seemed to commiserate as he stood by Jesse's side, his soft fur rubbing against the bare skin of her left leg. She sighed heavily. After stuffing her things into her backpack along with her hairbrush and her MP3 player, she slipped into her faded old blue jeans, bikini top and soft leather moccasins. She took one last look around and leapt into the sky. Along with Felcore, she joined Lodi and Wes where they waited up above.

The four of them arrived at a small village just as dinner was being served and sat down to a hearty meal. Wisps tended to have incredible timing when it came to food. It was a different village from the first one she had visited, but the layout was similar and meal times seemed to have a universal set up. Wes and Lodi introduced Jesse and Felcore to several wisps as they lounged around after dinner and listened to the band. Wes had borrowed Jesse's MP3 and the musicians attempted several aborted tries to duplicate the music. They finally accomplished a reasonable facsimile and then gave it up, promising Wes they would try again some other time. Jesse was relieved they did not make any further attempts at slaughtering rock and roll; extremely and completely relieved.

Hammocks were provided for their comfort that night and Jesse was able to enjoy sleeping under the stars once again. Felcore spent the night beneath her hammock, being disinclined to use a hammock himself. By the time morning peaked its brilliance over the horizon, Jesse was ready to begin the day, refreshed and looking forward to starting her training.

After breakfast, Lodi and Wes put on clothes, consisting of long pants, bountiful jackets, custom designed to allow for protruding wings, and thick leather boots. Lodi brought Jesse a similar jacket, which was anything but bountiful on Jesse's larger body. Lew showed up, coming suddenly from out of the sky, also dressed and ready to go. The King of Elysia knelt down to pet Felcore in greeting.

"Where are we going?" Jesse asked as she shouldered her backpack.

Lew stopped scratching Felcore's ears and stood up. He said, "To the northern village. It is high up in the mountains where it snows almost constantly. Felcore will be all right, won't he?"

Jesse eyed her dog, who was presently engaged in chasing his tail. With his wings flapping, he would lift off the ground as he turned, and land as he came close to the tip of his tail, adding a whole new dimension to the game. Jesse laughed as she appraised the long shaggy reddish golden retriever. "I think he'll be okay. He may be a desert rat like me, but he does come with his own fur coat," she pointed out.

Wes lifted a short way off the ground and summoned them, "Okay, let's get going. Lunch should be ready by the time we arrive if we hurry."

Jesse tried to see below her as they flew, but they were going so fast that it was mostly a blur. She could make out colors as they soared over dense forests and ice blue lakes, the vibrant greens and blues standing out distinctly. The cold moist air of the mountains touched her face as they climbed in altitude, indicating to Jesse that they were nearing their destination. The smell of smoke was evident before becoming visually noticeable up ahead.

It was snowing heavily and Jesse had a difficult time maintaining her balance as they descended toward the sparkling white frosted village. When they reached the ground, they were met by a crowd cheering Jesse's name. She waved at them shyly and looked around at the beautiful village. Tall "A" frame buildings surrounded them on all sides. Smoke emanated from each chimney, softly curling upward until it disappeared into the cascading snowflakes. Felcore, who had never seen snow before, ran back and forth snapping at the flakes as they fell and every so often buried his nose in the fluffy piles of ice crystals. He hesitated occasionally to glance friskily at them and "rrowf" as if to say, "Come on. Play with me."

"Let's go get some lunch. I'm hungry," Wes said, as usual, thinking of his stomach before all else and anxious to find the nearest meal.

"No. No. We have business to take care of first, Wes. It won't take long and then we can eat," Lew said. He started off toward the tallest of the A-framed buildings at a steady pace, leaving a snake like trail in the deep snow. Jesse wondered why he didn't just fly considering the snow was nearly over his head. Felcore followed Lew, as did Wes and Lodi and finally Jesse at the tail end.

They entered the building through a set of huge double doors and stood in a foyer resplendent in gleaming wood. Rich wood covered the floor, the ceiling, and the walls. It ran up a massive curving staircase with an ornately carved railing and served as furnishings in the form of high back chairs and small decorative tables.

Lew shook the snow off from his head and shoulders and stomped his feet, leaving tiny puddles to form in his wake as the discarded little snow piles melted. Heedless of the trail they left, Lew, Lodi, and Wes headed to a doorway to the left of the foyer. Felcore shook his white coat back to golden and followed after the three wisps, leaving Jesse staring after the party, wishing she had a towel or a mop to clean up after her careless friends.

"Come on, Jesse," Wes summoned as he turned around to find her still standing in the foyer with a frown on her face. "Come on," he motioned with a sweep of his arm as he waited for her to follow.

Jesse looked down at her own feet, noticing the puddle forming under her own moccasins, and sighed. "Don't you think we should clean this up first?" she asked.

Wes didn't seem the least bit concerned. "Don't worry about it. Come on!" he said impatiently. He turned and disappeared through the door. Jesse reluctantly followed, looking back once or twice to view the mess left behind.

The door she went through led into a room that seemed like a museum of sorts, except the only display in the room was a glass box on a wooden pedestal. As Jesse approached, she could see that the box enclosed a single sheet of paper. It was lit from above. Lodi stood by Jesse's side as she gazed at the piece of paper and explained, "The document you see here is the 'App Endix', left to the wisps to remind them of their duties and obligations as guardians of the gate. When you read the text you will find that we are sworn to maintain a passive role in the control of the gate and the places and peoples it serves. It is important that you read and understand the document before we go further."

Jesse stepped up to the display case and read the Appendix from start to finish . . . twice. Even though it was written in some other type of language with a foreign alphabet, she had no problem reading it. She looked questioning at Lew, who was watching her intently. "It is very straight forward, a simple and well organized reference page. What I don't understand is what happened to the rest of it?"

The three wisps in the room exchanged glances of utter confusion. Lew approached Jesse and took a look himself into the display case. "What do you mean? This is the document we travelled here to show you. There is nothing missing," he said.

Jesse replied, feeling slightly foolish about having to point out the obvious, "It says 'Appendix' right there at the top. There must be more to it if what is written right here is an appendix. The previous pages must be missing."

Lew laughed in relief at Jesse's mistake and said, "No. No. No. That is the document's title. You are confused. There can be no more to it than that."

Wes and Lodi giggled uncomfortably in support of their king, but they exchanged dubious looks.

Jesse didn't give in, "The document clearly states 'Appendix'. I'm afraid you are missing the whole main body of the document, which probably has a separate title altogether. Look down there on the bottom is a page number, page 321."

Lew looked unsure and said, "No. It can't be."

"I'm afraid so," Jesse replied, as she reached out and put a comforting hand on the king's shoulder.

"Oh my! What are we going to do? How could we have made such a big mistake?" Wes raised his voice in panic.

Lodi spun around on her heel to face Wes. "Don't panic!" she said as she turned to Lew in panic, looking for answers from their king.

Lew began to pace the room, back and forth, with his hands clenched firmly behind his back. He stopped suddenly and addressed his companions, "Okay, here's what we'll do. Don't tell anyone about this. We don't want this to get blown out of the sky and for chaos to take senses away from our fellow wisps. We will have to do some research into this matter and find out if what Jesse is saying is true. If it is . . . if it is . . . well, let's just start there. Remember, not a word about this to anyone."

"I wonder . . . " Jesse said. She pulled Gabriel's diary out of her pack and thumbed through it until she found the paragraph she was looking for. "You know, there is an instruction manual to the gate on Risen. It is mentioned right here." She pointed to the text in her grandmother's handwriting. "I wonder if the page you have displayed here came from that book. Do you think that it is possible?" she asked.

Wes began to tug at his clothes uncomfortably and said, "This is just terrible . . . What are we going to do?"

Jesse began to head toward the distressed wisp, but was intercepted by Lodi, who said, "There is no point in worrying about it, Wes. If the book does rightfully belong to the wisps, we'll simply have to retrieve it. If it is still in Gabriel's possession, we'll ask her for it. We will do what has to be done to correct this situation. In the meantime, we are here to celebrate Jesse's arrival on Elysia and to grant her wisp magic. This matter will have to be resolved later." After a drawn out stare at Wes and Lew, which indicated that the matter was closed for now, Lodi took Jesse's hand and led her up a small almost hidden set of stairs in the far corner.

Wes and Lew followed after the two females and the dog with Wes grumbling, "Everything is always later with her. Later . . . I wonder when lunch will be ready. I'm hungry. Probably later."

Jesse followed Lodi up and up the closed-in staircase that continued on without interruption as they ascended what Jesse gauged to be several flights. The top of the stairs ended at an open door. The expansive room they entered was illuminated with a multitude of spotlights in the domed ceiling. A spacious expanse of open area stood empty save for a few wisps who lingered in quiet conversation. They glanced up only briefly, curious to see the human in their midst, before returning to their sober discussion as they walked slowly across the surface of the polished wooden floor.

Lodi turned and smiled keenly at Jesse. She looked like a wisp with a secret bursting to be let out. Fluttering her wings, Lodi flew gently up toward the ceiling, encouraging Jesse to follow her with a wave of her hand. As Jesse ascended, she was joined by Felcore, who touched his nose firmly against the palm of her hand. She reached down to ruffle his fur and gazed down below. The work of art below her took her breath away.

A mural was assembled in colored stones and various types of wood upon the floor depicting various aspects of the gate and the galaxies it serviced. Centered boldly in black and gold was the shape of a lightning bolt. The gold itself would have been enough to pay off the national debt. Constellations, made up of in-laid diamonds, partnered with planets in a variety of forma-tions, shapes and sizes surrounded the lightning bolt spreading out in all directions, covering every inch of the floor. They were too numerous for Jesse to count, but she thought she remem-bered that Gabriel had written in her diary that there were two thousand eighteen separate galaxies, each appearing through the gate once a week for a period of about five minutes. Jesse searched for the Big Dipper, skimming over the floor, a short distance off the surface. The diamonds sparkled brilliantly as she moved. She located it near the wall in front of her and landed to take a closer look.

The stone in-lays, colored blue, green, brown, and white, showed in incredible detail the continents and oceans as viewed over the western hemisphere. The diamond stars making up the Big Dipper hung over the top of the planet in a pattern very familiar to Jesse. She reached out to touch the beautiful work of art and was surprised at the smoothness of the surface.

Rejoining her friends in the air, Jesse searched for the Condor and found it a short ways over from Earth, in the corner. Risen, the third galaxy, was almost as beautiful as Earth, with the sparkling representation of the Condor seemingly suspended over the blue and green world.

"Where is Elysia?" Jesse asked Lodi, who was watching her intently.

"You will not find it here," Lodi replied. "Come, I will explain." Lodi landed softly and took a seat on the floor near the center of the lightning bolt. Jesse, Wes, Lew and Felcore followed, each taking a seat on the floor, forming a small circle.

Lodi began her explanation in a narrative tone, "The creation of the gate by the one we deem the Creator took place long ago when the universe was still fresh and new. The purpose of the gate was to allow all of the creatures to share in each other's lives. It was the expectation of the Creator to bring the fellow beings together so they could all benefit from each other's accumulated knowledge. Representatives were chosen from each culture to meet in a place fashioned precisely for that purpose in the midst of the gate.

"The day came, but the meeting did not go as planned, with jealousy and resentment turning the hearts of some of the creatures as they communed. The Creator was amazed at the un-characteristic behavior of his beloved creatures. After sending the beings back to their respective homes, the Creator tried to find the answer as to why some of his creatures had reacted to the others with corrupted hearts.

"The essence he had used to create his creatures came from his own heart. The Creator knew that he was not only made up of goodness and love, but also of anger, joy, sorrow, passion, pity, compassion, and much much more. The blend was necessary to experience the best of being. But, he also discovered there was opposition in the universe to his love. An entity of corruption had taken on a life of its own in the midst of his creation. It was a spirit that incorporated only the scornful aspects of his being and none of the virtuous. The opposition was out of balance and intended to corrupt his goodness. If he didn't come up with a solution the Creator believed he would have to destroy all that he loved or risk the opposition debasing it forever.

"The Creator arrived at the only remedy he thought might help his beloved creatures. He created one more world and one more creature to watch over the gate within the gate itself, Elysia and the wisps. To the wisps he gave unlimited power but also a stringent set of rules so the wisps could not become dominant. The rules were written down and left on Elysia in the High Tower of Galaxia so all wisps could read and know their heritage. All knowledge of the gate was hidden from the other creatures of the universe so the chances of hate and jealously developing further would be suppressed."

Lodi paused a moment and thoughtfully caressed the wooden floor with her fingers. She continued, "Of course, the Creator is known by different names in different worlds, but the power is the same everywhere and in all things. He *is* love and it is love that we serve. If you have ever looked into someone's eyes and seen love, you have seen into the eyes of the Creator. It is necessary that we continue to fight against evil and embrace what is good. If not, everything, as we know it, would cease to exist on the plane of reality, replaced by a nightmare of extremes. The opposition thrives on chaos."

Lew's voice surprised Jesse as she contemplated Lodi's words. His bright blues eyes captured and held her gaze with profound intensity. "We are in great danger of having that happen as we speak. Decay is spreading throughout the universe. Never before have we seen the power being used so skillfully or so ruthlessly. The balance has already shifted enough to allow decay to leak into Elysia, as it never has before, . . . never! The tree at the edge of the gate cries out . . . " he bit off his words. Lew's small fists clenched and his eyes flashed with anger.

"The tree . . . " Jesse gaped at Lew. "I felt it," she said incredulity. "The terror . . . and the pain."

Lew looked surprised for only a moment and then accepting. "Yes, of course you would feel it. You are the one. You must help us, Jesse . . . help us overpower the corruption before it is too late."

"I don't know what to do," Jesse proclaimed with sincerity, not out of lack of drive, but out of a desire to be assigned the task so she could get on with it. "Where do I start?" she asked.

Lodi put a gentle hand on Jesse's knee. She said, "Continue on the path you have chosen. At all times do what you think is right. Follow your instincts and have confidence in yourself. If you believe, the Creator will help you. Trust in your heart."

"But, what if I make a mistake?" Jesse asked.

"Everyone makes mistakes. Just do your best. Act out of love. It will be enough. Do you believe?" Lodi asked with a smile, beaming confidence and emanating hope.

"Yes," Jesse said.

Wes used extravagant eye motions to get Lodi's attention. "Can we pleeeease go eat now?" he asked. Lew stood up and stretched his back, extending his wings in all four directions. "Not yet, Wes," he commented lightly. He extended his hand to Jesse and politely helped her to stand. Lodi and Wes stood up as well, both wisps reaching out to touch her affectionately on the hand before the group stood back away from her. As usual Felcore remained by his mistress's side.

Jesse opened her mouth to speak, but before she could utter her question, the room melted to blackness. The humming of many voices harmonized pleasantly in Jesse's ears. Suddenly the ceiling overhead blazed with blinding radiance. A single beam of light hit Jesse where she stood in the middle of the lightning bolt symbol. The gold outlining of the symbol burned like molten lava. In its midst, Jesse and Felcore stood transfixed.

Euphoria swelled up inside Jesse until she was bursting with joy. A feeling of freedom, more ultimate than anything she had ever experienced before washed through her spirit, as if everything that had happened in her past occurred only to strengthen her character, to solidify the virtue that was an integral part of her soul. Her spirit soared.

As the light faded, a sharpened awareness became evident to Jesse. Her instincts were amplified. She could tell that Wes, Lodi and Lew still watched her intently, but she couldn't see them, only feel their eyes upon her. It was obvious to her that they felt love and respect for her, although she didn't understand how she knew this. She became aware of Felcore's steady breathing beside her and knew instantly that the golden retriever had experienced the same sensations that she had. Total darkness enveloped them and Jesse heard in her mind whispered goodbyes as they transcended into the unknown.

Chapter 2

TEMPEST

The cave Jesse entered was dark and without life. She felt the presence of Felcore beside her only by instinct. Elysia was no longer physically tangible and neither were her wisp wings. She was spellbound by the void for only seconds when she noticed the faint trace of glowing light in the coals that remained from a wood fire in the center of the cave. It was her own from over two weeks before when Felcore and she had left the cave to venture on to Risen, but ended up on Elysia.

Had time been somehow suspended while she was in the land of wisps? It appeared as though she had been returned to the point in time at which she had previously vacated Earth. Although, in sequential time she had experienced events that would change her forever, here she was, right back where she started from. The possibility seemed highly questionable. Jesse gazed through gate's opening and reached for Felcore, who pressed his furry head against her hand in response to her touch. "Well, boy, it looks like we'll have to wait . . . Wait a minute! There's the Condor!" Within the lightning gate the constellation shaped like a Condor shown through the opening brilliantly.

Pausing only a moment, followed closely by Felcore, she quickly stepped through the gate. The musky scent that Gabriel had described in her diary met Jesse's nostrils, tantalizing her senses. Although she had never experienced the scent before, she knew that it was dragon and she found it quite pleasant and comforting. The feelings the aroma evoked were those of security and warmth, a complete sensation of love and belonging. For some reason she thought of the inviting, special feeling she experienced as a child on Thanksgiving day back home. It began with the wonderful scent of roast turkey as the house filled with family. The hustle and bustle in the kitchen as preparations were made for the large family dinner was a happy memory. Her father and a contingent of sports fans settled in the living room to watch football. She and Jacob ran around the house with the rest of their cousins, being pretty much ignored by the adults. Even though she and her brother Jacob always had to sit at the kids table, a card table set up at the end of the big dining room table, the occasion was fun. Anytime Jesse smelled roasted turkey, the memories of those family gatherings subconsciously made her feel good and happy. The heavy musk of dragon made her feel the same way.

The musky perfume filled the air as she walked slowly forward into the pitch blackness of the cave. She knew the entrance had to be somewhere in front of her, but she couldn't see anything. "Ouch!" Jesse cried out as she stepped on a sharp rock with her soft moccasins.

"RRAAAAHGRRRRR!" the rock bellowed and moved in front of her, looming large and forbidding. Hot breath almost knocked her over as it slammed into her with tremendous force. She impulsively took a step back from the glowing red eyes that opened, suddenly drenching the cave in an eerie mystical light. Jesse's mind filled with angry words that were not her own. *"Clumsy clod. You stepped on my tail. Get Out! How dare you trespass in my cave? Stupid girl! Get out and take your mangy gold wolf with you!"*

Jesse was stunned and then enraptured by the big scaly creature who lay on the cave floor before her. The dragon held her head in the air towering high above Jesse on a long snaking neck. A similarly long spiked tail curled around the dragon's glittering body, coming to a significant point at the end. Jesse didn't move as she watched the dragon peruse her with swirling eyes. She overcame her speechlessness and managed to murmur, "I'm sorry."

The dragon began to raise her massive body with fluid motions, her chest heaving in raspy labored breaths from the effort. Large leathery wings extended partially, hitting the sides of the cave and causing the ground to shudder under Jesse's feet. The long neck extended the head up, close to touching the ceiling, and then darted quickly back down to come face to face with Jesse. The voice in her head said, *"If you do not leave me alone now, I will have to eat you and your puny wolf, too. Get out! Get out!"*

Felcore ran up under the dragon's chin and started barking boldly and loudly, challenging fool-heartedly the mammoth creature to just try and make it past him to his mistress. The dragon bared her teeth at the dog, exposing fangs that individually were as large as the golden retriever's head. Felcore did not retreat, however, but continued his foolhardy assault, snapping and biting at the dragon's ankles vainly. The dragon thrust a taloned hand down, sweeping it harmlessly past Felcore. Terrified for her dog, Jesse stepped forward and proclaimed her indignation with mental force, saying, *"Don't hurt my dog! He can't harm you. I didn't mean to step on your tail and I already apologized. I thought dragons on Risen were supposed to be good creatures, not monsters."*

The light emanating from the dragon's eyes dimmed perceptively and the big creature swayed as if drunk and then faltered, dropping severely and heavily to her forelegs on the hard stone floor. She groaned in misery and lay down. Jesse noticed her breathing came in noisy gulps and mucus drained heavily from her wide nostrils dripping in ghastly pools upon the ground.

Felcore whimpered in commiseration and bravely drew closer to the dragon, pushing on the tough scale armored flesh of the dragon's neck. Jesse advanced with slightly more caution, being careful to avoid the disgusting puddles, all the while keeping an alert eye on the dragon's dull expression.

She reached out tentatively and touched the long neck, being surprised by the smooth texture of the scales and the vibration that hummed through her hand from the dragon's coarse breathing. *"You are sick. Can we help?"* she asked.

"No, human! There is no help for me. Magic did this . . . magic and cruelty. I have been this way for a very long time. I only want to be left alone to die now. To suffer any longer is beyond my endurance. Please, just leave me alone," she pleaded. The dragon blinked her eyes, plunging them all into darkness for a moment.

"Who did this to you?" Jesse asked.

"A human. He lured me into a trap and then held me captive in a cold and dark cellar; exposing me constantly to dragon bane left me weak and virtually senseless. After I was rendered helpless, he began injecting me with potions, once a day and sometimes twice. The concoctions seemed to keep me in a state of fogginess, but also intensified my anger and my terror. It was awful . . . the nightmares

. . . *the daymares, relentless and terrible. The pain was torture. I do not want to remember anymore,"* she cried.

Jesse's mind was bombarded with the horror of the dragon's ordeal with penetrating clarity. She found that tears were running freely down her cheeks as she listened to the voice inside her mind.

"I don't know why he did this to me. He seemed to get joy out of hurting me. But, why go to all that trouble? Why? I asked myself over and over again why he would do this to me. I am a good dragon. Finally, after many seasons had passed, I was able to gnaw through my bonds and escape my confinement; those horrible, horrible chains that cut into my flesh and kept me from flying were at last off! My only thought was to get away. I flew up to the mountains and found this cave. I have been here ever since. Now I only wait to die. Leave me alone so I can die in peace," she pleaded.

Felcore whined and lay down with his head on his paws, his eyes blinking up at the dragon with what appeared to be sympathy. The dragon closed her eyes and groaned, the walls of the cave repeated the deep rumbling ominously. Once again, plunged into the depths of darkness, Jesse kept her hand planted firmly on the dragon's neck. Mentally, she said, *"Let me try to help you. I am a healer."*

"No, please leave me. I want to die," the dragon said.

Instead of listening to the suffering dragon, she began to take from the wisp magic, now ingrained with her entire being, to inspire the freecurrent power to make the dragon well. She felt the gold pendant upon her chest grow hot as the freecurrent surged through her and into the dragon where their flesh met at the base of the dragon's neck. The exhilaration from the flow of power soon turned to excruciating pain as Jesse absorbed the corruption from the dragon and sent it scattering into her surroundings. Fire ripped through her body, starting at her fingertips, searing through her stomach and down through her legs to her toes. There was no time to scream. It took only seconds.

She gulped air, her knees buckled, and she hit the ground as the impact of the past few moments caught up with her. Soon the pain was only a memory, to be conveniently and thankfully forgotten, stored in a place where fear feeds freely off from discarded horrors. She marveled at the power, a part of her craving to feel it again. Before Jesse could analyze her thoughts, Felcore came to her and pushed his way into her arms. The dragon opened her eyes and lifted her head. "RRAAAAHGRRRRR!" *"I am whole again! My pain is gone. What is your name, healer?"* she asked.

"My name is Jesse. This is Felcore."

The dragon stood up and stretched, lifting her head, she let out another mighty "RRAAAAHGRRRRR!" The ground shook and dust fell in torrents from the ceiling. Jesse crouched down next to Felcore, protectively, taking most of the dust that rained down upon them on herself. They watched as the dragon walked to the cave entrance. She turned her head and spotlights from her large eyes fell upon the girl and her dog, illuminating them in red. *"My name is Tempest. I shall be your friend, Jesse. You are my Jesse and I am your Tempest. And, I will not eat the golden wolf you call Felcore . . . not yet, anyway."*

"You bet you won't!" Jesse declared firmly.

"Not yet," Tempest remarked stubbornly.

"You are my friend and will not eat my dog at all! Never! Nada!" Jesse told the dragon. She stood up and approached Tempest with Felcore at her side.

"He probably would not be very tasty anyway," Tempest said as she turned and walked out of the cave with Jesse and Felcore following. The two of them stayed far enough behind the dragon to avoid her long and dangerous tail.

A new day's sun was beginning to send beams of radiance shooting through the thick forest growth, giving them natural light to see by. Jesse saw Tempest's true coloring for the first time and marveled at the dragon's beauty. The purest snow was not as white as Tempest's shiny scales. They covered her body from nose to tail tip, ranging in size and shape according to their location on the dragon's massive body. As Tempest moved, her scales shimmered with an iridescent dispersion of hues. She was a prism of color, beautiful beyond anything Jesse had seen before. The female dragon stood proudly, with head and tail held high as she drew deep breaths of fresh air into her lungs. Tempest turned to look at Jesse with what appeared to be a smile on her reptilic face. *"I feel wonderful, Jesse! Thank you . . . Thank you . . . Thank you! Would you like to go hunting? It has been some time since I have had a good meal. A ripgar would really hit the spot right now,"* she said.

Felcore barked as if in agreement and Jesse wondered if the golden retriever could somehow understand the mental dialogue. She watched him curiously for a moment but he just wagged his tail and lolled his tongue in a supposed happy state of canine oblivion. Jesse turned her attention to Tempest and said, *"You go ahead. Felcore and I will wait for you here."*

"Very well." Tempest immediately launched herself in the gold dawn sky and quickly disappeared from view. Jesse and Felcore nibbled on left-over road rations while they waited for Tempest to return. She thought of Wes and knew that this meager repast would be far from satisfactory for the wisp's ever-present appetite. A smile crossed her lips and she took another bite of cracker and took a sip of tepid water from her bottle. Before the dew had dissipated from the trees, the dragon was back, announcing her arrival so as to not alarm them. *"Greetings, little ones. Are you ready to go?"* she asked.

Jesse grinned at the satiated dragon. *"Did you have a good breakfast?"* she asked.

"Certainly. A big fat ripgar, tender and juicy. I am afraid there was nothing left to bring you. Would you like me to kill another to share?" Tempest asked.

"No! No, thanks. That won't be necessary," Jesse replied. Gabriel had described a ripgar as being a creature with a savage array of teeth, brandishing four-inch fangs on the top jaw and three inch fangs on the bottom jaw. It had a bear-like mouth and deep set eyes surrounded by heavy ridges and had a special craving for human flesh. Jesse had the distinct impression that a ripgar was large, mean and nasty. She had no desire to see one, let alone taste one.

"Are you sure? You look kind of scrawny," she said. Tempest shifted her weight to her hind legs and tilted her head back as she played with a butterfly that dangerously flittered around the dragon's nose without regard for its own safety. *"Ahh-Choo!"* Sneezing, Tempest sent the butterfly into turbo-drive and quickly out of sight. Felcore started barking and Tempest glared at him with annoyance and what Jesse hoped was not hunger.

"Felcore hush! Come boy!" Felcore quieted and pranced eagerly over to his mistress. She knelt to scratch her big dog lovingly behind the ears before she gazed up at Tempest with a serious knit to her brow. *"Can you take me to the man who hurt you? I would like to meet him,"* she said gravely.

A rumbling sound issued forth deep from within Tempest's long throat and her eyes twirled a deeper red, the color of blood. *"Corruption darkens his heart. I know where he lives, but why do you wish to meet him?"* she asked.

Jesse pondered Tempest's question before she answered. When she had first decided to travel to Risen, she had thought only of escaping a situation on Earth in which she felt Felcore's life was threatened. Now that she was here she knew she had a purpose. The experience on Elysia had fused the inner force within her together with the newly obtained knowledge about how to tap the freecurrent power in order to make a solid foundation in Jesse's being. She could no longer proceed through life wrapped in obscurity. Jesse was driven to act, to heal, to use her powers to make a difference. A part of her fought against this fate and desired to ignore the responsibilities that came with the power. However, she accepted those feelings for what they were, mostly fear of failure, and set them firmly aside, choosing instead to follow her Grandmother Gabriel's lead and do what she must. With a solid foundation laid, experience would help build her into what she would become.

She responded to Tempest's question, *"The man who hurt you must be held accountable for his actions. I intend to find out what manner of threat he may pose. I have a gut feeling about him."*

The rumbling in Tempest's throat grew even louder. *"My gut feeling is to stay as far away from him as possible. But, I can see that you are determined to meet this human. I will take you to him,"* she replied.

Tempest lay flat on her stomach and extended a wing to accommodate her novice passengers' mounting. Jesse and Felcore crawled carefully up the leathery wing until they reached the crest on Tempest's back. The wing flesh was almost translucent and although it appeared ethereal and delicate, Jesse found it surprisingly tough. She settled into a fairly comfortable position behind Tempest's neck, between ridges. It felt like they were made for each other. Felcore established himself in front of Jesse, where he squirmed and whimpered in agitation.

She grabbed onto Felcore and Tempest as the dragon stood up, swaying her great body as she rose. Not finding a good hand hold, she leaned over Felcore, wrapped her arms around

Tempest's neck and clung there with a prayer on her lips. In one fluid motion Tempest spread her great wings and launched herself into the bright morning sky. They ascended over the forest with the dark green tree tops skimming just below Tempest's shear white belly. Upon reaching cruising altitude, Jesse was able to loosen her grasp and relax as she balanced with her knees while still holding onto Felcore around the stomach with her left arm. She looked down at the land that was foreign to her with a heightened sense of excitement. Echoing Jesse's feelings, Tempest raised her head and bellowed loudly, "RRAAAAHGR-RRRR!" announcing her return to the world.

Chapter 3

WAYFAIR MANOR

Warm as it was, the handsome young man savored the chill that ran through him as he watched the fish flop on the beach, its gills working in and out as it tried to breathe water, but suffocated in the air. Its struggles became weaker as its gills burned red with blood and it started to die. The pleasure it gave the man to watch the animal's suffering didn't seem unusual, or in any way depraved to him. For all of his thirty years he had known there was gratification to be gained from the pain of others, even if it was only in a subtle way, he believed it to be advantageous. He watched as the fish took its last breath before kicking it viciously back into the lake.

Having had a successful day of fishing, the man packed up his pole and bucket of worms and headed down the well-trodden trail that lead to his father's house. Although fishing had been his favorite pass time for years, lately he had found that it was becoming more and more boring. Bigger and better things were waiting to be had and he was ready to move on. It was well past time to begin putting his plan into action. The only thing holding him back was his over-cautious father. *"Zeth, it is important to have every detail precise and correct. Patience, my boy, patience."* He could hear the words repeating over and over again in his head. Nagging, always nagging, until Zeth thought his head would burst from the pressure.

As he came around the corner, a massive gray stone mansion came into view. The residence was surrounded with a tall iron and stonework fence that was overgrown with grass and brush that had long needed trimming. The gate in front of the mansion stood perpetually closed. Except for the few times Zeth had left the manor on some specific errand of his father's, the two men remained almost completely reclusive. His father had a small number of men he kept on staff as guards, but they were mean and anti-social and kept mostly to themselves. Even throughout his childhood years, Zeth could recall having little, if any, contact with the outside world. He had never had a friend. His father was practically the only person he had ever spoken with. He was virtually a prisoner in his own home.

The path led to a small gap in the fence that had been there for as long as Zeth could remember. He and his father had moved into the mansion when Zeth was just a baby. It was the only residence he had ever known. The former owner had been an associate of his father's years ago. Back then the large estate had been kept in immaculate condition; trimmed lawns and shapely hedges graced both the front and back yards, with water fountains spouting and clean flag stones winding in wandering paths through brightly colored gardens. When the previous owner was killed in a sword fight, the mansion had sat empty until Zeth's father moved in with his small son. Since that time the maintenance had been sorely neglected. Zeth's father had very little interest in the monotony of gardening. Zeth had even less interest in tedious maintenance regimes.

Entering through the large gourmet kitchen, also in a consistent state of disrepair, Zeth deposited his fishing pole and bucket of worms on the counter. He crossed the room and passed through a swinging door into the dining room. No longer a dining room in practice, the elegant table was cluttered with books, scrolls, and paperwork, along with collected pieces of this and parts of that, left there in a disarray of abundance. At the end of the table sat an old man, gray and wrinkled beyond his years. He squinted through the dimness at a parchment that lay on top of the books that surfaced the table in front of him. Without looking up, he grumbled an inaudible greeting to his son as Zeth entered the room.

"Father, you shouldn't be reading in the dark. Here, let me open the draperies for you." Zeth walked over to a large glass paned window and flung open the heavy drapes to let the sun stream into the room. "What are you studying?" he asked.

The old man cleared his throat and looked up at his son with a shrewd dark stare. "I have found it. Finally, I have found it," he proclaimed as he grasped the parchment tightly in his hand, which shook with enthusiasm.

"What is it, father?" Zeth asked. He sounded tolerantly bored by his father's announcement, as if he had heard this revelation many times before.

The old man glared at his son with fiery eyes that flashed with power. "Even though you let that dragon escape your grasp, there is still a way to make the plan work. I have found the way," he said.

Zeth felt the barb hit home and he cringed, using all of his effort to curb his tongue when speaking to his father, in a controlled voice he asked, "How?"

"We will have to travel to the Tower of Ornate. There we should find the final piece to the puzzle that will complete the spell. That old witch Shareen kept a book of spells that she passed down to Gabriel. In it I believe we will find the answer we seek. I shall have my victory yet," he said. The old man's dark eyes shined as they focused on another time and another place.

Zeth also felt passion quicken his blood. He had been so close to discovering the secret ingredient needed to complete the spell when that wretched white dragon had escaped. He should have cut off the dragon's wings and left her crippled when he had the chance and then she never would have known freedom again. Now, his father had perhaps found the last piece, or at least found out where they might learn about the last piece of the puzzle. He had to work hard to push back the anger that came from possibly having to concede this one victory to his father. Zeth clenched his fists and stared back at the old man's eyes. "Why don't you let me go alone, father? I wouldn't want you to get sick again," he said.

"No. We will go together. I am not dead yet, Zeth," the name left his lips like the hiss of a snake.

Zeth knew better than to argue. After a long stare that betrayed silently the brutal savagery in the struggle for power that was a constant battle between the two, Zeth asked, "When are we leaving, father?"

The old man rose from his chair, his heavy black robes draped loosely on his feeble frame. He stared out the window, taking a rare interest in the outside world. "We will have to prepare. There are things that need to be attended to before we go. Inform the guards that we will be gone for an extended period of time. It is essential that they don't go into the basement and disturb the egg under any circumstances." Turning his hawk-like gaze at his son, the old man almost caught a glimpse of the anger that boiled just beneath the surface of the younger man. "It is important that every detail be checked and double checked before we go." Seeing the look of annoyance escape Zeth's closely guarded mask, the old man chided, "Patience, my son, patience. Your time will come."

Zeth, seething with pent up frustration, kept silent. He walked quietly over to the table, sat down, and started going over his charts and records. Many years of discipline had taught him excellent skills of concentration, but today he was having a difficult time focusing. Usually, it was no effort to drown out the grinding anger in his head when he was studying. "*Discipline, my son, discipline,*" his father used to say. The words echoed in his brain until he felt it would split wide open. Maybe he would go fishing once more today. He needed to vent and fishing provided him that chance. "*Discipline.*"

Carry On

The time had finally come to leave their home and seek the power that had been taken from him so many years ago. His power had been stolen by that usurper Landtamer and his Wingmaster bitch. He would have it back. Now was the time to act. Their days in hiding were at an end. Once they had the dragons under their control, it was only a matter of time before they conquered every bit of Risen.

Candaz wasn't sure his son was ready yet, but he could wait no longer. He was almost seventy years old and time was slipping away. Already he suffered from the ailments of old age, not to mention the curse of old injuries on his aging body. Although the use of freecurrent had slowed the process, the rigors of battle and lack of physical activity over the recent years had taken their toll. Time was running out. It was now or never.

As he gazed out the window, he reached a hand into one of his many pockets and caressed the silk wrappings on his beloved's severed hand. He took comfort and strength in knowing he had a piece of Molly with him. It was a love that never had a chance. She was ripped from his life like he would rip apart the lives of the present kings. They would know what it is like to lose everything and everybody that they ever loved. He would savor the revenge.

His son did not yet understand what he had endured. The boy was weak. Gabriel's blood made him weak. He would have to work harder to toughen the boy up. Patience was required for the ultimate victory. Patience and discipline.

Uncle Zeth

Tempest spoke to Jesse throughout the entire trip. The dragon told her how she had grown up being largely ignored by the other dragons because of her small size. She explained that it wasn't because they disliked her, but they didn't want her to get hurt. They wanted to protect her and unintentionally left her out. After a while she was easily forgotten as she remained on the sidelines. When she reached maturity she was only about half the size of an average female dragon. Instead of being discouraged with her size disparity, Tempest took wing and flew east. She wanted to see the world. In the hopes of finding a human to bond with, the white dragon visited Castle Gentlebreeze. The king's dragon, Balls of Fire, ordered her to go back to the dragon breeding grounds where she would be safe. In bitter disappointment, Tempest disobeyed B.F. and flew north. Half blind with her inner turmoil, she flew straight into the corrupt human's trap. *"Everything seemed so hopeless . . . and then you came along, Jesse,"* she said. Tempest started to descend toward a crystal clear lake. Jesse could see many houses along the shore as they approached, but one stood out, set off by itself, a massive estate. Low rumbling began in Tempest's throat that Jesse could feel more than she could hear. Veering off to the left, the dragon landed them on the grassy edge of Blue Lake. Tempest was shaking uncontrollably as her passengers climbed off her back and down her wing to the ground.

Jesse patted the frightened dragon on her side and told her, *"Why don't you stay here, Tempest? Do some fishing. Felcore and I will take care of things. Don't worry."*

"That's probably a good idea. If I saw that human again, I would probably eat him and eating a corrupt sorcerer would surely give me a terrible case of indigestion. A golden wolf would be much more palatable, perhaps," Tempest licked her dragon lips with an impressive tongue and gazed at Felcore.

Jesse smiled tolerantly. *"You are not going eat a golden wolf . . . dog, I mean. We'll be back in a while."* she said to Tempest. To Felcore, she said, "Come on, Felcore." Jesse patted her thigh and Felcore automatically healed at her side as they walked up the river bank.

"Be careful!" Tempest called after her as she left.

"We will be. Happy fishing," Jesse replied.

They intersected with a path that seemed to lead in the direction that Jesse wished to go. As she turned to follow it, she spotted out of the corner of her eye someone down by the shore fishing. Changing directions, she approached the morose man. "Having any luck?" she asked.

He turned at the sound of her voice. The man was tall and slim. Thick black hair curled gently away from the etched features of his face. High cheek bones and a jutting square chin gave his face a long and lean impression. His proportionate nose and full lips complimented the rest of his face. He was very handsome to look at. Coppery brown eyes, that could have been Jesse's own, appraised the young woman and revealed an instant attraction as well as curiosity when he noticed her blue jeans, moccasins, cotton tee and backpack. A hint of wildness that Jesse sensed in his persona made him intriguing. His build was not large but strong and sinewy, like that of a long distance runner.

Jesse gestured to the fishing pole in his hand and asked, "Catch anything?"

He looked down at the fishing rod in his hand as if it were foreign to him, seemingly having totally forgotten the reason he was standing on the bank of Blue Lake. Returning his gaze to Jesse, he emerged from his confusion and stated, "No, nothing worth the trouble, anyway." She noted a strange gleam in his eyes and suddenly felt uncomfortable; a tingle of premonition ran icy fingers down her spine. Felcore remained glued to her side, his eyes not leaving the stranger unattended. The man stepped forward and bowed slightly before introducing himself, "I am Zeth. How can I be of service, my lady?" he asked. The exquisite smile he offered her was disarming with charm.

Pushing aside her trepidations, Jesse smiled back and extended her hand, "My name is Jesse and this is Felcore. Perhaps you can help me." Instead of shaking her hand, as Jesse expected, Zeth lifted it gently in his long graceful fingers and brought it up to his lips. With unexpected tenderness he lingered with his lips pressed to her knuckles. Embarrassed, Jesse snatched her hand away as soon as he released it. With her cheeks flushing and

Felcore insistently pressing up against her leg, Jesse regained her equilibrium and boldly asked, "Do you know who lives in that big gray house on the hill?"

He hesitated before answering her, "Yes, that is where I reside? Have you business there?"

Jesse was beginning to think that Tempest had shown her the wrong place. Perhaps in the dragon's debilitated state, she had made a mistake about her captor's whereabouts. The man that stood before Jesse seemed relatively harmless. Felcore seemed tense at her side, but not aggressive. "I'm afraid that perhaps I have inconvenienced you for no reason. I am looking for a man, a sorcerer."

"A sorcerer?" he repeated.

"Yes. Do you know of him?" Jesse asked.

Zeth looked thoughtful for a moment before answering, "No. But, perhaps my father has heard of him. Please, accompany me to the house and you can speak to him about this matter. It is just a short walk."

"All right. Thank you for your help, Zeth," Jesse said.

As they walked along the path, side by side, Zeth asked Jesse about where she was from, inquiring subtly about her unusual clothing and the golden wolf who accompanied her. She was evasive, offering only that she was a traveler from another land. Jesse could feel his eyes boring into her as they walked, but each time she turned to address him, his eyes darted to look ahead, down the path. She was feeling uneasy again, but didn't know why. Instincts were shouting at her to beware. Felcore walked quietly by her side, but his stature remained tense and his tail remained passively down.

They walked past the closed front gate and headed along the fence toward the side yard. Jesse read the rusted sign that was done in iron-work over the gate. It read, "Wayfair Manor." This was the place where Kristina and Rew had been held captive by that horrible man. What was his name? Rew had suspected that the man who owned the home at that time had somehow been connected to Candaz. She stole a glance at Zeth who turned to her and smiled with his amiable grin. Her suspicion waned slightly, but her caution persisted.

They entered the yard through a gap in the iron and stone fence and made their way through a weed-ridden garden to an entrance on the side of the house. Zeth opened the door, turned to Jesse and cast his eyes down at Felcore. "The wolf can stay out here while you talk to father. He has never liked animals."

Felcore growled so low in his throat that Jesse felt rather than heard the rumble against her leg. "My dog comes with me everywhere," she said.

Zeth smiled sweetly, "I am afraid he can't come in the house."

Jesse hesitated before acquiescing. To Felcore she said, "I'll be all right. Wait here, boy." She patted him lightly on the head.

Watchful, she followed Zeth into a large kitchen, through a set of swinging doors and then through a cluttered dining room. He led her into a living room that was dark because the draperies were closed and no light fixtures illuminated the area. The room smelled of dust and disuse. Elegantly furnished in a style similar to Victorian, the decor did nothing to inspire comfort.

Zeth turned to Jesse and gazed into her eyes with a pene-trating stare. Feeling suddenly threatened, Jesse wanted to back away, but didn't. He reached out and touched her cheek with a cold hand and seemed about to lean in and kiss her, but did not follow through. She gulped her relief. It was a strange exchange and very awkward. Her face surely gave away her aversion even though she tried to mask it. "Wait here," he said and then abruptly turned and left the room, shutting and locking the door behind him.

Jesse paced back and forth, waiting what seemed a very long time. She was anxious as she considered Zeth. Initially, she found him somewhat attractive, but when he touched her just moments ago she had felt fear and an overwhelming sense of revulsion. There was a deep coldness in him like frozen steel, with a knife edge sharpened precisely so when the fatal cut was made it would not be felt. She couldn't believe the audacity of him. Her pacing became more agitated. She was beginning to feel like a wild animal trapped in a cage. Jesse knew now that Tempest had not misled her and that she had indeed come to the right place. Zeth's sweet smile showed teeth that likely had a very vicious bite infused with venom.

Rubbing the gold pendant between her thumb and finger, Jesse wished for Felcore to come to her. She was not surprised to feel him press up against her leg and push his wet nose into the palm of her hand. "Good boy!" she said, bending down and ruffling the fur on the top of his head. Hugging him to her, she felt a sting of heat against her skin where his dog tags touched her arm. She had her suspicions about them and when she inspected the tags more closely she found the reason why. Felcore had worn them for as long as Jesse could remember, one dog license, one rabies tag, and one tag that had his name "Felcore" with her father's home phone number etched into it. The gold name tag was the one that was radiating heat. When she turned the tag over, she saw etched in the center the lightning bolt symbol, identical to the one etched in the pendant that she wore around her neck. She looked into Felcore's shining eyes with wonder.

The lock clicked and the door slid open.

Zeth entered and gave Jesse an appraising look, noting with genuine surprise and obvious disapproval the presence of her dog. Coming up behind Zeth, framed in the open doorway as he approached, was an old man, both tall and dark. Jesse felt the tiny hairs on the back of her neck rise.

He turned, "Father, I would like to introduce you to . . . "

Zeth's father cut him off, "Gabriel?"

Jesse felt her stomach tighten and her throat clench. For a moment she was unable to speak. The old man who moved ghost-like toward her had the darkest eyes Jesse had ever seen. They seemed to devour the light and, as she gazed into them, they attempted to dig into the core of her being and possess her soul. Jesse wrenched her eyes from his hold with considerable effort. Chancing a look at Zeth, who now stood behind the old man, Jesse caught his grave expression.

She put a hand firmly on Felcore's soft head to stay him as he moved to intercept the old man with a growl beginning in his throat. Avoiding his eyes by focusing on his bony chin, Jesse said, "You are Candaz."

A smile cracked thin lips revealing straight white teeth. "Yes, but you are not Gabriel." He was close enough that Jesse could smell a trace of mint on his breath. Candaz shifted his eyes down to her side and glared at Felcore. The dog quit growling and whimpered while leaning closer into Jesse's leg.

"My name is Jesse," she said. Again, he cast his dark eyes into her face, but this time she returned his gaze boldly.

"You have my son's eyes . . . Gabriel's eyes," Candaz remarked. Jesse gasped in disbelief at Zeth who moved to stand next to his father. She understood now. Gabriel had given birth to Candaz's son thirty years ago and had named him Jonathon after her late husband. Was Zeth that child? Was Zeth her uncle?

"Zeth is Gabriel's son?" she asked. The question was directed at Candaz although Jesse continued to stare at the handsome young man who seemed annoyed by the whole situation.

Anger swept Candaz's face in an instant. He growled, "Zeth is my son! He was born of my seed and raised by my hand!"

Zeth put a restraining hand on Candaz's shoulder. "Father," he said one word, pleading the old man to calm himself.

Candaz shrugged the hand off from his shoulder and turned away from Jesse. He strode back toward the door, his long black robes billowing dust as they dragged on the hard wood floor. Jesse watched him, ignoring Zeth, who gazed at her with a mixture of longing and malice. The old man swung around and came at her again, also ignoring his son. "What do you want?" he asked.

Jesse did not falter under Candaz's scrutiny. She said, "A dragon named Tempest was held here and cruelly abused. Are you responsible?"

"Ah, the white she-dragon," he responded. Candaz's eyes flared at his son, saying nothing and yet making Zeth cringe visibly.

"So, you admit it?" she asked although she already knew the answer. Jesse felt Felcore begin to growl as he pressed against her leg.

Candaz's voice was velvet. "My son's experiment. He was using the she-dragon to test potions. Had she not escaped, he would have found the right one. He was on the verge of finding the ingredient that would have granted control of the dragons to me! It would have put them completely under my command! Now we must gain the information elsewhere. Foolish boy, letting her escape."

Zeth's face was scorched with anger as he said, "Father! Next you will be telling her where we plan to go. If I ever get my hands on that she-dragon she will wish she had never been born."

Jesse wheeled on Zeth, having lost her temper, "How dare you?! Tempest was nearly dead when I found her. She has suffered horribly under your hand. You will pay for your cruelty!"

Felcore prepared himself to launch at either one of the men if they showed the slightest aggression toward his mistress.

Zeth was livid. He raised his hand to strike Jesse across the face, but delayed the action when his father intervened. Jesse put a hand on Felcore keeping him from attacking the man who threatened her.

Candaz laughed harshly and said without humor, "What do you think you can do, little girl? Your life was forfeit the minute you walked through that door."

"Father, no. Let me deal with her," Zeth tried to persuade his father. The two men stood eye to eye in silent combat.

Jesse figured it was time to leave Wayfair Manor. She felt she was not yet in a position to challenge Candaz and she wasn't quite sure what she should do at the moment, anyway. Although she had come to take vengeance of the man that had hurt Tempest, she had found more than she had bargained for. Now was the time to make herself scarce. She hesitated. There was something bothering her that she just couldn't identify. The two men were presently involved in a power struggle. It was time to go. Jesse nudged Felcore and started quietly toward the door.

She was almost through it when they noticed her. Zeth shouted, "Stop!"

Candaz started toward her, "You aren't going anywhere, little girl."

"Oh, yes I am," she said as she ran forward and plunged herself at Candaz, knocking the old sorcerer off his feet. He landed with a heavy thud in a cloud of billowing dust. At the same time Felcore went after Zeth, pouncing and landing squarely in the center of the man's chest, bowling him over, as well. Before either man could recover his feet or his wits, Jesse bounded for the door with Felcore at her side. They ran through the dining room, into the kitchen and out the side door. "Tempest!" Jesse called and in seconds the white dragon swooped down and grasped her passengers firmly in strong talons, taking them high up into the air and away from Wayfair Manor.

"*That was quick!*" Jesse commented as she pushed ineffectively against a sharp talon that was jabbing lightly into her side.

"*I feared you might be in trouble so I was circling overhead in case you had need of me. I would appreciate a little more warning next time,*" Tempest complained.

"*It was the best I could do,*" Jesse responded defensively.

"*You can't expect me to always be there at a moment's notice. A little consideration goes a long way,*" the nagging tone Tempest took was reminiscent of Jesse's father.

"*I didn't think we were in any danger until it was already too late,*" Jesse said.

"*I suggest you be more careful next time. You could have been killed,*" the dragon said. Tempest headed to a grassy spot and carefully landed, setting her passengers down gently on the ground to their great relief.

Jesse looked around and found that they were in an isolated field. She approached Tempest and started scratching her eyes ridges, causing the dragon to coo softly. "*I am sorry I worried you. I'll try to be more careful,*" Jesse said, remembering having said something similar to her father on several occasions.

"*I will not have found my human bond mate, only to lose her. Do be more careful in the future,*" Tempest said.

Tempest's serious concern touched Jesse. She felt chagrined for her annoyance at Tempest's nagging. She said more sincerely, "*I'm truly sorry, Tempest. Next time, I'll be sure to stay in communication.*"

"*Yes, yes. That would be good. But, I don't think there should be a next time.*" Tempest said as she lifted her head high in the air and sniffed the wind. Her eyes twirled red with excitement as she looked back down at Jesse. "*There is someone approaching.*"

Old Flame

Candaz didn't stop Zeth as he walked out the door. He wanted time to think without his son distracting him. The girl looked so much like Gabriel at first he thought she *was* her. Those old feelings of attraction were suddenly surging through him again. She had been his for a time. He remembered it well. Of course, Gabriel would never have given herself to him willingly. He had to take what he wanted. She was his enemy and he knew that she would not hesitate to kill him. Likewise, he would not hesitate to kill her if given the chance. Maybe someday that opportunity would arise; maybe soon.

That girl would be a problem. They would no longer be safe at Wayfair Manor. No matter. They would be gone before sunset tomorrow. But, she *did* know of their plans to enslave the dragons. He guessed that really didn't matter either. She didn't know where they were going or anything else about what they had planned. His secrets contained within these walls would remain safe. The guards he left behind could protect the property from any unwanted intruders while they were away for as long as they needed to them to.

He should have killed the girl. The insolence of bringing a dog into his home! Given a second chance, he would not delay the death of her or her golden dog too.

Distasteful Attraction

Zeth walked down the path toward Blue Lake with his eyes searching the sky. He had left his fishing pole and bucket of worms back at the mansion, having only one purpose in mind . . . to find her. Jesse. He repeated the name over and over again in his head, dwelling on it to engrain it in his memory for all time.

Never before had he seen a woman so beautiful, even if she was wearing men's clothing. Zeth had never known a woman who could light his fire so quickly, both touching and angering him at the same time. He wanted to kill her. He wanted to love her. He wanted her to love him and he wanted her to fear him.

The first time he had seen her standing along the shoreline of Blue Lake he knew she would become special to him. Her eyes had glowed with confidence as she stood next to her beautiful golden wolf, both of them full of pride and beaming with dignity. He had so easily fooled her into believing he knew nothing about the sorcerer she sought. She had no idea he was a powerful sorcerer himself, much more powerful that his father had ever been. He could have killed the wolf and her right then and there had he wanted to. No, that would be wasteful. He would rather savor the game, let the anticipation build. Once Jesse had learned to fear him, it would be so delightful to watch her beg to be near him. The victory would be exquisite. He couldn't wait to see his father's face when that occurred. She would be his.

Zeth had seen his father's own hunger for Jesse as the old man laid eyes upon her for the first time and called her, "Gabriel." Jealously had brought Zeth close to openly defying his father in front of the girl. When she guessed that the old man was Candaz, it had surprised Zeth and made him realize that the girl was more than she seemed. His appeal for her had grown by the moment as he watched her stand up tall against the old man, his desire . . . and his anger. All of his life Zeth had been forced to live under the shadow of the old man, catering to his needs, doing his bidding, being a good son. Never talk back. Never question. Zeth hated Jesse for doing what he had always wanted to do but could not.

The sky was turning a hazy pink as the sun began to sink low over the horizon. Zeth still watched the sky, hoping to catch a glimpse of Jesse on the white she-dragon. He remembered the passion in her eyes when she had turned on him in anger, yelling and threatening him. Oh! She was beautiful! He had almost struck her. The thought of following through with his stroke, the back of his hand against the soft flesh of her face made him tremble. If only his father hadn't gotten in the way.

Taking a seat, Zeth took off his heavy boots and let his bare feet dangle in the cool water. *Jesse.* The name ran through his head like a cadence. She would look at him with respect and admiration when he brought the dragons down before him. He shook with the emotions that filled him. Dampening his aspiration, but not extinguishing it was his father's voice, always in the back of his mind, nagging, *"Patience, my son, patience."*

Chapter 4

FELCORE'S KENNEL

Jesse knew right away that it was a wisp who approached them. How she knew, she didn't know, but she knew it to be a fact none the less. Unable to see clearly the small creature who bobbed up and down and all around the dragon, Felcore, and Jesse; pinching skin, looking under ears, lifting tails, touching hair--scales--fur--fingers--and toes, Jesse waited patiently for the wisp to calm down and introduce himself. Tempest wasn't as patient as Jesse. The dragon snapped at the wisp with her mighty jaws and used her long forked tongue to try to hinder the wisp's flight pattern. Felcore barked excitedly and spun in circles, leaping and trying to fly with wisp wings that were no longer there.

The wisp settled to the ground suddenly and introduced himself, "Hello. My name is Rew. Rew, son of Lew, Prince of the Wisps. Welcome to Risen, Jessica Gates and Felcore." The wisp's bright blue eyes were dazzling as he gazed at Jesse. His appearance was generally similar to that of all the other wisps Jesse had encountered, curly blond hair, pointed ears topped off with tufts of golden fur. He reached a height of approximately one and a half feet and had four iridescent wings crisscrossing his back. He was practically nude except for a G-string pant and a pair of leather sandals.

"Pleased to meet you, Rew. You know my name. May I ask how?" Jesse didn't mean to be rude; she just was taken by surprise.

"I am Rew," he stated, as if that explained everything.

"I don't understand," Jesse said.

"I am a wisp and you are the one, of course." Rew smiled with an impish grin and waved his hand in Felcore's direction. "Not only that," he said dramatically, "but, as a very good friend of your grandmother's and guardian of your guardian, I have followed your adventures on Earth very closely."

"You protect Felcore?" I asked.

"And you through him," he said.

"How?" I asked.

Rew sighed and rubbed his forehead with a small hand. "You ask a lot of questions," he said.

Jesse laughed and said, "I guess I do. I have one more question. Do you know where my grandmother is? Can you take me to her? She is still alive, isn't she?"

It was Rew's turn to laugh. "That was three questions. I have only one answer for you, however--yes. Yes, yes, and yes. If we leave now we should be able to make it there by dinner time," he said brightly.

Felcore barked appreciatively at the mention of dinner and strode to Rew and nudged him affectionately with his nose. Rew hugged the big dog around the neck and tolerantly let Felcore lick his face. "What have you been feeding him? He's as big as a horse."

"We just spent two weeks on Elysia. I'm surprised I'm not as big as a horse," Jesse commented lightly.

Rew's face lit up as he gazed admirably at Jesse. "You are big, but not as big as a horse, more giraffe-like," he said.

"*Although I am as big, in fact bigger than a horse, I am small for a dragon and I find all this talk of size a bit bothersome. Shall we fly?*" Tempest asked, considering them with her swirling red eyes. Her luminescent white scales reflected the subtle pink tint of the sky as the sun began to set.

Rew rose off the ground, fluttering his wings until he was parallel with Tempest's nose. "*You are quite an extraordinary looking dragon. Very compact. Would you like to race?*" he asked.

Tempest swirled her eyes faster with excitement. She answered, "*Yes, yes, let's race! Jesse, Felcore, mount up! Let's go!*"

Jesse knew Tempest was eager. She had even forgotten *not* to use Felcore's name. In Tempest's childhood she had never been invited to race with the other dragons and she had felt very left out. Although the dragon could never expect to outfly a wisp, Jesse hoped that she would enjoy the challenge.

Felcore and Jesse climbed up Tempest's outstretched wing and settled on her back. They hung on tight as Tempest launched into the darkening sky and followed the wisp. Rew stayed in the lead, but Tempest kept up with him, flying faster than Jesse could have imagined possible for the bulky animal. They flew northwest toward the high mountain range known as the Skyview Mountains. Rew started to descend over a semi-dense forest, heading for a clearing down below that was only visible as a small dot from their altitude. Tempest spread her wings as wide as they would go and let her weight carry her down in a kamikaze glide. Jesse held her breath and closed her eyes as she clutched Felcore and Tempest with a death grip. They passed Rew, whose eyes held wide fascination at the speeding trio. Bracing herself for the ultimate impact, Jesse said a prayer and opened her eyelids to take a peek. The ground was coming at them like they were a hurtling meteorite. Before a scream could escape Jesse's lips, Tempest leveled off and touched the ground gently without a jolt or a jar. Rew joined them seconds later. Jesse and Felcore used that time span to recover what was left of their scrambled wits.

"*I won!*" "RRAAAAHGRRRRR!" "*Did you see that, Jesse? I won!*" Tempest gloated.

"*Believe me, I saw. Congratulations,*" Jesse commented to the dragon wryly.

Rew planted himself on Tempest's nose and began a friendly debate with the dragon which ended in Tempest challenging Rew to another race. By the devilish grin on Rew's face, Jesse suspected that was exactly what he was counting on.

Jesse looked around at her surroundings from atop the dragon's back. They stood in the center of a large clearing, about the size of a football field. In the deepening dusk, brightly colored gardens that graced the walkway took on a hazy tone. The small cabin that stood on the edge of the clearing was quiet with smoke wafting lazily from the natural stone chimney. The peaceful atmosphere was shattered when the door burst open and a short woman strode out onto the wooden porch with her hands on her hips and spirit in her brown eyes. Jesse guessed that she was the banderg huntress named Anna. She wore a pink robe that hung to her ankles and had long shiny silver hair. "What is the meaning of all that noise? You'll spook my goldens," she said as she squinted her eyes in an effort to see them better. A look of understanding crossed her face. "Rew, I should have known you would be behind this. Who are your friends?"

As the banderg woman approached them, Jesse and Felcore dismounted Tempest. Rew remained on his perch upon the dragon's nose. "Jesse," the wisp said, "I would like to introduce you to Annalibijobahuntresshisheart."

Before Jesse could stop him, Felcore made a running leap and tackled the banderg woman to the ground and began licking her face as if he were a puppy. She struggled playfully with the dog before pushing him aside and regaining her feet. Before extending her hand to Jesse, she wiped it on her pink robe. "Nice to finally meet you, Jesse. What did you name him?" she asked. The woman stroked the golden retriever's head affectionately as she waited with her eyes focused on the girl.

Jesse's face plainly showed her confusion and she answered with a hint of hesitation in her voice, "Felcore."

"Hmm. Strange name, but I like it," she said.

"'Felcore' is a fictional character in a movie, a luck dragon," Jesse explained.

Tempest snorted loudly, *"You named that scrawny wolf after a dragon. How insulting!"*

"He's hardly scrawny, Tempest," Jesse returned to the dragon as Anna replied, "He is almost as big as a dragon. What have you been feeding him?"

"Just dog food, human food lately . . . and a lot of love." Jesse smiled as Felcore barked and wagged his tail happily.

"Well, I can see that. He's very healthy and obviously well loved. I was there when he was born, you know. My bitch, Taffy, gave birth to a litter of eleven puppies that day. Felcore was the biggest and the smartest of the bunch. Of course, Gabriel picked him out of all the rest and had him delivered to you, with a lot of special arrangements . . . magic and such," she said.

Jesse stared at Felcore in disbelief for a moment before the dog came up to her and nudged her hand in a most familiar manner. She remembered Felcore's special ability to show up at her side, even when locked doors or geographic distances separated them, and the golden tag he wore with the lightning bolt symbol etched into it. She knelt beside him and looked into his eyes, seeing the wonderful loving gold pools that had always been a source of strength and joy to her. Now that she thought about it, it didn't surprise her a bit.

Anna was watching intently with a gentle look on her face. Gazing past her, Jesse could see the slim figure of a woman silhouetted in the doorway of the cabin. Jesse stood up slowly, keeping her eyes locked on the woman who was now walking toward her. Strikingly similar in appearance to Jesse's mother Marguerite; the woman could have passed for her older sister. Had Jesse's mother not died almost six years ago, Jesse might have mistaken the woman for her. Dark brown hair was twisted and tied in a bun at the back of her head. A jade green gown graced her slim figure and complimented her copper-flecked brown eyes. The pretty face that smiled at Jesse was smooth with the wrinkles of age evident only around the edges of her eyes and mouth. She exuded power; warm and sparkling and beautiful.

Tears came to the woman's eyes as she reached out her hand and grasped Jesse's own. "Jesse, I am Gabriel. I am your grandmother," she said.

Jesse felt her own eyes fill with tears. Her grandmother stood before her. She was overwhelmed with a sense of love for the woman she had just met. Jesse was overjoyed to have finally met the woman she had always felt more akin to than anyone else. With a voice cracked with emotion she said, "Grandmother?"

Gabriel pulled the girl into her arms and gently stroked Jesse's long auburn hair. "Jessica, Jessica, I have waited so long . . . so long. You are finally here," she said.

"I cannot believe it, my Grandmother," Jesse said.

Jesse pulled away from Gabriel's embrace and looked her squarely in the eyes after wiping the tears from her own.

"Tell me how you got here. Did something happen between you and your father? I assume you found my diary," Gabriel said.

"Yes. I read your diary. The rest is a little complicated and a long story," Jesse said.

"How long have you been on Risen?" Gabriel asked.

"I just arrived today. Tempest was in the cave and we bonded after I healed her. We then travelled to Wayfair Manor to find the man who hurt her. I met Candaz and your son, Zeth," Jesse said.

Gabriel's knees seemed to give out and she almost collapsed to the ground. All of the blood ran from her face turning her cheeks porcelain white. Anna caught hold of her elbow to sustain her and Rew jumped from Tempest's nose to assist her. Anguish swept across her face like a storm front with a strong northeast wind behind it. "Alive?" was all she could manage to vocalize.

"Yes, I met them both earlier today," Jesse said. She waited for a response, startled at Gabriel's reaction. Hadn't she prior knowledge of her son's whereabouts? She had assumed that her grandmother had already known that Candaz and their son Zeth presently occupied Wayfair Manor. "You didn't know? I'm so sorry. Are you okay?" she asked Gabriel.

"Zeth?" Gabriel tested the sound on her tongue, her eyes far away as she repeated the name over and over again. She literally shook herself physically and looked back up at Jesse. "My son is alive? Candaz is not dead? They are together?" she asked.

"Yes. They are together. Zeth has your eyes," Jesse replied, feeling terrible. She had no idea she was dropping a bomb shell. Poor Gabriel.

"It is not possible," Gabriel shook her head in denial.

"I'm surprised you didn't already know. I'm so sorry to have dropped it on you like this. Are you okay, Grandmother?" Jesse took Gabriel's hand away from Rew and squeezed it gently.

"It's not possible . . . Are you sure?" she asked.

"Yes Grandmother. I'm sorry," Jesse replied.

Anna motioned to them all with a wave of her hand and said, "Come, let's go to the cabin and get comfortable and then we can discuss this."

Gabriel and Jesse talked as they walked hand in hand up the garden path. Anna and Rew accompanied them, keeping a short distance behind. Felcore took off, pursuing his own interests. Tempest lay down on the same spot where she had landed and closed her eyes. Breathing deeply, the dragon was soon fast asleep.

Gabriel talked about how she had lost her son thirty years earlier, "Candaz was holding me hostage at Castle Xandia. My son was conceived. Jonathon was born while I was still a prisoner of Candaz. The date was May 27, 1984. I named him Jonathon Theodore Thomas."

Jesse knew the story from her grandmother's diary. She said, "'Jonathon' after your husband; 'Theodore' after Prince Theodore Wingmaster."

Gabriel smiled, "Yes, only it's King Theodore Wingmaster now. After they took Jonathon away from me, Rew and Theo came to my rescue."

Rew cleared his throat when he heard his name mentioned. He said importantly, "All in a day's work, Mistress."

Casting an amused glance over her shoulder, Gabriel continued, "Theo and I sought out Candaz. I demanded my baby back. He declared him dead. He attacked me with magic and Theo ran him through with his sword. As Candaz was dying he caused an earthquake that shook Castle Xandia down to its foundation. The whole place was destroyed within minutes. It was a true miracle that so many escaped. I searched for my baby, but finally I had to accept the fact that he was dead, buried under a ton of rubble along with his father, Candaz. Now you tell me they are alive. I should have never quit searching." She quickly wiped the tears from her eyes. "I should have never stopped looking," she repeated.

"You did what you had to, Grandmother. You had children waiting for you at home. They needed you too," she said. Jesse patted her grandmother's hand in reassurance as they stepped up onto the porch.

The inside of the cabin was as warm and as cozy as little cabins in the woods can get. Soft pink cushions and draperies colorfully decorated the hard wooden furniture and glass paned windows. Vases filled with fresh flowers stood in various corners. A blazing fire crackled in the black stone fireplace dancing shadows across the floor.

A banderg woman entered the living room. She was leaner than Anna and a much taller. She could have passed easily for a petite human woman. Brunette hair was braided into a rope that hung down the middle of her back all the way to her hips. Instead of a robe, she was dressed in tan pants and a green tunic that hung down to her knees. It was tied at the waist with a beautifully tooled leather belt. Tan skin stretched smoothly across her round face. Her dark brown eyes sparkled with vitality.

Anna introduced her to Jesse, "I would like you to meet my niece, Kalimoryvernahuntressmyheart."

Jesse stepped forward and shook the banderg's hand and said, "Hi, I'm Jesse."

She smiled a smile that could brighten the darkest room. "I'm happy to meet you, Jesse. Call me Kali."

"Jesse is my granddaughter," Gabriel told Kali proudly. "The granddaughter of a sorceress. Do you have the gift as well, Jesse?" Kali asked. Jesse noticed Gabriel watching her with intense interest.

"That's a long story," Jesse answered obscurely.

"I can't wait to hear it," Gabriel eyed her granddaughter curiously. "You must tell me how your father is doing. I know it was devastating for him to lose Marguerite." Gabriel paused and cleared the lump that suddenly formed in her throat. "I hope he has found a way to accept it. How's my grandson, Jacob? You have much to tell me."

Before Jesse could answer, Anna interrupted, "Please have a seat, Jesse. I'll prepare something to tide us over until dinner." Anna disappeared into the kitchen.

Rew followed after her. "I'll help. I'm starving."

Jesse sat with her grandmother on the couch. Kali excused herself and went to help Anna and Rew in the kitchen. Jesse told Gabriel all about their family, her assault and subsequent departure from New Mexico and the trip through the gate. Gabriel's eyes sparkled with delight when Jesse told her about how Jim McCaw had rescued her. Her grandmother was completely surprised when Jesse related the story about how she had been granted wisp magic on Elysia. Her recitation of her meeting with Tempest brought a smile to Gabriel's face. "I was motivated to confront Tempest's kidnappers," Jesse related, "if only to find out who was behind her abduction. I couldn't believe someone could be so cruel. When I first met Zeth on the shoreline of Blue Lake I judged him to be a decent man. I couldn't have been more wrong." Jesse saw Gabriel flinch at her comment.

Anna, Kali and Rew returned from the kitchen with platters of appetizers and five tall glasses of lemonade. They made themselves comfortable and listened to Jesse continue, "I began to figure out that I had been mistaken about Zeth when he locked me in a room to wait for his father. A cold iciness ran up and down my spine. When Candaz walked in, I knew immediately who he was, the corrupt sorcerer you named in your diary. It could have been no one but Candaz. At first he thought I was you," she said to Gabriel.

"You suspect Jonathon . . . I mean Zeth of being on the side of corruption?" Gabriel's turmoil was evident. "Are you absolutely sure that it was them?"

Jesse hesitated for only a moment, feeling her grandmother's distress, but she said, "I'm sorry, Gabriel, but yes. I'm afraid Zeth follows in his father's footsteps."

Rew stated the obvious, "It was inevitable. Zeth was raised by Candaz. It was out of your hands, Mistress."

Gabriel clung to a hope and expressed her wish, "I must rescue him from his father as soon as possible. There is still a chance to save him."

"No. You don't understand." Jesse felt a twinge of impatience with her grandmother. Despite Gabriel's relationship to Zeth, she had to make her grandmother understand. "He is corrupt. He plans on enslaving the dragons, using them to conquer Risen. He is his father's son," she said adamantly.

"He is my son, too," Gabriel asserted stubbornly.

"I am sorry, Grandmother," Jesse said with true compassion.

Gabriel hesitated. In her mind she gazed back in time to the innocent little child she had held in her arms, the baby boy who was stolen from her so many years ago. "We must warn Theo," croaked from her throat, anguish evident on her face. "Do you know what their next move is?"

"I only know that they needed more information to complete their spell. It seems unlikely they would remain at Wayfair Manor now that they have been exposed." Jesse took a sip of her drink and tried to remember if they had given her any more clues.

Rew commented cryptically, "I know I wouldn't stay there, even for one day. What a place! Nope! After being chained to the floor in the cellar and given nothing to eat or drink for days and days, I never want to see that place again. You know a wisp can starve to death if not properly fed at least five times a day."

Kali laughed and got to her feet and said, "If that was a hint, I whole-heartedly agree. Dinner has been delayed way too long. Come on, Rew, let's see what we can put together." The two walked hand-in-hand into the kitchen, nudging and teasing each other as if they were siblings.

Gabriel smiled and shook her head. Getting back to the subject, she said, "After we warn Theo, we'll stop by the Tower of Ornate and then head on to the dragon breeding grounds. Candaz and Zeth's most likely destination will be the dragon library on the Island of Zedra. Unless we learn otherwise, I think that will be our best bet. As soon as this is over, Jesse, I want you to go back to Earth and set things straight with your father. Believe me, I have never forgiven myself for leaving things the way I did with your mother and uncle. I should have had the confidence in them to confide the truth, at least part of it. Regrets are pesky little things that seem to increase with age."

Jesse knew her grandmother was right, but she was afraid for Felcore and afraid of the emotional confrontation that would be inevitable if she did go back. She was in no hurry to go back home.

Noticing Jesse's discomfiture, Gabriel insisted more strongly. "You must do this, Jesse. I know from experience that if you leave loose ends, you will eventually get tangled up in them."

Anna offered, "You can leave Felcore here if you wish."

"Thank you, Anna. I will consider it." Speaking of Felcore, where did he go? Jesse silently wished him to her and the golden retriever came trotting up to her from the kitchen a few minutes later. She reached down and petted him as Anna and Gabriel watched the exchange with a certain amount of pride. "Tell me Grandmother, what's the story behind Felcore? Can you tell me his story?" she asked.

Anna replied with a grin, "Well, here on Risen we call it a 'tale'."

Jesse smiled and laughed.

"Do you remember the day you found the gold medallion?" Gabriel asked.

"Sure."

"On my instructions, Rew planted it there while you and Marguerite were finishing lunch. Wisps can travel through the gate at will, but you probably already know that. The storm that drove you into the cave in the first place was encouraged by magic. The whole situation was orchestrated to put you or your mother in possession of the medallion. I was testing you both to see who was meant to have it, to find out which of you was meant to follow in my footsteps. When I discovered that you were the one, I immediately started making plans to guide you in the right direction. After your mother died, I thought you needed something extra to love and some added protection. I asked Anna for one of her golden puppies and she gave me the largest male in the litter. A simple enchantment gave him the ability to always sense when you needed him and the gift to transport to your side, wherever that may be should you call. The gold tag Felcore wears is very similar to yours. It focuses the freecurrent power like a lens. On Christmas Eve, Rew delivered Felcore to your father's house, playing at being one of Santa's elves. I asked Rew to keep an eye on you, which he did through

Felcore, using the sight water to establish the contact with the dog and sometimes even making personal visits back to Earth so he could observe things first hand."

Jesse gazed into Felcore's warm gold eyes and hugged him close. She said, "Thank you for him, Grandmother. Thank you very much."

"You're very very welcome, sweetheart." She leaned over and gave Jesse a warm hug. "I'm so happy you're here."

Kali and Rew came into the living room and announced that dinner was served. They adjourned to the kitchen and feasted on a juicy grilled blue fish fillets, steamed vegetables and spiced rice. After dinner Jesse went outside to check on Tempest. The dragon was still sleeping deeply. She was feeling very weary herself. It had been a long day. After paying her respects to Anna and Kali for their hospitality and the wonderful meal, she hugged her grandmother goodnight, went to the spare bedroom and fell fast asleep.

In the morning when Jesse arose Felcore was not in her room. She went in search and him and found him in back of Anna's cabin where a kennel lay hidden in the woods. Although it was fenced in, the gate stood open. Kali came around the corner with buckets in both hands and greeted Jesse, "Good morning. I've been feeding and watering the goldens. I went ahead and fed Felcore already. I hope that's okay."

"Sure. Thanks. Can I help you with anything?" Jesse asked.

Kali smiled with her eyes and lifted a bucket. "Take this and follow me."

The kennel was a large fenced in area with separated runs for each dog. All of the dogs were golden retrievers. Felcore greeted Jesse with a sharp bark. He was frolicking with a bitch in her run and Jesse suddenly knew where he had been all night. Kali spoke to Jesse as she distributed food into individual bowls from the bucket. "Anna breeds goldens for hunting. They are wonderful animals and skillful as retrievers." She nodded at the bucket in Jesse's hand and said, "You can start at the end and give each golden one scoop in their dish." She continued working by refreshing water dishes. "Anna's been teaching me. I will inherit the cabin and the kennel from her someday. Every now and then Gabriel adds to Anna's breeding stock by bringing in a dog from Earth. The one Felcore is with now is one such golden. Her name is Tica. She is the dog I have been working with. They will have beautiful puppies, don't you think?"

"Yes, indeed," Jesse replied as she emptied her bucket one scoop at a time and went to pet Felcore and the dog he was with. She was very beautiful with bright intelligent eyes and an endlessly happy face. Jesse helped Kali finish the rest of her chores and then they washed up with cold water from the pump in the back yard and joined the others for breakfast.

The rest of the day was spent in preparation for a long journey. Road rations were packed in water tight bags. Assorted cooking utensils and medical supplies were tucked snugly into packs. Water skins were filled. Anna fussed constantly about Gabriel's lack of attention to details such as bringing along appropriate hunting weapons. Gabriel easily deferred those preparations to Kali. It was well into the evening before Skymaster arrived.

Tempest trumpeted loudly in front of the cabin and told Jesse, "*Master Skymaster is here.*" A louder trumpeting sounded from the sky, as Skymaster announced his own arrival. Tempest added rather hastily, "*He is surprised I bonded with a human.*"

"*We'll just have to show him.*" she said to Tempest. "Excuse me," Jesse said to everyone else and got up from the dinner table and joined Tempest, taking the time to scratch her eye ridges and nose as she gazed in amazement at the massive dragon mage with shiny silver scales. Tempest cooed softly and let Jesse tend to her various itchy spots.

Gabriel walked out, dressed in leather pants and tunic, and introduced Skymaster to Jesse. It surprised Jesse to hear the voice booming in her head, a mental voice distinctly different from Tempest's, as the High Mage of Dragons addressed her, *"It is my pleasure to meet you, Lady Jesse. Gabriel has told me much about you, but she didn't tell me you were such a lovely girl. Should you ever need a ride I would be most honored to convey you wherever you need to go.*

"Thank you, Master Skymaster. I am so honored to meet you. I appreciate your gracious offer. Tempest and I are all set for now, though. She is an awesome flyer!" Jesse told him. Tempest puffed up with pride at Jesse's words.

Gabriel said something to Tempest that Jesse couldn't hear and Tempest replied, *"I can see where Jesse gets it from."* Jesse wondered what she meant by that but she didn't ask.

With Anna's help Gabriel strapped a saddle on Skymaster, using a ladder to reach his back, and secured a traveling bag on one side and a pack belonging to Kali on the other, along with the young banderg's hunting weapons and a special pouch for her dog. Kali was going with them to Castle Gentlebreeze and, to Felcore's delight, so was Kali's dog, Tica. Anna, however, had to stay behind to care for her goldens and other such matters. Once they were all packed and ready to go, Gabriel mounted Skymaster and helped Kali into place behind her. Tica was strapped into a saddle bag that reminded Jesse of a side car for a motorcycle. Jesse and Felcore climbed up Tempest's wing and settled themselves comfortably behind her neck. A niche between ridges was the perfect spot to sit, like it was made just for her. They waved good bye to Anna and launched into the cloudy dusk. The dragons trumpeted loudly.

Rew flew next to them and Jesse heard him ask Tempest, "Race?"

Tempest bellowed "RRAAAAHGRRRRR!"

Jesse got a firm grasp on Felcore and held on tight.

Chapter 5

DEPARTED

The clear water of Blue Lake made a soothing noise as it gurgled by the slow moving boat. It was large enough to accommodate the three-man crew and on occasion one or two passengers who may have business up or down stream on Blue River and could afford to pay the price. Mostly they transported goods from the busy commercial dock on the south side of Skyview to Lakeside and down to Vinnia, the southern-most city in Brightening. They made a healthy profit dealing in perishable goods, enough to keep food in their families' mouths and maintain a comfortable, but far from luxurious lifestyle. Dealing with passengers was bothersome so they avoided it most of the time, but if someone was willing to pay the price, they would not turn the opportunity down.

Zeth was anything but lulled by the gentle sounds of the lapping water. The crawling pace was making him anxious and irritable. Father had insisted that they pay the exorbitant fee to the crew for the use of their boat and for safe transport to the opposite shore of Blue Lake. It wasn't the boat's normal route so the men raised the priced even more. There had been other boats available, faster, sleeker boats, with larger crews that catered to their passengers with white gloves, but father demanded they remain inconspicuous. They dealt under the table, behind closed doors, a few words spoken and jewels passed from closed palm to closed palm. Zeth didn't see what was so important about remaining elusive. Nobody would know or care who they were anyway.

His hands clenched the side of the boat, white knuckles showing his tension. Zeth gulped down his anger as his father leaned over and said, "Patience, my son, patience."

Zeth turned to face his father and spouted, "It seems we are cursed, having to travel by means such as this while others fly by dragon, covering ground in days that will take us weeks. The dragons should be ours by now."

"They will be, son. Have patience in all things. Patience will reward you when the time has come."

Patience wasn't something Zeth had in any measurable amount; he had long ago used up his quota. A hollow ache started in his stomach and ran down to his groin as he thought of the future he desired. Saberville and all of Risen would be under his rule. All the riches of all the races would be his to command. They would all fall to their knees at his feet and honor his wisdom and supremacy. At his side would be Jesse, radiant in her gold and silks, attentive to his every need, worshiping him as her king and cherishing him as her husband. The days would be filled with audiences and conferences, as well as banquets and luncheons where flirtatious beauties would fawn over their king and he would be free to be his own man. The nights would be his and Jesse's alone. She would be waiting for him every evening and she would be his to do with as he pleased.

He would have it all, but he wouldn't wait until he was an old man to have the ultimate power. All of his life Zeth had waited for his father to meticulously iron out the details of their plan. Now was the time to act. They would take control of the dragons and then conquer all Risen. The wait was over. Patience no longer applied!

The black tower jutted up from the shoreline like a giant rook alone on a chess board. The Tower of Ornate was home to the Master Sorceress of Brightening. Built for Shareen Wingmaster more than sixty years ago after the death of her husband, King Theodore Wingmaster II, the present king's grandfather, the tower presently housed Master Sorceress Gabriel Thomas. Shareen had the tower built after the death of her husband so she would have a place to study away from the toil and pressures of castle life. Shareen had given up all her powers as Queen, although she had retained the title, and become virtually a recluse at the tower until her death at the hands of Candaz. It had been her refuge. To Gabriel it was home. She lived there alone, doing her own cooking and cleaning, feeling free to eat and sleep when and if she felt like it. Her priorities often involved studying before taking care of her own creature comforts. Often times she would have guests stay at the tower and they would comment on her erratic schedule. She would smile and go about her business leaving them to throw up their hands in resignation and learn to fend for themselves.

There was no dock on this shore so Candaz and Zeth had to clamor awkwardly from the boat to the grassy shore as they disembarked. Zeth helped his father, lending the older man a strong arm on which to balance himself until Candaz found solid ground under his feet. Zeth slipped, soaking his left boot and cursing his ill fate. The men aboard the boat tossed Zeth two traveling bags, one his own and the other his father's before thankfully leaving their passengers behind. They didn't like the feeling that surrounded the two dark haired men, although they were happy to take their money; they were also relieved to have the two strange men off their boat.

Zeth and Candaz walked boldly over the grassy plain up to the front of the Tower of Ornate. Whether or not the tower was currently occupied was not a concern of Zeth's. If Gabriel was at home they would simply kill her and take what they wanted. However, Zeth had a feeling that she would not be there. When he was a little boy he used to dream about the meeting between them. She would scoop him up into her arms and cry with joy and laugh at nothing in particular, just for the sheer joy of being with him. As he grew into a man he set that dream aside. His father had told him all about his mother the sorceress, how he had been conceived and born to Gabriel in her captivity. Candaz told Zeth how he had rescued him as an infant boy when his mother had held Zeth as a babe out an open window, high up in the tower and threatened to drop him to the boulders on the ocean shore far below. She was out of her right mind. Candaz let Zeth know that he was responsible for Zeth's life because he had pulled him from the hands of death that day. Zeth still secretly hoped that his mother would take him in her arms and proclaim her love for him. He wanted to meet her, but he was also terrified of that encounter.

The late morning sun was hot on his back as they stood at the door to the tower and activated a spell that would slip the lock open. Candaz chanted softly words that Zeth knew by heart and pried with a long pick at the lock. Zeth leaned casually on the side of the tower watching his father, his hand resting on the leafy green ivy that covered the black marble surface of the structure. Small purple flowers dotted the twisting vine, tiny buds with star shaped pedals and bright yellow centers. As Zeth became more impatient, he began to pluck individual flowers that were within easy reach and crush them between his thumb and forefinger. The crushed flowers gave off a strong floral scent. Reflexively his father's continuous badgering rang in his head, "*Patience, my son, patience.*" He ground another flower to a pulp and let it fall to his feet before reaching for another.

The lock clicked and Candaz pushed the door to the Tower of Ornate open. Cool air rushed out from the opening, brushing seductively against Zeth's hot cheeks. Stepping inside the threshold, he let his eyes adjust to the dark interior. All of the window coverings were drawn, keeping the hot sun from violating the cool interior. It was quiet. Nobody was home. Mixed emotions flooded through Zeth faster than he could sort through them. Disappointment at not being able to meet his mother competed with relief that he would not have to confront her. The part of him that sought violence and bloodshed was dissatisfied, but that displeasure was dulled by a quirk in that he did not really want to murder his mother, did not want her dead, but wanted instead for her to love him.

"This way," Candaz said as he motioned with his arm for Zeth to follow him. They climbed a flight of stairs and quickly searched through the bedrooms before ascending to the third floor. They immediately found a cluttered library, with books and scrolls lining the shelves on the walls and stacked on chairs and on the floor. A plain wooden table stood in the middle of the room. It was clean with the exception of a large book that lay open. Candaz paid no attention to it, but scanned the shelves, up and down, meticulously looking for the volume he sought. It was a leather bound book about the size of a man's hand and had scrolled in a woman's handwriting "Shareen's Spell Book" on the cover. He took his time and went over each and every bound manuscript while Zeth stacked and restacked books as he searched through the piles that were on the floor.

The afternoon came and went but they came up with nothing. Candaz sat down in the chair at the table and sighed heavily. Idly he turned pages of the large book before him. "It is not here. We have only one alternative left, son."

Zeth stood up, stretched his back and turned to his father. "Zedra?"

"Yes. We will travel to the Island of Zedra and see if we can find our answer in the ancient dragon library in the Temple of Neeg. Should that fail us, there is still yet one more legitimate possibility."

"Father?"

"We will capture Skymaster the High Dragon Mage. Surely we can elicit the answers we seek from him," Candaz said.

A spark of excitement ran through Zeth. Now, that would be fun. He had enjoyed using the white she-dragon, but the dragon high mage himself would be entertaining!

Candaz suddenly started reading the text in front of him with avid interest. He turned the page and read some more and then began flipping through it and reading indiscriminately. His voice was pitched high with excitement, "Do you know what this is?! Do you know what this is?!"

"What is it, father?" Zeth asked in annoyance.

"Oh, my boy! This is a find, indeed!" Candaz beamed.

"What is it father?" he asked with a heavy sigh.

The old man hit the book with the palm of his hand and slammed it closed with a wide diabolical grin on his somber face and said, "This, my boy, is the instruction manual to the gate."

"The gate?" Zeth asked. He had heard something about the gate from his father, but knew very little about it. He knew that it was a threshold to other places, but he didn't know where it was located or where it went.

"Yes, the gate! Here," Candaz handed him the heavy and bulky book, "put this in your bag. We can study it on the road to Zedra."

Zeth packed the heavy book away along with the rest of his meager possessions. They left the Tower of Ornate as dusk was settling over the land. They found a tiny fishing boat pulled up on shore that they commandeered and took across the lake. A damp scent on the breeze promised of rain to come. Shouldering both bags, Zeth strode beside his father as they headed west on foot. They walked briskly, with purpose, hoping to put miles behind them before they rested for the night. Zeth was driven by more than just that goal, he was driven by ambition, an ambition that ate at him even while he slept, pushing . . . always pushing to possess the ultimate power. He wouldn't stop until he had it all. Time was running . . . always running. Faster. Faster. Faster. Driving him harder. His father's litany pounded at his brain. *"Patience, my son, patience."* No! *"Patience."* No! *"Patience."* No!

Chapter 6

CASTLE GENTLEBREEZE

Moonlight filtered through the sheer panels that hung over the window, glowing in silver shades down to the plush burgundy carpet on the floor. The prince's room took on a dreamlike quality when drenched in the nighttime glow. The prince, who was in the habit of rising with the sun, could be seen a shadowy figure where he still lingered in his bed. He had been there all day sorting things out in his head. This was not a typical day for him by any means. Since he was old enough to have his own room he had been an early morning riser. This day, however, Nicholas had remained languishing in his room since dawn. Rolling over onto his back on the soft warm sheets, he gazed up at the canopy of white linen that was draped between the high wooden posts and contemplated the future. His stomach growled with hunger, but he resolutely ignored it.

He was well into his seventeenth year and had recently completed his basic curriculum studies and graduated at the top of his class. His father, King Theodore Wingmaster III, wanted to start tutoring him in the intricacies of governing and the art of war. Nicholas shied away from those subjects; not because he didn't want to become king someday, he just felt he wasn't ready to give up totally on his freedom yet. He knew that once he truly started taking on the all of the responsibilities of being the crown prince that it would mean the end of his independence, what little he had left anyway. He wanted to be a boy for a little while longer, although at seventeen, physically he was closer to being a man. An internal struggle existed for him between childhood and manhood and he wasn't sure of the best course to take to avoid the later for as long as he could without incurring the wrath of his father. But, of course, growing up wasn't an issue that could be resolved. Manhood was going to take away his childhood with or without his permission and sooner than he endorsed. His mother and father were quickly losing patience with his lack of focus on the future. When the king was his age he was already in charge of his own squadron, as Nick was frequently reminded. But Nicholas knew that once he went down that road, there would be no turning back. So, he had spent the day in bed fighting with the inevitable.

"Nicky . . . " his older sister Natina walked into the room without knocking, "So, this is where you've been hiding out. Are you feeling all right? Should I call mother? It isn't like you to dawdle all day, not to mention most of the night." Natina looked a lot like her mother, long thick red hair, tall slim figure, but she had her father's bright green eyes. This evening she wore a cream colored gown that was extravagantly trimmed with lace. As always, she looked beautiful. She suddenly blushed prettily, "Oh my. I'm not interrupting anything, am I?"

Nicholas rolled regretfully to the side of the bed, sat up, and stretched his arms over his head. Defined muscles bulged in his shoulders and across his chest and stomach as he moved. He ran a hand through his shaggy blonde hair, combing it carelessly into place. "No, Nati. Everything is fine. Turn your head," Nicholas said, as he watched her focus her bright green eyes on him and smile playfully.

"Oh, don't be bashful, Nicky. I've seen it all before. I used to diaper your bare bottom when you were a baby."

"That was a long time ago, Nati. Now turn around," he ordered.

"Oh, all right," she said. Absently, Natina started picking up discarded clothing from off the floor and folding the items neatly before placing them on the coffee table in the sitting room. The prince's quarters consisted of a large wooden four poster bed that sat on a pedestal at the far end of the room and a sitting area with a couch, two high backed leather chairs and a coffee table near the double door entry. The rich burgundy and gold decor didn't really suit Nicholas's taste, but he didn't spend enough time in the room to bother changing it. When he saw that Natina's back was turned, he padded across the floor in his bare feet and retrieved a soft pair of leather leggings and a dark blue shirt from his wardrobe. He pulled them on and cinched a richly tooled leather belt around his waist.

Natina turned and addressed her brother seriously, "Gabriel and Skymaster are on their way here. Apparently something big is up. Father will expect us all present for the audience. He would not be happy to know you are still in bed at this hour. Goodness, have you really been in bed all this time? Are you sure nothing is wrong? I'm afraid you can't be excused from this meeting, no matter what, dear brother."

Nicholas appraised her shrewdly while he finished adjusting a brown fitted overcoat on his shoulders. He grabbed his brown leather boots and a pair of socks off from the floor, walked over and sat down on the couch. A look of disgust wrinkled Natina's face as Nicholas nonchalantly smelled the socks before he put them on. Ignoring her question, he said, "That isn't the only reason you came to see me, Nati. What is it?" He pulled on his boots and waited for her to respond.

She lowered her eyes demurely before she spoke. "I have information about you that father would want and you have information about me that I would rather be kept from him and mother." She looked up and smiled coyly as she sat with a stiff back in one of the leather chairs. "I know you went to see Grandfather Shane yesterday in Colordale. Although mother would not take you to task for visiting her father, our *father* would not be at all happy about your flying into Colordale to hunt with the old man. You know that father would not understand. He is not a kendrite."

Nicholas's gold eyes flashed for a brief moment with indignation and then softened quickly with amusement. "Tell me if I have this right. You will not tell father about my trip to Colordale if I don't tell mother about the young man you've been-- well, shall we say--seeing. Is that it, sis?"

She tried to read his expression for a moment before she answered, "Yes."

Even though Natina was several years Nicholas's senior, she lacked the common sense that he had in abundance. "Natina, you do realize that you would be disowned from the family should anyone catch you carousing. You *are* a princess. Does a life of servitude sound good to you?" he asked.

Natina's cheeks flushed rosy red. "I assure you, little brother, I take every precaution. You just mind your own business," she said.

Nicholas laughed and said, "And you mind yours, sis . . . and, please, do be careful. I don't want to see you get hurt." Natina stood up, strode to the door, and flashed her sparkling green eyes at him. "I know what I am doing."

Nicholas grinned at her, before replying, "I'm quite sure you do. Oh, and don't worry about me mentioning anything to mother about your little téte à téte." He had never even considered mentioning the subject to either his mother or his father. Nicholas believed in being discreet. If he thought there was cause to worry about someone's actions, he would take up the matter with them personally, not to someone else behind their back. Unlike his sister, Natina, he would never use 'intel' against someone he loved for his own gain. He loved his sister dearly, but was not blind to her character flaws.

Natina's smile was dazzling as she sealed her end of the bargain, "Your hunting trip will be our secret as well. Gabriel should be here soon. Are you coming?"

"I'll be right there. You go ahead." Nicholas sighed as Natina closed the door behind her. He hoped she truly knew what she was doing. Cavorting with the staff was bad enough for the men in the castle and easily frowned upon, but she was a princess and such behavior would not be well received, especially by their mother and father.

Nick had two older sisters, Natina and Nedra. Natina was the younger of the two, and at twenty-three years old, remained single and unattached. Nedra, on the other hand, had a husband, Trevor, and two beautiful children, Bryce, a girl, and Kyle, a boy. As beautiful, if not more so, as her younger sister, Nedra was stable and down-to-earth. Where Natina was more likely to act on her passions, Nedra always thought things through care-fully before taking action. Neither of his sisters had inherited their mother's kendrite power to shape change. They both had their father's green eyes.

Although Nicholas had been born with the kendrite gold eyes, he was surprised when at thirteen, a very late age, he dis-covered that he had inherited the kendrite power. At first he was apprehensive about it. But after a short time and some coaching from his mother, he delighted in the ability, finding it extremely freeing to change at will into a wolf and run fast and sleek, or an eagle and glide endlessly on the breeze. As a dolphin he and his mother had played joyfully among the waves and explored the world beyond the realm of man. Nedra's daughter, Bryce, also had her grandmother's gold eyes and both Jessabelle and Nicholas secretly hoped that she too would someday partake in their kendrite heritage.

Nicholas got up from the couch and left his bedroom, making a quick stop in the kitchen to snatch a bite of left over dinner from Sweeny, their family cook before he made his way to his father's library. The door stood open and a crowd stood just in-side talking quietly, making introductions. *I'm late,* he thought, as he stuffed the rest of a dinner roll into his mouth and entered the room. Gabriel was there along with Rew, as were his mother and father, Natina, Nedra, Kali and Tica, as well as a human girl he had never met before. The girl had a golden, like Tica, who sat silently next to his mistress. She turned to look at him as he walked into the room and he felt something shift deep inside him. Nicholas paused to drink in her features and his knees seemed to grow weak as her sparkling copper brown gaze fell upon him. He felt his cheeks flush under her surveillance and he suddenly grew uncharacteristically flustered. "Excuse me," he said, smiling a crooked and very charming grin that he was completely unaware of, "Sorry I'm late."

Conference

The first glimpse Jesse had gotten of Castle Gentlebreeze was merely a blurred concept of the white stone structure from atop a speeding dragon. They had landed in a stadium of some sort on the grass field behind the castle. Again, Tempest gloated about her victory over Rew until she was insufferable. Jesse, Gabriel, Kali, Rew and the two dogs left the dragons and headed on foot to the gate.

A fairy tale castle couldn't have been more like the towering structure Jesse beheld. Four large towers stood at the corners of a square courtyard, with smaller turrets on both sides of each tower. Standing six stories high was the main building in the center of the courtyard. Long windows ran the entire six story height at architecturally appealing places. Lights lit the windows in an inviting manner. A massive rampart surrounded the entire castle and grounds. A marketplace lined the gravel streets, now deserted because of the late hour. Jesse could smell approaching rain in the air and she shivered reflexively.

Uniformed guards greeted Gabriel with warm hails as they passed through the gate and walked down the street to the main entrance. Once inside, Gabriel announced to the door man that they were there to see the king and asked that his highness be informed at once. They were asked to wait in the library. Gabriel led them there without delay.

King Theo and Queen Jessabelle appeared a short time later holding hands and dressed casually. After embraces by Gabriel, Kali and Rew, Jesse's grandmother introduced Jesse to them. Theo and Jessabelle greeted her warmly. She was also introduced to the princesses Nedra and Natina, who smiled politely, at the same time discreetly examining Jesse's unusual costume. She felt a presence behind her and she turned to find a young man staring at her with bright gold eyes, the shining color of luminescent amber just like the Queen's. He was handsome and although a quality of youth still remained about him, his build and stature were very masculine. A good haircut could do much to tame his appearance, Jesse thought as she suppressed an urge to brush back a stray lock from his face. There was something oddly familiar about him. A crooked grin touched his face that made her forget for a moment everyone else in the room.

"Excuse me," he said, "Sorry I'm late."

"Nicholas, come in," Theo motioned to his son with a wave of his hand. The king casually put his hand on Jesse's shoulder. "This, my son, is Jessica Gates. She is Gabriel's granddaughter. Jesse, Nicholas," he said.

Jesse noticed the subtle heat in Nicholas's cheeks as he took her hand and kissed it with a feather-soft touch of his lips. She felt her heart beat quicken as she looked into his eyes and he said, "I am delighted, Lady Jessica." His gaze seemed to penetrate through to her very soul. She lowered her eyes to keep from melting into his.

With much effort, she fought the feeling of vulnerability. "Your highness," she said simply and slowly took back her hand.

"Why don't we all have a seat?" Jessabelle suggested, indicating for them to retire to the two bulky leather couches in the center of the room. A tray of cheese and crackers and steaming pitcher of spiced wine had been placed on the coffee table along with cups and napkins. Jesse took a seat beside Gabriel. She accepted the cup of spiced wine offered by Jessabelle graciously and enjoyed the warmth it brought.

Gabriel seemed reluctant to start. She stared into her wine for a long moment before she looked up at Theo. "Candaz lives," she finally said.

The king' visage crumbled. Jessabelle gasped.

"That's not possible. He was bleeding to death when the castle came down on top of him," Theo addressed Gabriel. The two of them could have been alone in the room.

"He lives. There is more. My son lives also. He goes by the name of Zeth. Candaz and he are working together," she said.

"To what end?" he asked. "He has nothing left. Saberville has returned to Landtamer rule and has prospered under Serek's guidance. Candaz's authority is gone. Does he still have ambitions to dominate all of Risen?" Theo stood up and began pacing as he waited for Gabriel's answer.

Jessabelle commented with a calm voice that belied the tension that filled the room, "Worse than anything this news is. Time has not eased the evil that he intends you can be sure. A son raised by Candaz cannot be good and could be just as dangerous, or more so than his father."

Jesse could see her grandmother's struggle to maintain a hold on her emotions. As she grasped Gabriel's hand to lend her support, Jesse provided the information that she had recently acquired. "They intend to put the dragons under their control. A she-dragon named Tempest was captured by Candaz and Zeth and tortured unmercifully. They used her as a lab rat to experiment with various potions while they held her in a room protected by magic. She was unable to cry out for help. After her escape, we became friends. I sought out her captors and found Candaz and Zeth. They are looking for a way to enslave the dragons. Apparently, they don't know how to do it . . . not yet. They are seeking information. We think they'll go to the dragon library to get it. We intend to stop them."

Theo raised his eyebrows at this last announcement. His expression softened only slightly when he noticed the serious look on Gabriel's face. "The three of you plan to stand up against the most corrupt sorcerer Risen has ever known--alone."

"Four," Rew corrected.

Theo shook his head, but said nothing. Jessabelle was watching her husband with unspoken words crowding her mouth, but she remained silent as well. Time dragged on. Jesse yawned. It was well past midnight and she was very tired.

Finally, Theo spoke, "Do you really think that this scheme of Candaz's can be successful?"

"There is a spell in Shareen's spell book that would fit the parameters to accomplish just what they intend." Gabriel's expression was grim. "I don't know, though; there is a lot involved in getting all the conditions in place to pull off something that colossal and the dragons lend a whole new variable to what that specific spell anticipates."

"The spell book, where is it?" The question came from Jessabelle.

"It is at Ornate. I had no idea that we were in this kind of danger or I never would have left it there when I went to visit Anna. Peace has reigned for so long that I have let my guard down. We had better move quickly. We'll go to Ornate first and then we'll seek Candaz out." Gabriel's voice was laced with poison as she added, "Personally, I have a score to settle with him," she paused, "and I still have hope for Jon . . . well anyway."

Natina and Nedra exchanged glances that spoke volumes silently to each other. They were well aware of Gabriel's history with Candaz.

Nicholas spoke urgently, "We should leave for the tower immediately. Tomorrow might be too late. The sooner we depart the better."

Spell Dispelled

Rain pelted the ground with force, coming in sheets of bone-drenching moisture. Any attempt to keep dry was futile. Zeth slogged over the saturated ground with mud-caked boots seeming like an apparition. His white skin took on a milky semblance next to his jet black hair. He ground his teeth and looked back to discover his father had fallen even further behind. Why couldn't the old man keep up? Zeth fumed with internal combustion. If they could just make it to the forest's edge, they would have some protection from the accursed rain. At the rate they were going, it would be high-night turn before they could stop and make camp. "Come on, father!" Zeth shouted, although Candaz had no chance of hearing his son's voice through the downpour. The older man struggled to take each step with his old injury aching with renewed vigor in the cold wet chill.

With a deep groan of frustration, Zeth turned and continued his march. His pack was heavy with the addition of the book they had stolen from Ornate and the straps dug painfully into his shoulders. Instead of distressing over the pain, Zeth used it to his advantage to drive him step-by-step forward toward his goal. Keep moving. Just like the gnawing, nagging, ever-present voice in his head that motivated his actions, the pain was something to draw nourishment from to feed his ambition.

As always lately, his thoughts went to Jesse. In Zeth's imagination he envisioned the feel of her skin as he traced her face with his fingertips. The warmth of her breath touched his lips as she brought her mouth up to kiss him. He shivered uncontrollably. Zeth knew he must possess her. He would have her for his own.

Awash in his fantasy, Zeth had slowed his gait. The burning in his blood abruptly ceased as he felt a heavy hand on his shoulder. He knew without turning that it was Candaz. His father's icy presence left no doubt as to his identity. Zeth stopped walking and faced his father, noting without fitting sympathy or concern the drawn and dark markings under the old man's eyes and the blue tint to his lips. After his injury at the hand of that sniveling King Theo, the old man had never fully recovered his good health. Uttering in a voice that was filled with a chilling sonorous power, Candaz said, "I cannot continue at this pace, my son. We must find some transportation soon."

Zeth shrugged the hand off from his shoulder impatiently. "We are almost there, father. If you can just go a little further, we can settle in the forest for the night."

"Yes. I can make it. The forest will offer protection," he agreed.

"Yes and tonight we will summon a dragon. I have an idea that just might work," Zeth said. He saw clearly his father's skepticism and felt his own rage burn fresh. "You don't think I can do it, do you?!"

Candaz turned away from his son and started walking. Zeth followed briskly behind him. The old man said in an even tone, "It is too early. We must know all of the facts. Patience, my son, patience."

In an unprecedented act of rebellion, Zeth turned on his father, "Tonight! Tonight I will summon a dragon, and not just any dragon, but the dragon high mage, Skymaster! You will see. You will see, father." *He will see who is the greatest sorcerer on Risen,* Zeth thought to himself as he turned away from the infinite blackness of his father's gaze.

Finally, they crossed into the sanctuary of the trees. The canopy of the forest absorbed a majority of the heavy downpour although moisture weaved its way down to the floor in the form of a heavy mist. All was quiet. The wind did not rustle the leaves. The mystical lyrics that usually whispered through the forest were mute. Silence. Forest animals huddled in warm, dry dens or had long ago found their beds in private hidden niches out of the rain. The hush seemed unnatural . . . forbidding.

In a clearing, Zeth sat down his pack and started collecting dead fall to make a fire. Everything was wet, but it would not be a problem for a sorcerer of his caliber to start a fire with wet wood. Soon he had a warm blaze flaming and he added branches until the fire roared. Candaz watched his son work with penetrating scrutiny. Zeth was very aware of his father's stare and felt cold sweat trickle down his back as he labored to ignore the old man. He stripped off his heavy cloak and hung it on a nearby limb to dry by the fire. Taking road rations of jerked black deer meat and dried apple slices from his pack, he handed half to his father before finding a seat on a large rock beside the fire. The flames licked his thoughts as he stared into the fiery depths.

The spell he intended to use was complicated and Zeth knew he must clear his mind of all else and concentrate on its content. Candaz chewed on his own private thoughts as Zeth began to gather what he needed from the plentiful forest. He would have to use dry powders that they had brought with them for the items he could not gather fresh. Obviously, he preferred fresh ingredients, but some items were only available in specific areas of Risen. Dragon bane, for instance, grew in abundance around Skyview, but was otherwise nonexistent throughout Risen. The hours just past high-night turn were drenched in darkness and the rain had ceased by the time he was ready to begin.

With great care, Zeth removed a small pot from their gear, positioned it on a flat rock beside the fire and began adding the fresh ingredients he had gathered. First he added water, a precise amount and then fluid from a dragon egg, two leaves from the sour root plant, four leaves from the split leaf tri-pod tree, a male night shade beetle, a pinch of red moss, and eight legs from a live black barbed spider. Zeth had almost been stung by the lethal spider when he had removed the legs, plucking them out one at a time as the spider squirmed in his tight hold. It was necessary that the spider remain alive when removing the legs to stimulate an adrenalin-like substance in the pain-ridden creature and to keep the juices flowing properly into the remaining limbs. After removing the legs, Zeth dropped the rest of the spider to the ground where it would eventually die.

Zeth glanced up at his father as he added the dry powders into the pot and gave it a good stir. Candaz continue to observe his son with the same cold stare and a mask of glossy marble. He hadn't said a word to him since Zeth had announced his intention to summon Skymaster earlier. A dread spread through Zeth that was connected back to some childhood memory long ago hidden from his conscious mind. It was a feeling that instilled a deep fear. The feeling was smothering in its intensity. He gulped down the panic that the fear brought with it and continued his meticulous work. With his back turned to his father, Zeth took the pot in his hands, ignoring the heat that was tangible but not enough to burn his flesh, and poured the simmering contents in a complete circle around the base of his feet. Without further thought he discarded the pot with a careless toss.

A chant arose from the base of his throat, deep and resonant, growing with power as the night dragged on. Calling. Calling. The power that Zeth tapped surged through him with such tremendous force that it made his hair stand on end. The chant changed in cadence, becoming faster and more insistent. As he became one with the deepest, darkest, and most vile of all that is and all that will ever be, Zeth felt whatever might remain that was good within him succumb to corruption. He did not pause to mourn its passing. Still he chanted. Calling. Calling.

In the dark night sky before him a blue cloud of mist began to form, surging and writhing as it grew in front of Zeth. He continued to chant, watching, waiting, and calling for Skymaster to come forth. Candaz rose to his feet and moved one step forward, an expression of surprise and awe dominating his features. Zeth's voice rose in urgency as red swirling eyes came toward him from the center of the cloud, growing larger and brighter with every heartbeat.

Silver scales glinted in the midst of the blue cloud.

Zeth chanted . . . calling.

The cloud was now twenty times larger than Zeth. The swirling mists parted and Skymaster was there. The mighty dragon mage sang out his rage with a furious roar. Flashing teeth bit the air. Long talons shot out and sliced at Zeth, missing him by only inches. Zeth wailed in terror as he felt his face burn with the heat of the dragon's breath. Skymaster's red eyes washed the young sorcerer in savage light. Instead of completing the attack, however, the monstrous dragon abruptly retreated back into the mist. The sound of a base voice echoed heavily in Zeth's mind, seeming to split his head two, "*What have you done? What have you done?*"

Zeth felt his body fall limply to the wet ground. His breathing grew shallow and the world spun wildly around him. He was aware that Candaz came to him. A dry woolen blanket was wrapped around his body. Words were whispered urgently into his ear, but Zeth could not comprehend their meaning. His head was spinning. Around and around the world went. And then everything went black.

Resolution

Jesse felt a sudden tightening in her stomach. She tried to breathe to alleviate the nausea that swept over her but the air seemed too thick to inhale. "There's something wrong," she gasped. Felcore was whining and seemed to be having the same trouble breathing as Jesse. Rew had his hands clamped tightly over his ears. Tears were streaming down the wisp's cheeks. Meanwhile, Theo stood up and ran quickly to the window, where he threw open the sash and cried out loud, "B.F.?"

"What's wrong?" Jessabelle took Jesse's hands in her own, even though Jesse tried unsuccessfully to pull away. She could see the terror in the girl's eyes. "What is it, Jesse?" The Queen turned to Rew, "What is it? What's going on? Theo?"

The pressure on Jesse's chest grew steadily heavier. Her whole body cried out in pain. Tears rushed out of her eyes as she heard in her mind a tremendous bellow. "It's the dragons. Something's wrong," she managed to blurt out.

Theo spun and headed for the door and then stopped and turned toward them. "Gabriel? Do you hear anything?" he asked.

Gabriel didn't answer right away. The expression on her face was far away. After a moment she looked up at him with alarm wrinkling her features. "I can't reach Skymaster or B.F. They are closed to me," she said.

"Good Creator! What has happened? I can't contact B.F. either," he said. Theo came to crouch down in front of Jesse with terror in his eyes. He looked into the girl's tear-streaked face. She caught her breath and examined his bright green eyes that were presently clouded with fear. "Can you tell me what has happened?" he asked.

The nausea was passing and she took deep breaths to steady herself. "The dragons are gone . . . just gone. I don't know. This feeling of horror . . . "

Rew interjected, "Yes, it was corruption at its worst. Whatever it is that has happened to the dragons, I know we must hurry if we are going to help them. We have to go to Zedra immediately. The ancient dragon library may be our only chance to find out what has transpired and put it right."

Jesse heard a voice in her head, *"Jesse! Jesse! Are you there? They are all gone. All the dragons have gone."*

A blankness washed across Jesse's face to those observing as she communicated with the she-dragon, *"Yes, I know, Tempest. You are still here? Are you safe?"*

"I am here and yes I am safe, although I feel rather ill. My stomach hurts. I'm afraid I threw up my dinner," she said.

"Do you know what happened to Skymaster and B.F.?" she asked. Jesse had last seen all three dragons together in the stadium behind the castle.

Tempest answered, *"I do not know. One minute the two big males were here and the next they were not. I heard them scream . . . all of them and then there was only silence. They do not answer me when I call. I'm so afraid."*

"I know. I'll be down in just a little while." She looked up and noticed everybody watching her. "Tempest is still here," she said as her eyes once again filled with tears. "But she doesn't know what happened. She said one minute Skymaster and B.F. were there and the next they were not. Rew is right. We must go immediately."

Theo stood up and started pacing once again. "We must warn Serek and Kristina," he said.

"Breezerunner is gone too. All of the dragons are gone. All except Tempest," Rew stated flatly.

Jessabelle spoke with compassion, "Serek will be sick with worry. Perhaps I should fly to Castle Xandia and tell them what little we know."

Rubbing his chin, Theo said, "No, Jessabelle, I need you here with me. We will send Nicholas to Castle Xandia."

Nicholas immediately stepped forward and addressed his father with a furtive glance at Jesse, "Father, I think I should go with Gabriel and the others. They may need a warrior with them."

Theo replied with an edge of teasing although it was evident he was brimming with pride and affection, "A warrior! Nicholas, you have barely spent an hour a day practicing your sword."

Ignoring his father's manner, Nicholas plowed ahead, "I am very good with a sword, father."

Smiling at his son, Theo said, "Indeed you are. However, I need you to go to Saberville to see your Uncle Serek. You can join up with Gabriel later after you go there and deliver our message. How inconvenient it is not having the dragons to expedite communication."

The thought popped into Jesse's mind, but she kept it to herself, *Yeah, try life without your cell phone.*

Gabriel put a comforting arm around her granddaughter before speaking to Nicholas, "Yes, and without the dragons we will have to go on horseback, so you should be able to join us before we get to Farreach. I don't think it is necessary though, Nick. This is sorcery we're dealing with. I doubt we will have need of a sword arm."

Nicholas was not to be deterred. He said, "I would prefer we opt on the side of caution. After I travel to Saberville I shall join you within a couple of days." He found his eyes once again seeking out the gorgeous foreigner who was busy petting her dog.

Jesse had no idea the young prince was taking such an avid interest in her. She was both emotionally and physically exhausted from the recent attack on her senses. As usual, she took solace in stroking her dog. Besides being deeply concerned about the dragons, a feeling of dread had worked its way into her heart. Dismissing the feeling as just fatigue, Jesse listened silently as plans were made for their coming journey as she lay in the crook of Gabriel's arm.

Heir

After an hour long strategy session the meeting finally broke up. Nicholas slouched on the comfortable leather couch as he watched Jesse leave the room with his sisters, her ever present golden trotting lightly beside her. He wanted to speak to her alone, but Theo had asked him to remain behind so they could talk. There had been a few girls he had taken an interest in over the last few years, but none of them had ever stirred his insides the way this beautiful stranger had. Part of him felt like it was drowning and instinct compelled him to fight to stay above the water line, but another part of him wanted to dive in head first and let the water envelope him, to drown in the wonder of whatever this was. He smiled at himself for being so infatuated; amused that he could even think so seriously about any one girl, but he couldn't seem to shake her from his mind. The draw was so powerful.

Theo walked back into the room and took a seat across from Nick. "Pretty girl, huh?" he asked. The smile on his father's face clearly showed that Nick had not hidden his feelings as well as the young prince would have liked. He scowled at his father's amused expression. With a heavy sigh Theo automatically became serious again and said, "I want you to be extra careful of this man Candaz. He has stayed hidden a long time, but I'm sure his ambition has not waned over the years. Watch over Gabriel. Her emotional ties in this situation may interfere with her better judgment. It's been thirty years since she was kidnapped and forced to have a child by Candaz. At that time the bandergs were enslaved by him. Although I worked to procure their freedom immediately after it occurred, I failed. I failed Gabriel. Father called me back home after the battle at Skyview and ordered me not to pursue her, thinking that she had gone back home. I should have known better. Even though I defied him and looked for her anyway, I gave up much too soon. I should have continued to investigate her disappearance until we found her. There is so much I would have done differently. We were formulating a strategy to free the bandergs from Candaz, but the activity was too slow, leaving the bandergs enslaved for far too long. Meanwhile we were making wedding plans and going on with our lives while she was being held by that scoundrel. Gabriel has forgiven me, but I have many regrets about my actions during that time. I should have followed my heart. Always follow your heart, Nicky. Be careful of Candaz. He's a slippery skunk."

He was not at all surprised by his father's counsel for caution. It was hardly necessary for him to tell Nicholas who they were dealing with. The young prince was very well informed about the events of the past and had excellent instincts. He grinned warmly at Theo and asked, "Is there anything else, father?"

Theo's eyes sparkled and he returned Nicky's grin with a severe countenance. He said, "Just come home safe, son. I wish I could go in your place. Unfortunately, my responsibilities lie here, at least until I wrap up some business that needs to be addressed before I can be freed up. As you know, B.F. is my best friend and I do not intend to take his disappearance lying down.

You can be sure I will do everything in my power to get to the bottom of this."

Getting up off from the couch, Theo walked over to the weapons case in the corner of the room and took out a sword. The shiny blade glimmered as it hit the light. Nicholas had seen the sword many times before. His father always wore the weapon with his full dress uniform. Emeralds embedded in the gold hilt flashed as facets angled toward him. At the age of fifty-eight, Theo, who maintained a strong physical presence, handled the heavy weapon with ease. The green eyes that flashed at Nicholas as Theo turned toward him were brighter than the encrusted emeralds. "This sword was presented to your great grandfather, Theodore II, by your great grandmother, the sorceress Shareen on their wedding day."

He already knew the history of the sword; had indeed heard the story many times before, but he listened to his father with quiet patience.

"An enchantment was put on the sword to seek out and destroy corruption. For more than a generation the magic was nullified, cursed to remain so until the next Sorceress of Brightening laid her hand upon the blade. About thirty years ago Gabriel touched this very blade while standing in her barn in the twenty-third galaxy on the planet known as Earth." As Theo ran his finger down the lightning bolt engraving, a tiny blue spark followed the contact, barely visible to Nicholas where he sat on the couch. "The curse was lifted and the sword's enchantment was restored."

As Theo approached, Nicholas instinctively stood up. A hint of sadness was subtly visible in the tight-woven mask the king wore, evident to Nick only because of the close relationship he shared with his father. The sword rested on Theo's up-turned hands as he raised his eyes and held Nicholas captive with their magnetism. "Take it," he commanded.

Nicholas reached out and brought his hands up next to his father's. His shining gold eyes shifted between Theo's face and the gleaming weapon. Theo let the sword go and the descending weight forced Nick's arms down unexpectedly. For a moment he thought he was going to drop it and humiliate himself in front of the man for whom he had such utter respect. He had never touched the sword before today. It was heavier than he imagined, but he maintained it. The steel felt cold against his skin. He ran his finger carefully up the blade and grasped the hilt firmly. A jolt of blue electricity engulfed his hand and again he almost dropped the weapon. The phenomena lasted only seconds but left his palm tingling slightly. He experimented with the grip, feeling the balance both in his hand and through his back and shoulder muscles. The fit was perfect.

He noticed the look of indulgent pride on his father's face as he lowered the tip of the blade down to the floor. "I will not let you down, father," he said.

Theo came forward and embraced his son in a display of affection that had lately become rare. "I know you won't, Nicky. You have grown into a wonderful young man. As your father and your king, I couldn't be prouder."

Nicholas hoped he could live up to his promise and his father's admiration. He suddenly felt as much a youth full of vulnerabilities as he did a man ready take on the world. In spite of his striving attempt to throw off the chains of royalty and dally in his waning youth, he had accepted a huge responsibility instinctively and maybe foolishly. As he turned to go, the sword felt very burdensome.

Chapter 7

MURDER

A cold cloth was pressed to Zeth's forehead when he awoke. It was morning. The forest was alive once again with the sounds of creatures pursuing their interests, mainly hunting and feasting. The rainy mist had ended late in the night. An occasional "kaplut" could be heard as water drops shook from the tree tops at the whimsy of the wind. The forest felt steamy with humidity. Zeth sat up slowly, feeling the pressure in his head increase with the motion. He winced, but did not lie back down. "Father?"

"I am here. How do you feel?" Candaz asked.

"I'll be all right," he said, finally being able to see his father in the dim light. As soon as he did spot the old man he had to look away. Those eyes. Those dark penetrating eyes bore into him without compassion or love. They were full of power and fervent to consume. As he slid out from under the blanket, he struggled to get up, taking care not to display his weakened condition to Candaz. He felt humiliated and very angry. Accomplishing the spell he intended should have worked and he could not figure out what had gone wrong. Perhaps his father was to blame for his failure.

"My son, the fool! Always impatient. Rush. Rush. Rush. See what your impatience has wrought?" Candaz fumed.

Zeth could feel Candaz's eyes on his back. He recoiled visibly.

"If you had only waited, like I told you to. Stupid fool!" Candaz was pacing in his agitation. Zeth watched him warily from the corner of his eye. This was going to be bad. His father never paced.

"Do you know what you did?" Candaz asked.

Zeth turned to face his father unwillingly and said, "Instead of summoning Skymaster to us, I sent him away . . . and all the rest of the dragons, too. I don't know what went wrong. I don't know where they are and I don't know how to get them back."

"You are a fool!"

With his blood boiling hot with anger, Zeth had a hard time controlling his voice, but years of practice made it possible. "We must continue to Zedra. I will find a way to get the dragons back and I will find a way to put them under our control."

Candaz shook his head in disgust and hissed between clenched teeth, "I see no other alternative."

The rest of the day neither man spoke to the other. Zeth continued seething within, adding more fuel to his ambition. He couldn't figure out what had gone wrong with his spell. It should have worked! Theorizing that if he could make the dragons disappear, he could likewise make them reappear, he continued to stew on the problem. He would find the answer. He would put the dragons under his sole control and make his father bow before him. The old man would have no choice but to fall to his knees and swear his loyalty to his son. Zeth would make the old man respect him. He didn't care if his father chose not to love him. What was love to him, anyway? Love was for fools. Power is what he craved.

The day dragged on as they traversed the forest, heading west toward the coast. In his mind he went over every detail of the previous night. Candaz walked in front of him silently, keeping a steady pace although the progress they made was slow. At this rate they wouldn't reach the ocean until much later in the week. This mode of transportation, namely walking, was intolerable.

Late that night, without having any dinner, he lay down, using his cloak for a pillow and closed his eyes. Visions of grandeur ran through his head. He sat on the throne at Castle Xandia with people all around him. The minions cheered his name and he offered them a smile and a wave of his hand. The prosperity the people enjoyed was all due to him. The miniscule taxation he imposed on them was nothing compared to the good life he had brought them. Life was good! He envisioned himself flying dragon-back with Jesse behind him with her arms wrapped tightly around his waist. They would soar over the land, his land, all of it. Zeth sighed as he enjoyed his fantasy. The cloud of euphoria was burst suddenly, however, when his father's angry words ran through his head like a speeding train, "Fool! *Stupid fool!*"

They started out the next morning heading west through the forest, again avoiding conversation. Before the morning sun had dissipated the dew from the ground, they came across three travelers on horseback, trappers by the looks of them. Making up a feeble story, Candaz and Zeth stopped the men and asked for their help. Although the three men were wary and their horses pranced about nervously, they dismounted and offered their assistance to the decrepit old man and his son. Once on the ground, Candaz made easy prey of them. A skillful killer, he brought his sword forth and struck quickly and without warning or mercy. The trappers didn't stand a chance against the powerful sorcerer's blade.

The first man's throat was cut and he was still falling to the ground as the flying blade drove through the second man's heart. Before the third man could react, the sword was turned on him and sliced a lethal gash between his shoulder and neck. He collapsed in a pile of flesh and quickly breathed his last. Candaz smiled as he wiped his blade clean on the first man's clothes.

With fascination, Zeth watched his father work. The old man seemed to move with uncharacteristic ease as he murdered the men. Blood soaked the ground around the victims as it left their bodies. Their eyes stared in surprise. He suppressed an uncomfortable urge to laugh out loud at the bizarre expressions on their faces.

It wasn't an honorable end for three hard working men. They were honest men who trapped animals for their furs to make a meager living in order to keep their wives and children fed. Their families would never see them again or know what had become of them.

Zeth claimed the dapple gray mare, throwing the dead man's baggage on the ground next to the corpse and securing his own travel bag to the saddle. Candaz mounted a chestnut colored gelding, using his sword to cut away a bundle of neatly gathered furs before securing his own gear. Although Zeth was hoping to find some food in their packs, a quick survey of the men's possessions showed nothing worth keeping. They rode off, leaving the three dead men lying in pools of their own blood.

Following the narrow path through the forest, they slowed only when thick foliage demanded it. Zeth felt his stomach rumbling with hunger. It had been a couple days since he had eaten anything of substance. He kept his eyes on the lookout for any game as he rode. When Candaz's horse scared some wild chickens out from a patch a brush, Zeth was quick to skewer two of them with his sword. They would eat well that night. His mouth watered with anticipation.

He was beginning to feel better, regaining some of his light-hearted disposition. He thought of Jesse as he rode and hummed along to a tune his father had taught him years ago. They found a hidden spot behind a rocky outcropping to camp for the night and soon had a fire burning and the chickens roasting on a spit over it.

The two men said little to each other that night and Zeth enjoyed being lost in his own thoughts of what he was going to make of himself. He let the images comfort him like a soft blanket. The angry nagging that constantly assaulted him, however, could still be heard in the background of his mind. *"Fool! Stupid Fool!"* He imagined himself touching Jesse's soft skin. *"Patience, my son, patience."* His lips met hers tenderly. *"Fool!"* His kiss became ferocious. *"Patience!"* His hand came across her face in a slap of pain and gratification. He would have everything he ever wanted. Jesse would be his queen and his father would be his crony. The future was his to command.

The Price Of Disobedience

He wanted to vent his rage at his son. How could the boy be so stupid? He had warned him but the boy did not listen. The dragons were lost. To where? How? The answers were not available. The anger that was building within him was about to explode. The heir that he wanted was turning out to be his bane. It was all Gabriel's fault. He never should have chosen her to be the mother of his child. Zeth was powerful. That much was certain. How powerful, he did not know. That was yet to be established. He was also very smart, but the choices he made were questionable. The boy tended to act emotionally instead of logically and the results were evident. The dragons were lost. The Temple of Neeg may hold the answers he needed to get the dragons back and to put them under his direct control. He knew it held many secrets and the knowledge of all the dragon mages throughout time. Dragons were creatures of magic and they were very difficult to comprehend. What the dragons may consider relevant may not hold any relevance at all. He hoped they would find what they needed, but he had his reservations.

His men had recently visited the Island of Zedra and brought him home his little treasure from the egg laying grounds. The egg remained preserved by freecurrent until the time he could use it. The time would come when it would be very useful, maybe even change everything. He could wait.

Another option that still remained a possibility was the book. There was a very ancient manuscript he once had in his possession that could have the answers they needed. If the library did not prove worthy they would have to go north to Saberville--to the catacombs.

A shiver ran through him as he thought of the men he had left for dead along the trail. He marveled at how easy it was to murder again. It actually felt good to exercise the compulsion to kill. The pleasure it gave him surpassed anything he had experienced for a very long time. His fingers ran the length of his sword and he could feel the corruption that remained infused into the steel of the weapon. He smiled. He was starting to feel alive again.

Chapter 8
RESOLUTE ACTION

Water droplets ran efficiently from Nicholas's well groomed golden-brown feathers. Rain shot into his eyes and his beak, however, making flying somewhat uncomfortable. He shook excess water off his head and sighted far down below to get his bearings. The Standing River glimmered as it snaked its way north directly under him. The landmark told him that he would be at Castle Xandia within a couple of hours.

He was looking forward to seeing his Uncle Serek and Aunt Kristina. The last time they had met was at Festival earlier that year in the spring season. Nick had visited Castle Xandia as a child many times, some times for as long three months, spending summers with his cousins. During his visits he had become very close to his aunt and uncle and two of their four children. They had two boys and two girls. The older two were Treves and Laurel, a boy and girl respectively. They had long ago married, moved out of the castle, and now had children of their own. Treves would become the heir to the throne of Saberville someday, but for now Serek allowed him to follow his own pursuits. Kristina and Serek's youngest son was only a couple of years older than Nicholas. His name was Stephan and the two of them were more like brothers than cousins.

Stephan's little sister Katia, or Kate as she was called was a year younger than Nicholas and had always followed him around like a puppy. Although sometimes it was annoying to Stephan, Nicholas enjoyed her company, finding her both intelligent and easy to talk to. The three of them were easy friends.

It was nearing dusk as the towers of Castle Xandia became visible up ahead. Nicholas had departed Castle Gentlebreeze almost immediately after leaving his father's library and flown the rest of the night before taking a much needed rest early in the morning, but only a short one. It took him the remainder of the day with as few breaks as possible to make it to Castle Xandia. He was lucky for the good south wind that helped him on his way or the trip could have been much longer and harder. Usually the journey north took him a couple of days of dedicated flying. He had made good time.

Before setting off he had only stopped to pack a few essentials and kiss his mother goodbye. The rain had begun in earnest as he stood on the balcony and shape changed into a golden eagle. His sharp senses picked up the scent of dragon musk and he had soared down and around to the back of the castle where he caught sight of the beautiful white she-dragon that had bonded with Jesse. And, sure enough, there was the girl and her golden standing out of the rain, under the protection of the dragon's large head. He had trilled twice, caught their attention, circled one more time bathed in the light of her eyes and flew away. Why had this particular girl moved him so profoundly? He couldn't answer that question, but knew it to be true. With the rain, the ocean took on a gray and forbidding tone as Castle Xandia rose up from the rocky shoreline, a gray stone building against the gray shore. Gray on gray. A series of three towers, one large and two small, jutted up from the rocks and pointed to the sky. In Candaz's time the castle had been destroyed. Since then, however, years of labor had restored the structure to its original form. Nicholas flew to the highest tower and went directly to the third window sill from the top that faced directly over the ocean. He landed on the sill, adjusted his wings on his back, and used his beak to tap on the window. "Tap Tap . . . Tap. Tap. Tap . . . Tap Tap."

A young man approached the window dressed in black leggings and a dark red military jacket, tailored to fit squarely on his broad shoulders and taper down to his slim waist where it was belted with a black and gold belt. A sash of gold and silver was draped from his left shoulder to his right hip, indicating his royal rank. He unhooked a latch and let his feathered guest in. "Nicky . . . what are you doing here?" he asked.

Shaking the rain off from his feathers, Nicholas began to shape change back into a man before Stephan's eyes. An amused grin cracked Stephan's handsome face when he saw that Nicholas, now a man, fully dressed and soaked clean through to the skin. A large puddle of water began to form around the young man.

"How about a towel?" Nicholas asked sardonically.

"No thanks, I'm fine, *dry* as a bone," Stephan replied as his grin broadened. "You're dripping on my floor." He amused himself at his cousin's expense for a few seconds more before going into the next room to get him a towel. He threw it to Nick from across the room and then sat down in a chair next to the bathroom door. The two young men couldn't have looked less alike. Nicholas had blond hair and gold eyes. Stephan had dark brown hair and blue eyes. Nicholas stood about six inches taller than Stephan, but Stephan was wider with shoulders like a linebacker and thighs like a running back. Other than that, they both tended after their fathers' features.

Undoing the clasp on his belly released the sword that was sheathed and strapped to Nicholas's back. He threw the heavy weapon onto the bed, where it bounced once before settling into the mattress. He spoke to Stephan in an earnest voice, "You know that the dragons have disappeared?"

"Yes. Of course. Do you know what's happened?" he asked.

"No. But, Candaz is back and he most likely has something to do with it. Candaz's son kidnapped a she-dragon named Tempest with the intention of finding out how he could gain control over the entire dragon population." After stripping off all of his wet cloths, Nicholas toweled himself dry and mopped up the unsightly puddle on the floor with his already wet towel, which he threw at Stephan who caught it deftly and threw it back. It fell wetly on the floor at Nick's feet.

"That sounds crazy," Stephan said.

"Yeah. But, Gabriel's granddaughter, Jesse, bonded with the she-dragon and when she went to find out who had tortured her dragon, she found Candaz and this other guy, Zeth." He hung up items of clothing at various likely locations around the room. Rubbing his arms from the cold, Nicholas asked, "Do you have something I can wear?"

"Gabriel's granddaughter?" Stephan got up slowly from the chair and went to a wardrobe, where he selected several items of clothing and handed them to Nicholas. "I want these back."

"Of course," Nick said.

"Except the socks," Stephan emphasized.

Nicholas rolled his eyes and started dressing. The attire Stephan had handed him was casual dress, very much in style for young men around Saberville. Subtle brown hues overlapped one another as each piece was layered, socks, baggy pants, under shirt, over shirt, vest, jacket, and belt.

Nicholas continued, "Gabriel, Jesse, Rew and Kali--Anna's niece, are on their way to the Island of Zedra to find Candaz and his son. They have the white she-dragon with them and two golden hunting dogs." The larger man's clothes hung loosely on Nicholas, except the baggy pants weren't so baggy because of Nick's extra height. They came up a little short at the ankle, but after he pulled on his boots it wasn't noticeable.

"Now, wait a minute. I thought all of the dragons were missing," Stephan said.

"Not Jesse's dragon. For some reason she wasn't taken," Nicholas said.

"Jesse is Gabriel's granddaughter?" Stephan asked.

"Keep up!" Nicholas chided as he retrieved his sword from the bed and strapped it on.

The serious expression on Stephan's face softened and his blue eyes sparkled suddenly. "What is this girl like? Is she pretty?" he asked.

Nicholas felt a rush of jealousy that he definitely thought was out of place, but could not be suppressed. "I guess," he answered vaguely, avoiding his cousin's eyes.

"She is, isn't she? And, you have a crush on her. I get it now," Stephan started laughing, banging his thighs with his hands as he doubled over. "It is written all over you face. Her, I have to see."

The playful appeal in Stephan's eyes made Nick all the more rankled. "I came here to talk to Uncle Serek and Aunt Kristina about the dragons and what we plan to do about it," he said, immediately trying to get back to the main subject.

Stephan's eyes were still alight with the fire of amusement. He walked over, clapped Nicholas on the shoulder and led him to the door. "Come on, I was just on my way to join them for dinner. They will be happy to see you, Nick. Kate and I were just talking about you yesterday and she mentioned how much she missed you . . . "

Trail Ride

"It's called rock and roll," Jesse told Kali, whose face was pinched together as the banderg girl listened to the ear buds she had finally managed to position correctly in her ears. A thin cord ran from the headset and attached to the MP3 player clipped to her belt. Jesse was pleased and amused when she discovered that the freecurrent energy she channeled was able to recharge her MP3 player. She wondered if it would work on her cell phone. Oh, how she missed her cell phone!

Kali's face grew confused as she looked questioningly at Jesse.

"Rock and roll," Jesse said more loudly. Her horse whinnied and shook its head. Jesse patted the white mare on the neck to apologize for being so resonant and waved her hand in the air indicating for Kali to "never mind".

They were traveling toward the Tower of Ornate on horses Theo had provided to them for the trip. Moving along the grassy shore of the Blue Lake as they rode south, Jesse watched the rain falling into the water, causing little spirals to form. It had been raining all day and she was weary of it, but the gray sky showed no sign of a break. They had a long way to go and the horses could not go as fast as a dragon on wing. She had gotten quite a tirade from Tempest when she had told the dragon they were going to stay with the rest of the group, which meant walking. Every so often the white dragon, who remained a short distance apart, would let Jesse know again what she thought of this ridiculous mode of transportation.

Kali removed the ear buds and said to Jesse, "It's noisy, but I think I like it. What did you call it, again?"

"It's called rock and roll," Jesse said.

"Hmm," was all Kali said as she placed the ear buds back in and moved her head to the beat of the music.

Jesse smiled at the banderg and kicked her horse to make it catch up with Gabriel and Rew, who were sharing a horse. "How far do we have to go, Grandmother?" she asked.

"At this rate it should take us another day to reach Ornate." Irritation was evident in Gabriel's tone.

"Tempest shares your frustration," Jesse said, smiling.

Gabriel laughed, "Yes, she has not been shy about letting me know her opinion on the matter."

"She thinks horses are to be eaten, not ridden. I assured her that King Theo would not be happy if she snacked on his favorite breed of pony. Things would be much easier if Tempest was a vegetarian."

This caused her grandmother to laugh again, "Yes, much easier."

They rode in silence for a while, when Gabriel said, "I don't understand how this could have happened to the dragons. If they are under some type of a spell, I would think we would still be able to communicate with them. Tempest says they just disappeared without a word or a sound. The question also remains as to why was she spared out of all of them?"

"Wisp magic saved Tempest," Rew surprised Jesse with his disclosure. He went on, "Jesse used wisp magic to heal Tempest back in the cave. That act bonded Jesse to the dragon and Tempest to Jesse more strongly than any normal human-dragon bond. When the corrupt magic took the dragons, Tempest had the authority to deny that power because of her bond to Jesse. It was a simple reflex on her part, an involuntary action like pulling your hand away from a hot flame."

"*The dragons are alive. I can feel them like I can feel the moonlight on my face. I can't locate them. But, I can feel them, in a slight 'snowflake on your tongue' kind of way.*" Tempest commented as she lifted her head and was about to bellow loudly.

Jesse stopped her quickly by saying, "*Don't! The horses will bolt.*"

"*But the other dragons might be able to hear me,*" Tempest protested.

"*Have you tried to communicate with them?*" Jesse asked.

"*Yes, many times,*" she answered.

"*And?*"

"*Nothing, but I know they are alive like I know that tree over there is alive. I can't hear them, Jesse, but I can feel them in my spirit. I fear for them all. They are afraid,*" she said.

Jesse could feel Tempest's deep concern. "*We will get them back, Tempest. I promise to do everything in my power to get them back,*" she told the dragon.

"*They were never my friends, but I would be lonely without them,*" Tempest said.

"*We will find them,*" Jesse promised again.

To Gabriel and Rew she said, "We know from Tempest that the dragons are still alive. Also we know that Candaz and Zeth intended to enslave them. If they were successful and they're still here somewhere, I would think that we would still be able to communicate with them. Unless . . . When Tempest was being kept hostage, she was unable to communicate with the other dragons, just like Gabriel couldn't communicate mentally when she was being held hostage by Candaz. A spell prevented them. So they could be here but unable to communicate for whatever reason. Let's assume that their attempt went terribly wrong and something happened to the dragons during the spell that was unexpected. Perhaps instead of enslaving the dragons they vanquished them. But to where? Where does one keep a wing of very large dragons? What if they were sent through the gate? If the dragons were transported somewhere through the gate would we still be able to talk with them?"

Gabriel deferred to Rew on the subject of the gate. He replied, "I guess that would depend entirely on where they went. More than likely we would not be able to communicate with them through the gate. It is very complicated involving the alignment of time, place, proximity and the intimacy of one's relationship with the person or in this case dragon one wishes to communicate with. Gabriel had success once using the sight water contacting her sister back home, but it was a dangerous attempt and could have left one or both of them with brain damage. I, of course, used the sight water to see through Felcore's eyes, but I am a wisp and he is a dog. My best guess is that if communication was possible, the dragons would have already spoken with us. But, using sight water *might* produce results. It's worth a try, anyway. The wisps of Elysia would know if a wing of dragons passed through the gate. Perhaps I should fly home to check with the wisps and see if they know anything about the dragons' disappearances."

Gabriel's face was speculative, "That might be well advised, Rew. Let's get to the tower first to see if there are any clues there."

On the third day out they arrived at the Tower of Ornate by mid-morning. Tempest and Rew were already there waiting when the rest of the party approached the tower. The two winged creatures had finally had enough dawdling and wanted to exercise their wings. Rew challenged Tempest once again to a race, obviously hoping to get the best of the dragon this time. As the rest of the party arrived, Jesse could hear Tempest before she could see the beautiful white dragon. *"I beat him again, Jesse. I am the champion!"* "RRAAAAHGRRRRR!"

Rew was in front of the door with a grim expression on his normally bright face. Jesse didn't think it was because the wisp had lost the race. Gabriel indicated that she knew something was wrong. "I can feel it", she told Jesse as they dismounted the white mares, leaving the horses to wander at leisure on the grassy plain. Jesse could sense it too. The extra awareness she had acquired on Elysia had not diminished at all, although she was becoming accustomed to it. Felcore and Tica sniffed around, blowing and snorting from rain-diluted scents. The bolt lock had been tampered with. Scrapes and scratches covered the antique brass all over. She noticed the lock was American made. Gabriel must have brought it with her when she had moved to Risen some years ago. Her grandmother confirmed the assumption, "This lock was one of the items I brought with me to Risen when I moved here permanently. Now it is ruined." She pulled on the door and it swung open.

"Look at this," Kali said, bending over and picking up something from the porch. They looked down into her palm at small crumpled purple blossoms. She dropped the purple balls into Jesse's outstretched hand.

She knew who had destroyed the flowers. "Candaz and Zeth were here. Not too long ago . . . three days maybe," Jesse told them.

They all looked at her remarkably. "Wisp magic," Rew stated simply as his bright blue eyes appraised Jesse with fondness.

"I was afraid of this." Gabriel said as she ran into the tower and immediately ascended the stairs. The rest of them followed her. She stopped first in her bedroom. The bed was made. Everything seemed to be where is belonged. Pictures of family lined the walls, Bill and Marguerite, Jesse, Jacob and a man who Jesse knew only from pictures of her own as Gabriel's deceased husband, John. Other pictures were displayed of people Jesse recognized as her cousin, Jon, and her Uncle Peter and Aunt Cindy. She wondered how her grandmother had come by the pictures of herself and Jacob, which were of them as babies and every year since, up until her senior picture which had just recently been taken this summer. Gabriel went to the bed stand and pushed a little button in the back. From the side of the small table opened a hidden drawer from which she took out a leather bound book. "Thank God," she whispered as she stuffed the spell book into the pocket of her riding cloths and left the room.

When they entered the library Jesse again sensed that it had been invaded. Felcore barked, telling Jesse in his own way that he felt the same. Gabriel immediately went to the plain wooden table in the center of the room and ran her finger over the vacant top. She scanned the shelves and the floor, but her eyes came to rest back on the empty table. Kali and Tica entered the room as Gabriel looked up at them. Her eyes were consuming as she said, "They took the instruction manual to the gate. We must get it back."

"The wisps' book?" Jesse asked as she came over to her grandmother and grasped her hand, getting her attention. "The instruction manual to the gate belongs to the wisps. It should be returned to Elysia. Now it is gone?"

Rew looked shocked, "I don't understand. We have a document called the 'App Endix.' I have read it. You have read it. There is no other book."

Jesse explained to Rew, "The 'Appendix' is only a portion of the book. You see, an appendix comes at the end of a book and tells you where to find things in the main body of the book.

Somehow, that one page was removed at one time or another and left on Elysia, while the main book was taken elsewhere . . . here, apparently. Now it is in their hands. This is terrible. We must get it back!"

"Oh my!" Rew said. "Oh my! We have to get the book back and return it to Elysia!" Rew spun around in agitation and then turned to face them, his eyes imploring them to do something.

Gabriel slammed her palm against the empty table top and said, "Let me get some things that I need and then we can go." She started out of the room, but turned quickly. "Wait," she said, "I want to check the sight water to see if I can reach Skymaster or B.F."

Jesse watched her grandmother ascend the stairs and disappear into the room on the top floor. She hesitated and then followed. Gabriel acknowledged her presence only briefly as she sat down at the table of water. She extended her hand and let her fingers rest gently on the surface. Jesse stood in the doorway and observed her grandmother go into a trance-like state. It lasted only for a brief period before Gabriel removed her hand and turned to Jesse. "I'm getting nothing," she said. "Maybe fear, but I can't isolate the feelings from my own."

They descended to the kitchen and joined the others for lunch. Even though they felt the need for expedience, Rew insisted that they break for lunch before they resumed their trek. Gabriel's pantry was sorely lacking in supplies, but a hungry wisp and a banderg together can easily manage to work around such obstacles. Within the hour they were well fed, cleaned up and back on their horses heading west.

Cousins

Nicholas looked back at Stephan who sat astride a shiny black stallion and wagged his tail. They had been traveling all day and Nick's pads were caked with mud. It had stopped raining late the night before, but the ground was saturated and the sun hadn't had a chance to dry things out yet. He had kept them on a path heading straight south of Castle Xandia, scouting ahead of Stephan. They had covered a lot of ground and he hoped they could rendezvous with Gabriel and the others within a couple of days.

Stephan reined in his horse beside the rust colored wolf and swung his leg over the saddle, coming to land firmly on the ground next to the big stallion. He patted the horse and turned to his cousin. "Do you want some water, Nicky?"

"Rrupp."

Taking a small cup from his leather pack, Stephan poured it full of cool, clean water and offered the cup to Nicholas, holding it in front of the wolf's nose. He lapped up the water greedily. "Rrupp."

"You're welcome," Stephan said as he poured himself of cup and drank it all down as well. "Conversation with you certainly improves when you're a wolf."

Nick showed his considerable teeth and growled.

They continued on the trail until after dusk, breaking only one more time before making camp for the night. As they sat around the camp fire and sipped on cups of banderg tog, Nicholas talked confidentially to Stephan about things that were on his mind. "Father wants me to learn how to run the government and become proficient at the art of war. I'm only seventeen. What's wrong with growing up first?"

Stephan smiled tolerantly at Nick before he took a sip of his tog. It wasn't the first time he had heard this complaint from his younger cousin. "You'll be eighteen this summer, right? When I was seventeen I was in charge of my own company of troops. It's important that you learn how to lead men, Nick. Like it or not, it is the position you were born into. It is your responsibility. Uncle Theo only wants to make sure you are ready in case something happens to him and Aunt Jessabelle. You wouldn't want to take charge and because of lack of knowledge undo everything they have worked so hard for all these years, would you?"

"Of course not. I know all of that and I am not bemoaning my lot in life. I appreciate the opportunity I've been given. I'm just afraid I'm not ready yet," Nicholas responded.

"Of course you're not ready. That's the point. Experience is the only way for a man to grow into a man. Some things that your father can teach you could be invaluable and save you some trouble in the process, but mostly you have to gain your own knowledge. I understand why you're fighting against growing up, but believe it or not you already have the worst part of it behind you. Relax, Nick. It's not like you have to become king overnight . . . not unless something happens to both Uncle Theo and Aunt Jessabelle . . . and hopefully that won't happen any time soon. There's really nothing to be afraid of. Being an adult does have *some* benefits," Stephan said as he gave Nicholas a knowing wink.

"I don't have any choice, do I?" Nicholas gave his cousin a resigned sigh.

"'Fraid not, cous." Stephan leaned forward and took on a conspiratorial tone. "Now that that matter is settled, tell me more about Jesse."

Nicholas groaned and rolled his eyes. He stood up, threw the rest of his tog into the fire and said, "I'm going to bed. Good night, *cous.*"

"What? What did I say?" Stephan exclaimed.

"Good night," Nicholas replied with finality.

Chapter 9

EMPTINESS

The air felt like ice crystals in the form of gas in stillness that was as absolute as the blackness enveloping Skymaster. He stretched his long neck up and scented the darkness with his massive and ultra-sensitive nostrils, picking up nothing more than a faint trace of dragon bane that was a remnant of the magic that had sent them to this place. The bands of light that shot out from his swirling red eyes illuminated infinitely the inky, endless void that surrounded him. The high dragon mage extended his wings and launched his bulk into the air, stroking and soaring through the cold nothingness until his breath became heavy from the labor and yet he went nowhere. Baffled, Skymaster settled once again on the surface below him. *What is this place?*

His fellow dragons were nearby. He could feel them. An inside knowing that was similar to the tingle of "knowing" someone has their eyes upon you and turning to look to find that very fact to be the case. Seeing the others, however, was impossible as was hearing them or smelling them. It occurred to Skymaster that his kin were stuck in the same kind of abyss in which he found himself so maddeningly entrenched. Their fear was oozing through the thick blackness to stab at him with daggers of panic. He trumpeted, hoping to be heard by the others and perhaps lend some comfort. The roar of his own voice sounded dull in his ears as it was muted by the nothingness.

Skymaster's dread increased along with his frustration. Again, he launched himself into the blackness and flew, this time in an ever widening circle, again getting nowhere. Getting out of wherever he was became more than urgent as he thrashed and fought against the unseen boundary. His exertions did nothing but increase his fatigue. Drained for the moment, Skymaster rested once more.

He suddenly remembered that it had been egg laying season during the last moon phase. The eggs couldn't survive in this cold place, and if they had been left behind in the warm sands of the dragon caves, they couldn't survive without proper care. The eggs had to be turned at least every few days or they would cook from the heat. Either way, too much cold or too much heat, the embryos could not survive. Grief gripped him and tore at his heart with steely talons. Skymaster bellowed his rage into the emptiness helplessly.

The face of the sorcerer who had wrought this predicament was clear in Skymaster's mind. Copper brown eyes resembling Gabriel's had been visible for just a short moment through the fog just before he was transported to this place. Yet, those eyes were cold and hateful unlike his mistress's own. The human had been attempting a spell that had been spoiled and mutated from its original intent. The remembrance of the power behind the spell formed a nauseous knot in the pit of Skymaster's belly. A swirling, double-vision had rolled and leapt with a cacophony of sounds and images before a flash of light preceded the plunge into darkness. It seemed to Skymaster almost as if he and his fellow dragons had been thrust into an alternate dimension, a place parallel, but yet hidden from the dimension in which they had lived all of their lives. It was cold and dark and lacking in life.

He pondered this for some time, hoping to find an answer hidden within the folds of logic and finding none. Skymaster knew he would have to try something soon. Inaction would kill them all. A dragon can only go so long without food or water and neither was available in the depths of this void.

Resurrection

Zeth was awakened abruptly by the howling of wolves. The fire had died out completely, leaving only the light of the first moon to see by. He knew that the night was only half through from the position of the quarter moon high in the sky and the absence of the second moon, altogether, the latter having not yet risen. Nearby the horses shuffled and snorted in agitation as they pulled against their tethers. Throwing off the blanket, Zeth rose to his feet and scanned the thick forest surrounding them. Glowing eyes looked back at him hungrily. Moving with caution, Zeth walked over to where his father slept, kicked the old man lightly in the side and whispered urgently, "Father, wake up."

Candaz grunted, glared up at his son and asked, "What is it?"

"Wolves."

The old sorcerer sat up slowly and said, "Start the fire. They won't come near it."

With his eyes on the glowing points of light that watched him from the cover of the trees, Zeth piled wood onto the cold ashes and ignited it with a freecurrent spark. The flames leapt quickly to life, adding their warmth and radiance to the pale moon light. He wrapped his cloak tighter around himself and crouched down beside fire. His wary eyes scanned the forest again, making out motion in the underbrush as the wolves moved to surround them.

The sound of his father's voice startled him. It was low and haunting, "They know me. Many years ago I corrupted a pack of wolves to use in the war against Brightening. Somehow, they know me. We are in great danger." Candaz threw his blanket around his shoulders and moved closer to the fire.

Zeth remembered the story his father had told him about the creation of the monsters he had named 'warwolves.' During Candaz's reign in Saberville, during the war between the Sabers and the Brights, Candaz used his corrupt power to mutate a pack of wolves into hideous killers, driven by blood lust to seek death and destruction as they ran wild across the land. The warwolves had long ago died off and could no longer be seen ravaging the countryside. It had been many years since warwolves roamed the land.

Zeth scoffed discernibly at his father's paranoia, "They couldn't possibly *know* you . . . that's impossible!"

Candaz's angry voice sliced through the tension of the night, "Even though you are a grown man, you are still a foolish boy! You will never be as powerful as me if you do not learn to listen!"

Hatred burned behind Zeth's eyes as he hid his rage behind a mask of submission. The old man had no right to degrade him. Zeth knew he was more powerful than his father could ever hope to be. He would show the old man. His time would come soon.

"Patience," he heard his father's grating voice inside his head. Zeth would show him patience. An idea tore through Zeth's mind and he sprang up to his feet from the mere attraction of it. The wolves cloaked in the blackness of the forest reacted to the movement with fierce growls of malice. Arrogantly, Zeth picked up a rock and tossed it at one of them, smacking the nose and making the animal let out a "yipe!" of pain.

"What are you doing boy?!" Candaz asked. The fear that crept into his voice made a tingle of pleasure run down Zeth's spine.

He picked up another rock and aimed it between two glowing red eyes. The animal sensed Zeth's intent and deepened its growl. Taking his time, Zeth let the rock fly. It met its mark causing another sharp "yipe!"

"Stop it you fool!" Candaz grabbed Zeth's shoulder and spun him around.

Zeth pulled easily away from his father's grasp and crouched down to the ground. The smile on his face clearly showed the madness his father had just accused him of. "Watch this, old man," he said.

Taking a burning stick from the fire, Zeth began drawing an intricate pattern on the ground before him. The rune was complicated and Candaz watched with fascination as his son correctly drew each spiral, line, zig and zag. Zeth had the uncanny ability to remember such things with exact detail after having seen it only once. He knew his father had always been jealous of him because of this ability. His genius would someday earn him great power and Zeth relished the thought of what that would do to the old man. The drawing finished, he tossed the smoking stick back into the fire.

"Don't do this, Zeth. I warn you, don't do this!" he growled. Candaz's face was infused with anger, dark and terrible in its sincerity.

"A rune drawn with fire must be quenched with blood," Zeth quoted from the spell book Candaz had compiled for his son's use many years ago. Zeth knew it by heart. He took out his knife and made a vertical cut down his forearm. Blood escaped from the self-inflicted wound and ran down his arm to his hand and dripped from outstretched fingertips. As the drops of blood splattered on the rune, the pattern began to burn like flowing lava. Hastily, Zeth wrapped a piece of cloth ripped from his shirt around his arm and shot his passion inflamed eyes into the forest.

A wolf with a thick gray coat walked slowly toward them out of the thicket. It was the dominant male from the pack, but he struggled to maintain his proud demeanor. His lope was hesitant and jerky as he fought against the magic that compelled him. The large head hung low and a vicious growl persisted in the back of his throat. His lips were curled back revealing long fangs and his ears were laid back flat against his head. He watched Zeth with sharp eyes as he approached with reluctance. An unseen force possessed the wolf to move forward one step at a time.

"Come on you big brute. Come on," Zeth persuaded the wolf to him with a soothing voice and a hand motion.

As the gray wolf drew closer a whimper replaced the growl.

"Oh, you are a tough one, aren't you?" Zeth said. A condescending tone overshadowed Zeth's previous soothing manner as he mocked the wolf. He poised his knife in the air above the head of his intended victim.

"Zeth, you must not continue this spell. It does nothing to further our cause. What do you intend by it?" Candaz's voice sounded far away to Zeth. He ignored the old man and brought the knife down, slicing across the wolf's throat with a quick slash.

The dying animal was strangely silent as life left its body in gentle tremors of death. His once bright eyes faded to gray. Drenching his hands in the warm blood that spilled from the wolf's throat, Zeth sprinkled it onto the fiery rune. Wet blood hitting the fire spit and spitted. It flared brighter. A vapor rose, black and oily, growing and taking on its own ether life. Snake-like, it wound up into the air, flowing from the rune on the ground. Up and out it went, dividing into many different tendrils as it undulated beguilingly.

Zeth watched in fascination as the vapor trails wound their way closer and closer to the forest where the pack of wolves paced anxiously. The writhing poison reached one wolf and innocently entered through its nostrils. All the other wolves were likewise delicately assaulted by the vapor. Within seconds howls rang out in horror and the once majestic animals began to change.

As the howls of terror turned in to wails of pain, Candaz grabbed hold of Zeth and spun him around. "This is our only chance. We must get out of here now!" he said.

"No. I want to watch," Zeth said. Sickness gleamed in his eyes.

With more strength than Zeth would have thought possible, Candaz dragged his reluctant son away from the scene and to the horses they had left tied to a nearby tree. Their terrified mounts were frantic to get away and tugged vigorously against their reins. Candaz quickly whispered a spell that tranquilized the horses so they could mount them. Bellowing sounds rose all around them as Zeth followed his father at a full gallop away from the nightmare that he had created.

Father and son rode the rest of the night and well into the next morning. The sky was bright and clear and the day promised to be pleasant and warm. Zeth felt exulted. He wondered what his father thought of him now. Never would the old man belittle his son's power again. The spell had worked perfectly. Wolves had changed into warwolves. It had been exquisite! Zeth wished he had been able to stay and see the full transformation. Their bestial cries had been horrendous in the blackness of the night. A tickle of carnality rippled through Zeth's body. He looked over at Candaz, who rode beside him, with a gloating smile that vanished when he saw his father's deep scowl.

"It was necessary, father," he said defensively, with a hint of a childish whine. "They would not have shown *you* mercy when they wrapped their fangs about *your* neck. Is that what you wanted?"

Candaz spat angrily on the ground and grunted audibly. "What do I care for mercy? You have no sense, boy! You use your power to satisfy your own demented nature instead of using it to further our cause. You have no sense!" he fumed.

Zeth wished he had let those wolves have a taste of his father's flesh after all. "I saved your life," he said defensively.

"I can take care of myself! You are a fool, Zeth," Candaz said.

They rode the rest of the day in mutual silence. Before dusk had fully taken hold of the land, they crested the high cliffs that hid the dragon caves somewhere down below. The ocean rushed in and crashed in violent bursts of frothing water against the rocky shore. Off in the distance the Island of Zedra could be seen, a tiny speck of green in a sea of blue. They camped the night where they stood.

The next morning, with Candaz in the lead, they took a narrow trail that wound its way down at a steep angle toward the ocean shore. Zeth's horse misplaced a hoof and lost his footing once, but managed to recover without breaking a leg. It took him considerable strength to keep the big horse in check the rest of the way down. He kept envisioning his brains dashed all over in messy array on the rocks below. By the time they reached the shore, the sun was high in the sky and he was exhausted.

To get out of the hot noon-day sun, Candaz and Zeth crawled into one of the abandoned dragon caves and finished off most of their road rations before settling down wrapped in their cloaks and easily napping.

Zeth dreamed of Jesse. Her sweetness filled Zeth with aching as they danced barefoot high atop a grassy hill. They held hands, spinning and twirling while they laughed and played like children, lost in the joy that they brought to each other. Suddenly, Jesse stopped and looked out over the plain. Her eyes filled with terror and she looked for a place to run and hide. In his dream, Zeth followed Jesse's gaze and saw a pack of warwolves running toward them. They were monsters with deformed ridges over their eyes and horns growing from their misshapen skulls. In their eyes was all of the world's hatred intensified by rage. When Zeth looked back, they had her. The warwolves tore the flesh from her bones in an eating frenzy as she screamed for him to help her. He was frozen, unable to move. He didn't realize he was screaming until he awoke from the dream.

Candaz was down on the shore, looking out over the ocean toward Zedra when he emerged from the cave. Recovering his wits, Zeth calmed his breathing and walked down to join his father. Everything seemed so quiet and peaceful. There were no gulls swooping through the air looking for fish. The dragon caves stood empty and silent. Even the ocean seemed to have lost its momentum to roar. Zeth recognized the feeling. He had experienced it continually throughout his entire life. Loneliness was his constant companion. He longed for Jesse. *"Patience, my son, patience."* The litany repeated itself in his head, blaringly, like a blow horn placed up against his ear.

Alone

As he gazed out over the cold gray ocean Candaz felt an empty aching loneliness. He remembered the day he and Molly had escaped his father's controlling world only to end the day with loss and pain. The vision of his Molly falling dead out of his arms haunted him still. He had tossed her body over the cliff into the pounding surf off the coast of Saberville. She had hit the rocks below with sickening brokenness. His heart went with her and his soul and although he wasn't aware of it, so did his sanity.

He reached into his left pocket, one of many in his voluminous cloak, and caressed for a fleeting second the hand of his beloved Molly. It was a mummified, dried out and wrinkled, blackened version of the beautiful warm and soft hand he had once held. The hand was wrapped in silk torn from the dress she had worn that day. The ring he had given her remained upon her middle finger. He could feel it through the wrappings. Broken dreams were contained within the old tattered grotesque package.

Was his son another broken dream? Zeth was so disappointing. He seemed to be destined to waste his gift to satisfy his own demented goals. Candaz was beginning to wonder if maybe he would be better off without him. Although he still desperately wanted an heir to inherit the power he was about to obtain, he wasn't sure that Zeth could handle the responsibility.

Conjuring the warwolves was an example of his lack of focus on their ultimate goal. There was no point to creating the vile creatures. It only served to satisfy his insatiable need to indulge his cruel nature. The spell was done from memory to perfection. That *was* impressive. Maybe he *could* mold the boy into what he wanted him to be. Maybe with a little guidance the boy could become a great sorcerer. As he heard Zeth approach him from behind, he decided not to give up yet. Not yet.

Lost

I fly until exhausted but still get nowhere, Skymaster thought to himself. *The only thing solid is what lies beneath me.* Experimentally, the dragon mage extended his talons and scratched at the surface of the ground he sat on. It felt like earth but did not smell like earth. He raised a sample to his efficient nostrils and sniffed. The trace was minute, but there. Dragon bane. He had noticed the scent earlier. But how? The smelly plant grew only around the Skyview Mountains. It must have something to do with the spell used that brought us here. Skymaster thought for a few more minutes, his analytical mind working through the possibilities. Making a decision, he raised his great body from the sitting position and brandishing his talons, began to dig.

Chapter 10

TRAIL OF TERROR

Jesse took a deep breath and gazed around attentively. The forest was dark and ominous as the company approached it from the east. Dusk was settling over them with a briskness that made the air seem crisp and clean, almost brittle, leaving a light taste of fall on the tongue with every breath. The gentle breeze that had kept them company all day departed suddenly, replaced by a stillness that made every single heartbeat seem to echo beneath the breast. She retrieved her jacket from her backpack and put it on.

Gabriel reined her horse in next to Jesse's and addressed her granddaughter without taking her eyes from the forest's deep shadows, "Tempest will have a hard time moving through that dense foliage. It would be better if she went on ahead. If you would like, the rest of us can catch up with you on the other side of the forest."

A tingle of dread passed through her as she examined Gabriel's stern countenance. Something lay hidden behind the sorceress's copper brown eyes that made her anticipate trouble. Gabriel seemed to have a way of "knowing", a type of prescience that was just part of her nature. Jesse wasn't even sure if her grandmother was fully aware of her ability, and this latest subtle hint for her to pass by the forest made her wonder what the reason was for the caution. Felcore approached at an easy lope as she pondered conflicting inner thoughts. Her grandmother was trying to protect her, but from what? She wasn't going to let Gabriel treat her like a child; she was made of sturdy stuff and would not be put off easily. Protection wasn't something she needed or desired at the moment. What she needed was to get to the bottom of the dragons' disappearances, and soon.

She looked over at Tempest, the radiant white dragon seemingly having dozed off while the company delayed. Rainbows of color danced of her shiny scales as the last bit of sunlight struck her with brilliance. "*Tempest?*" Jesse called silently and gently to the giant beauty.

Slowly, Tempest's large eyes widened until the red swirling balls illuminated Jesse through the dusk. "*Is it time to resume this redundantly tedious march?*" she asked in a bored tone.

"*How would you like to stretch your wings?*" Jesse asked.

The red in Tempest's eyes brightened and her massive tail thumped the ground involuntarily like a dog, causing the ground to shiver on impact. "*Oh, yes! Shall we go now? We could go hunting. Yes, let's go hunting, Jesse!*"

Amused by Tempest's child-like enthusiasm, Jesse laughed, dispelling for a moment her bleak mood. She replied, "*No, Tempest, I am afraid I am not going with you. The rest of us shall continue through the forest and meet you on the other side.*"

"No, Jesse! *I don't want to go alone,*" Tempest said. The big dragon's head weaved back on forth on her long neck.

"*I'm sorry, but I think I should stay with Kali and Grandmother and you are too big to proceed through the forest. You will be all right,*" Jesse assured her.

"*I'm afraid, Jesse,*" Tempest said. Her head tilted sideways and she stood perfectly still. *Wait! There is something amiss.*" The dragon emitted a bizarre humming sound from her chest. Her head began to swing from side to side in agitation. She closed her eyes before letting a massive crooning roar blast from her mouth. The images that invaded Jesse's mind were confusing and painful, a twisting tortuous cry for help; a type of helplessness, like falling in a dream and not being able to stop the descent.

"*Tempest, what was that? What's wrong?*" Jesse asked the dragon as she continued to huff anxiously.

Gabriel reached out and grabbed Jesse's arm before she said, "There's something wrong."

Tempest again made the pain-filled crooning roar and screamed mentally at them, "*The eggs are dying. I must go help them. I have to go now.*" Immediately, she launched into the sky and headed directly into the sunset, soon to be seen as just a speck in the western sky.

"*Tempest, be careful. We'll join you soon if we can,*" Jesse called after her. "*Let me know what you find.*"

As a last second thought, Jesse suggested, "Maybe Rew should go with Tempest." Her bright copper-colored eyes fell on Rew, who sat on Gabriel's horse where the two of them spoke to each other urgently.

A slight hesitation followed as Rew looked from the forest to the horizon and back again before answering, "I have no desire to go into that dark forest. I will gladly accompany Tempest. She might need my help. Will you be okay without me?"

Jesse replied, "Don't worry, we'll be fine. It would make me feel a lot better if you were with her, Rew." Jesse smiled uneasily, but after noting Gabriel's dour expression, bit her lip and looked down at her hands.

Gabriel spoke quietly and calmly despite the concerned look on her face, "If the dragon eggs have been unattended since the dragons' disappearance five days ago, they might not survive. The eggs have to be turned at least every four days to keep them from overheating in the hot sands of the egg-laying grounds. Tempest might get there too late to save them. Although I hate to lose Rew, I think it would be a good idea if someone was with her. We can't be there for a couple of days at best. What do you think, Rew?"

"I'll go with the dragon," he responded as Kali emerged from the forest.

Kali, looking casually at home in the saddle, materialized from the edge of the trees and started for them at an easy gait. Beside her, Tica had no trouble keeping pace with Kali's much larger horse.

Jesse and Gabriel dismounted and exchanged brief greetings with the slim banderg huntress. Kali's face was painted with a grim expression as she jumped down from the saddle. She removed a feathered shaft from her bow and reported to them, "I saw nothing out of the ordinary, but could not shake a feeling of . . . I don't know . . . it was . . . just not right. The trail is thickly overgrown, but we should be able to make fairly good time if we stick to it. I wouldn't recommend trying it tonight, however. Darkness in that forest would be thicker than Aunt Anna's stew. We should make camp and wait until day break."

Kali's eyes scanned the forest again, drawing all of their eyes to involuntarily to do the same.

"Did you see any sign of them?" Gabriel asked. There was no question as to whom she was referring when she said "them".

"Yes. Two men came through here at least two days gone by. They stuck to the path and remained on it for as far as I tracked," Kali replied.

"We must go on. If what Kali says is true, they are already a full two days ahead of us. There will be no camp tonight," Gabriel declared as she spun quickly and caught the reins on her horse before vaulting into the saddle.

Kali exchanged an uneasy glance with Jesse before she turned and whistled for Tica, interrupting the two dogs that were frolicking on a patch of grass nearby. Kali's golden retriever came immediately upon being beckoned and joined her mistress as she mounted and started toward the ever darkening forest. Kali again nocked the deadly shaft in her bow and kept her horse at a casual stride that seemed a sharp contrast to the cautious analysis she gave her surroundings.

Felcore nudged Jesse's hand with his nose and she looked down at him as he watched Tica and Kali's departing backs. His eyes glowed brilliant gold in the darkening evening light. Deep down from the base of his throat came a light whimper. Jesse bent down to hug him and whispered tender reassurances into the soft fur of his ear, although her own thoughts were far from comforting. Her body was a mass of tension.

Rew was hovering at eye level as he said his goodbyes. "I will see you all in a few days' time. Be very careful. I do not like dark forest paths, especially at night. Rew spoke in a conspiratorial tone aside to Jesse, "You had best be on your way, girl. Mistress Gabriel is not a patient woman."

Jesse found Gabriel watching them with impatience on her face. Her horse pranced uneasily, keying in on her rider's tension. From behind her, Jesse heard Rew's sweet voice turn serious, "I will do what I can to help the dragon eggs and Tempest. There is still hope."

"Hope can make all the difference in the world," she replied, as the wisp sped away faster than her eyes could follow him.

As soon as Jesse was mounted, Gabriel's horse headed into the forest at a break-neck pace. Jesse almost lost her seat as her mare fought to catch up with the elder sorceress. Felcore managed to easily keep pace with them, running behind Jesse's horse without seeming to touch the ground with his paws. The forest enveloped them. It was dark, a deeper absence of light than black velvet on a cloud-covered moonless night. The wind that whipped Jesse's face seemed tainted with a scent she could not put her finger on. She fought her unease, trying unsuccessfully to swallow the tightness in her throat.

The path was narrow and dense with undergrowth. Branches tore at her from every direction. She ducked instinctively as a large branch passed close overhead. Hugging her horse tightly around the neck, she buried her face in the mane and let the mare do the tailing. "This is crazy!" As the words were whipped from her mouth her horse slowed, taking its cue from Kali's mount up ahead. Without any further warning they came to an abrupt halt.

Shadows became perceptible in the darkness as her eyes adjusted and Jesse watched Kali suddenly vault from her horse and follow Tica off the path. She sat waiting and watching, trying to catch her breath and straining her ears to hear over the pounding of her own heart and the huffing and puffing of her horse. Gabriel turned and came up next to Jesse's horse. "What is it?" the older woman asked, her voice sounding distant and unreal.

"I don't know," Jesse replied. Whatever it was wasn't good. Felcore followed his nose and plunged into the dense growth where Kali and Tica had left the path moments earlier.

"Felcore, wait!" Jesse shouted.

She heard the dog hesitate at her command and then continue on his course.

"Shoot!" Jesse dismounted and quickly tethered her horse to the nearest branch. "Felcore," she called out, as she moved carefully, making her way to where she thought her companions had disappeared.

Gabriel was immediately with her and together they made their way into the forest. About one hundred feet into the trees was a small clearing. To Jesse, the oppressiveness was suffocating. She suddenly felt like an elephant was sitting on her chest. Her knees buckled and she fell to the ground, where she remained groping in the dirt to steady herself. Felcore was panting heavily beside her, but she couldn't find the control to put a comforting hand on him. After a moment she felt Gabriel beside her, bracing her with strong arms.

"What is it Jesse? What is wrong?" her grandmother asked.

She fought against nausea as she clenched Gabriel's arm. The world slowly settled back to its symmetry and she was able to look around. A fire pit stood coldly near the center of the area. Although it seemed harmless, a natural part of the scene, waves of contamination washed from it. It seemed to literally vibrate with bad chronology. Jesse managed to stand up with Gabriel's help. She approached the cold stone pit like someone would approach a frightened and dangerous animal. Felcore stayed where he was and whimpered quietly with his head upon his paws. Kali watched all this from the far side of the clearing with a look of curious interest on her face. Jesse was unaware of the banderg girl and was only marginally aware of Gabriel's assistance. Her emotions were awash in horror.

Visions assaulted her like a slide show where the projector is flashing its images at an accelerated speed, too fast for the human eye to comprehend, but not too fast for the subconscious mind to grasp. A face, wild with passion, perverted with obsession, staring into a thick mist. A spider, wriggles in pain as its eight legs are torn cruelly from its body. Black eyes, watching, judging. Fire. Steam. Mist. Skymaster, his eyes swirling red. Anger. Blackness. An utterly overwhelming feeling of loneliness struck her heart with sorrow. Jesse again sank to her knees next to the fire pit and began to weep. A warm wet tongue on her cheek brought her back to the present. She swiped a sleeve across her face and dried it of the tears that had spilled out.

Felcore trembled slightly as he leaned into Jesse. He had literally crawled over to her. Before looking up at her grandmother, she kissed the dog on the nose and recovered her balance. "This is the spot where Zeth made the dragons disappear. It seems that the dragons are somewhere in a void, a place of nothingness or absence of substance. The magic is strong. I'm not sure if we will be able to undo it. The corruption may be too complete."

"We will undo it! I will not fail in this, regardless of what it may involve or how long it will take," Gabriel fumed. "Can you tell me anything about the spell?"

Jesse felt a tightening in her throat. She didn't want to know. Swallowing her fear, she reluctantly pressed her hand against the cold ashes and concentrated. As the freecurrent took her through the remains of the spell, excruciating pain seized the muscles of her body. A small cry escaped her lips and tears ran once again unheeded down her cheeks. The gold of the medallion burned hot against her skin. At once she knew what had gone wrong with Zeth's spell. The foulness of it was repulsive and she reflexively pulled her hand away. Dry heaves wracked her body with violence. It felt as if someone was trying to pull her intestines out through her throat. She took deep breaths to steady herself. The power was amazing and dreadful.

Finally she recovered enough to talk. "The spell was a potion along with an incantation. Have you ever heard of a black barbed spider?"

Gabriel nodded. Her face was strained.

"He pulled the legs off the spider while it was still alive. He is cruel! He relishes it," Jesse said.

Impatience stole into Gabriel's tone, "What else was in it?"

"I can't be sure," Jesse replied.

"Tell me," Gabriel ordered.

Jesse shifted her balance and traced her fingers through the ashes. Her fingertips tingled from the residual power. "Leaves from a sour root and the split leaf tri-pod tree, a night shade beetle, male not female, red moss, powdered dragon bane, dried black spotted mushroom, crushed dragon talon, fire powder, fluid from a dragon egg. Something called black breath?" She looked at Gabriel for affirmation that there was such a thing.

The older woman nodded and said, "Yes, go on."

"That's it," Jesse said as she stood up and brushed herself off. She felt filthy and wanted desperately a hot shower and a tooth brush. The pain had subsided, but exhaustion took its place. She sank back down on her heels.

Gabriel scrutinized her with penetrating eyes and placed a hand firmly on Jesse's shoulder. She asked, "What went wrong? Why didn't the spell work?"

Jesse flinched and turned away from her grandmother's gaze. She said, "He corrupted it. The potion took on a different character. It was supposed to summon a dragon. He corrupted it and drove them all away."

"How?" Gabriel pressed.

"Depravity," she almost whispered.

"What?" Gabriel asked.

"His depravity corrupted the spell. It changed the properties. He is sick with it. He is beyond redemption."

Jesse could see the pain register on Gabriel's face. Instead of saying anything further she stood up and turned away, walking from the clearing as fast as she could into the dark of the night.

Kali caught up with her as she reached the path. "Jesse, wait," she said.

"I just want to find some place to sleep. I can't . . ." Jesse began.

Kali grabbed her arm and swung her around to face her. "You don't have to be so cruel to her. She is tough, but has a heart of gold. It has been very hard for her over the years," she said.

Jesse pushed the palm of her hand against her forehead as if she had a headache. After a moment, she said, "I didn't say it to be mean. I told her the truth. She has to face the truth about her son. To coddle her about it won't be doing her any favors. Eventually she's going to come face to face with him and then what?"

"You are right that she has to face up to what Zeth has become. It could be dangerous for her if she doesn't accept the facts. However, I find your tactics a bit harsh. I grew up with Gabriel as a friend and a mentor. She is probably more of a 'Grandmother' to me than she is to you. One of her faults is that she loves too much. Zeth is her son. She will not give up hope in finding some good in him. Try not to adopt Gabriel's resentment by openly displaying your hate for him," Kali advised.

Jesse sighed heavily and said, "I'll try being gentler, but I can't help the way I feel about Zeth. The power I have, or 'curse' might be a more appropriate word right now, makes me know things all the way down to the core of my soul. Not only do I know that Zeth is corrupt, I know that he is demented. I am afraid Gabriel will just have to accept that he is who he is. Hiding the truth from her won't help in the long run. It won't help us get the dragons back and it won't help her get her son back."

"There is always hope," Gabriel's voice spoke gently from behind Jesse. She jumped at the sound.

Kali agreed, "Yes, without hope we are lost."

Jesse shivered and drew closer to her horse for warmth. "Neither of you understand. It isn't lack of hope in the future or even in the power of love. It is *knowing*. Yes, I believe in miracles. I've seen God at work in more ways than one. But, Zeth is beyond . . . well, beyond hope, for lack of a better word. I am sorry, but that is the way I see it."

"I can't accept that," Gabriel said.

"You might have to, Grandmother," she said.

The silence that followed wasn't only heavy, but stifling. Without a word, Jesse crossed the space between Gabriel and herself and gave her grandmother a hug. Gabriel wrapped her arms around her granddaughter and hugged her back and then gave Jesse a kiss on the cheek. "We will do everything we can. It will be all right," she said quietly.

Jesse didn't respond. She wasn't so sure. Things were worse than she expected.

Off in the distance a howl arose, filling the night with heightened awareness. Like a siren, it continued on until it was joined by others, a chorus of wailing in a mournful melody. Cold fingers ran up Jesse's spine and she shivered again.

With a sense of urgency, they mounted their horses and continued at a fast and steady pace down the trail. Kali was in the lead and Jesse brought up the tail end of the group. The darkness still prevailed and it was difficult to keep track of the person in front of her. Jesse's weariness dragged at her eyelids until they would no longer stay open. Succumbing to her exhaustion, she snoozed in the saddle.

She was awakened suddenly when the horses came to a complete halt. Looking around as her eyes adjusted to the dark, Jesse noticed Kali, Felcore and Tica were once again gone. Gabriel was next to her with her eyes locked on a space between the trees in front of them. "Kali went to investigate whatever it is that spooked the dogs," she said quietly. They dismounted and stretched out their tired muscles. It had been a very long night.

Without a sound Kali stepped out in front of them with Tica and Felcore by her side. Her eyes seemed to shine of their own accord as she found them in the darkness. Jesse sighed and made her body relax under the banderg woman's serious but calm gaze. Kali's voice sounded strange in the quiet that surrounded them. "I have found something. Three men are dead. I'll show you," she said.

Gabriel glanced at Jesse and told her, "You stay here, honey. We'll be right back."

Her grandmother's well intentioned protectionism was beginning to rankle. She had seen a lot of very gory movies with her brother and dad over the years. For some reason the boys always wanted to watch death and destruction for their entertainment pleasure. Being the only girl, she was usually overruled on movie choices. "You don't need to protect me. I am a big girl," she asserted.

"You think you can handle it?" Gabriel asked.

"Yes," Jesse said.

"Very well, then. Come along," Gabriel said. The tone of her voice told Jesse that the woman clearly thought that she would indeed *not* be able to handle it, but was willing to let the lesson be learned. The older woman turned and followed Kali back into the woods.

Jesse hesitated slightly, took a deep breath, and followed her grandmother.

A short distance off the path they came across a small clearing. Light was able to filter down from the star-lit canopy overhead. It illuminated the area in an eerily silver light. Three men lay helter-skelter around a cold stone fire pit. The one face Jesse could see was oddly colored with blue-black lips and staring wide eyes. The man's throat had been slashed and a dark stain made a grotesque pillow under his head. Flies were making a feast off the dead flesh. The other two men looked as if they had been tossed in a pile on the ground, like a piece of clothing carelessly discarded on the floor after a day's wearing. Along with a large bundle of furs, their packs lay nearby, no longer of any use to their owners. The smell was strongly sickening-sweet. Jesse stayed on the edge of the clearing, willing her sudden uncontrollable shivering to go away. She hugged herself tightly and tried to breathe as little as possible as she averted her eyes from the human remains.

Kali and Gabriel walked cautiously through the murder scene, examining the bodies without disturbing them. They were silent and grim as they moved from one corpse to another. Kali's skilled eyes trained on something on the ground and she bent slightly to pick it up. "Gabriel, take a look at this," she said as she held out the object in her hand.

Gabriel opened the small leather pouch offered to her and sniffed. Curiosity propelled Jesse to Gabriel's side. She also sniffed the contents of the pouch. It was familiar and brought forth good memories of family breakfasts together with her father and Jacob in their kitchen back home. "Freshly ground coffee," she commented, fighting back the sudden urge to vomit.

"Dragon bane," Gabriel corrected quietly. She turned the leather pouch and pointed out the stitched inscription on the other side. A capital "C". "He must have dropped this. Candaz is responsible for these murders."

Pointing to the ground, Kali observed, "There are two sets of hoof prints leaving the clearing and heading back toward the path. Another horse went in the opposite direction without a rider." Kali glanced back at the dead men. "Do you think we should bury them?"

Gabriel replied, "If we had the tools, we could, but we don't. I can make a funeral pyre with freecurrent magic. That will have to do. Those poor men. Let's take their packs with us. Maybe we can deliver their belongings to their families with our condolences."

"At least they'll have some closure," Jesse said.

The three of them worked together and accomplished the very gruesome task of disposing of the men's bodies. They tied the extra baggage onto their horses as the corpses burned. Jesse said a brief prayer before they left the clearing for the final time.

The very tired party mounted their horses and began a slow procession through the forest with Kali in the lead and Jesse bringing up the rear. The sway of the saddle almost instantly started to lull Jesse into an uncomfortable sleep. Dawn was just painting the dark forest a deep indigo when she awoke with a start. Her horse had slowed to a very leisurely stroll, but she almost fell off when she realized where she was. Felcore looked up at her with glassy eyes that seemed to say, "Well, Jess, you've done it now. We're lost." Gabriel and Kali were nowhere to be seen. She dismounted and stretched aching muscles before giving Felcore a good scratching. "'Where's Tica, boy?"

Under her feet she felt the ground shake. She paused and looked up and around. Again, a tremble shook the packed dirt beneath her feet. Boom . . . Boom . . . Boom . . ! Whatever it was, it was getting closer.

The sun suddenly crested the horizon and sparkles of light dashed across her vision. Out of the glimmering light stepped a giant horse. Mounted on the giant horse was the hugest human Jesse had ever seen. No, not a human, a torg! Jesse stared down the path at the approaching mountain of humanity without moving. She felt her roots were sank so deeply that she couldn't have moved if the world tipped upside down and tried to shake her off.

The male torg stopped his horse in front of her and dismounted. He towered over her. If she looked straight ahead she would be staring directly into his belly button, which was only half concealed with curly red hair. He wore only some leggings and when Jesse looked up into his face, he was smiling.

"You look like Mistress Gabriel when we first met many turns ago before the freeing of the torg nation. I am Kaltog," he said with a voice that would have come from a very deep cave if a cave could speak.

"I'm . . . I'm Jesse," she replied, sounding shy to herself. "Um. This is Felcore."

"Woof!"

Kaltog looked curiously at Felcore for a long moment, a gentle expression settled on his rugged face. "You are the granddaughter of Gabriel. What are you doing in the forest all alone?" he asked.

She glanced around behind her looking for the rest of her party and then back at Kaltog. "I wasn't alone. Gabriel and Kali were with me, but I fell asleep as we rode last night and must have gotten left behind. It was really very asinine of me, but I just couldn't keep my eyes open. I used to have that problem in school sometimes. No matter what I did, boom, my eyes would shut during a lecture or a movie. I don't think toothpicks in my lids can even help when I feel like that."

The giant torg looked suddenly worried. "You wouldn't stick toothpicks in your eyes would you?"

Jesse laughed. It was a great release and felt wonderful after a tension-filled night. "No, I wouldn't do that. It's just a figure of speech. You know, one of those old sayings like, 'I'm so hungry I could eat a horse.'"

The serious reaction this statement induced made Jesse laugh all the more. Kaltog said in all seriousness, "You would be better off eating your golden than your horse. Walking always hurts my feet."

"No. No. I wouldn't eat either one of them. Felcore is my friend and I must agree that walking can be hard on the feet. Besides, I could never eat a horse." She thought of Tempest, knowing that the dragon would not have such qualms.

The pounding of hooves sounded behind Jesse and she turned to find Gabriel and Kali along with Tica coming down the path toward them. Gabriel swung from her horse the minute she reached them and ran to Kaltog, who bent low, picked her up and let her hug him. Then he sat her down on the ground and Gabriel adjusted her cloths and hair absently. She smiled as she said, "It is so good to see you. How is your father? It has been far too long since I've been to Farreach. Everything is all right, isn't it?" she asked.

"Yes, except there has been a ripple in nature. Something has been thrown out of balance. I have come to investigate the source," Kaltog said. "It could be as simple as flooding from the recent rain. But, I have the feeling that it is not caused conventionally. Have you seen anything out of the ordinary?"

"Well, Kaltog, I assume you already know of the disappearance of the dragons," Gabriel replied.

"The dragons are gone? Where did they go?" he asked.

Kali, who had dismounted and was stretching carefully answered, "We don't know where they are. That is what we are trying to find out. What we do know is that Candaz and his son Zeth are responsible. A spell was used and somehow mismanaged and now the dragons are gone."

"Candaz is alive? Are you sure?" he asked as he appraised Kali curiously.

"Unfortunately yes," Gabriel replied. "My son lives too."

"That is impossible. Where have they been all of these years?" Kaltog asked.

"Right under our very noses. They have been living at Wayfair Manor in Lakeside," Gabriel told him.

"That is unfortunate," he said as he scratched his beard in thought. After a moment he asked, "What is your destination?"

Gabriel answered, "We are heading to the Island of Zedra. So far we have tracked Candaz and Zeth in that direction and assume that is their destination. They seek information on how to enslave the dragons. They have left a trail of blood behind them. In the forest we found three trappers murdered. We intend to intercept them and put an end to this travesty. Hopefully, the information on how to find the dragons will be available on Zedra. Would you like to accompany us?"

Kaltog ran his fingers through his curly red hair before he answered, "I was on my way to Castle Gentlebreeze to consult with Jessabelle about some trade issues, but it can wait. It would be my pleasure to help you find that sleazy sorcerer."

The group made a small fire in a clearing and heated some water for tog. Road rations were distributed among them, making a dismal breakfast after a long night of travel. As soon as they were refreshed, they stomped out the fire and continued down the trail toward the western coast of Risen.

Chapter 11

A FISH OUT OF WATER

They needed a boat! The Island of Zedra stood just off shore beckoning them to come but was unattainable. Candaz threw more wood on their fire and prodded his son awake with his boot. "Zeth get up," he said.

Zeth rolled over and looked up into his father's solemn face before crawling out of his blankets. They were just inside a small opening on the western shore inside an old dragon cave. They had been there for more than a day, trying to decide what their best option was for obtaining a boat for their use. Farreach was to the north and Colordale was a longer trek to the south. Since they had arrived, they had seen no one.

"I want you to head south today and find us a boat. Get going. We are wasting time here." Candaz threw Zeth his knife, which the younger man caught easily.

He got up and without another word to his father or pausing to eat; he started walking to the south. The shoreline was rocky and the way was not easy. It was midday when he spotted a small sail boat anchored just off shore. A woman was tending a small cooking fire on which she was roasting a freshly caught fish. Her back was to Zeth and she wasn't aware of his approach until he spoke. "That smells delicious," he said. He was hungry and he was being honest about the aroma. His mouth watered.

She jumped and immediately had a knife in her hand while she turned and crouched in a defensive stance. "What do you want?" she asked, keeping her eyes on him. Short dark hair framed her face, which was pretty in a way, although at the moment it dramatized fierce suspicion. Her eyes were an unusual light brown, almost the color of caramel.

Charm seeped from Zeth as he addressed her calmly, "I'm sorry I frightened you. My name is Zeth. Please don't be afraid. I won't hurt you." He eased his way toward the fire and reached out his hands to warm them and to display to her that he did not have a weapon and posed no threat.

The girl held her position, watching him warily. "Be gone. Your company I do not wish to have," she said.

"I'm sorry to bother you, but, I'm afraid my father who is crippled and dying is waiting just north of here. There is a plant that grows only on the Island of Zedra that we require to make medicine to ease his pain. I see you have a boat. Would you be willing to convey us to the island? I would be happy to pay you. My poor father suffers so. I'm afraid that he will not be able to withstand too much more. It is so difficult to watch," he said. Zeth's eyes filled with tears and he looked away to discretely wipe them away. When he returned his gaze to the girl, her stance had relaxed and a look of compassion filled her strange colored eyes. He had her!

"Your father I'm sorry about but I am not for hire," she said as she held her knife loosely in her hand and reached down to turn the stick gently that the fish was roasting on. Zeth could kill her now, but he withheld his hand. She intrigued him.

"Would you consider renting me your boat? I promise to return it to you undamaged by this afternoon," Zeth said.

"No. I couldn't. Sorry I am. Sit. I will share my fish with you. Terese is my name," she said as she sheathed her knife. Zeth sat down and smiled warmly. "Thank you. I am hungry." They ate the roasted fish with their hands, picking pieces of the tender meat directly off the bones. It was good and it filled Zeth's empty belly, making him feel satiated and happy. He decided once again to delay killing her. "My father has been suffering with a disease that eats away at his muscles a little bit at a time. The pain can be excruciating, but he never complains. Years ago my mother died in a tragic accident when she drowned after our boat capsized in the middle of Blue Lake. Although father dove after her over and over again, he was unable to locate her until it was too late. She was already dead. He has never gotten over the loss. They were so in love. Such a tragedy. Now, father has this debilitating disease and I watch him stoically suffer in silence day after day. If we could just get the plant we need to ease his pain, he could have some comfort," he shared his tale. Tears welled up in Zeth's eyes and this time he looked into Terese's eyes before looking away.

"Okay. Take you I will, Zeth. I too know of anguish," she said. She did not offer anything else, but stood up, put out the fire and headed for the boat.

It didn't take long for them to reach the spot where Candaz was waiting. After beaching the boat, Terese and Zeth climbed the rocks until they reached the campfire. "Father, this is Terese.

She is going to take us to the island so we can look for the plant for your medicine. Terese, this is my father, Cal."

Candaz greeted her cordially, "So nice to meet you, Terese. Thank you for helping us." The eyes he turned on Zeth were full of danger, but he maintained the charade for Terese.

She smiled a beautiful smile that Zeth had not yet seen and inclined her head. "My pleasure it is," she said.

They headed to the boat with Zeth "helping" Candaz carefully down the hill. Candaz grumbled to his son, "Why didn't you just kill her?" Zeth didn't answer. He wasn't really sure of the answer to that question but it irritated him that it was even asked. The trip to the Island of Zedra was fairly quick. Terese's boat had a small sail, which she handled with an expert hand.

The Island of Zedra was a tiny speck of land that had grown out of the ocean when an ancient volcano, now dormant, spewed forth its inner-most liquefied rock, making itself propagate into a small island. A beautiful sandy beach leads up to a jungle that surrounds the remains of the volcano's cone. The cone itself houses the dragons' Temple of Neeg, an ancient and seldom used natural room inside the mountain where very old texts are carved into the hardened rock wall faces, the years of knowledge etched into the stone by the dragon mages themselves.

The soft sandy beach offered an ideal place to land the water craft and the three of them disembarked; Candaz with Zeth's unwanted help. Terese asked the obvious question, "The plant, what does it look like? Can I help?"

"Why don't you stay down here on the beach and relax? The plant we are searching for is pretty tricky to spot and looks very much like many of the others in the jungle. Father and I will seek it out. I'm sure it won't take us too long. Relax. Enjoy the sun. We'll be right back. I'm sure it won't take long," Zeth assured her, taking Candaz's arm and walking with him into the jungle while Terese watched them go.

When they were out of sight, Candaz pulled his arm roughly away from Zeth's touch. "What are you doing, boy? You should have simply killed her and taken the boat. Why the elaborate charade?" he asked.

Zeth didn't think it necessary to tell his father that he didn't know why he had kept the girl alive so he made up an excuse. "We need her to sail the boat, father. She can be killed after we are back on the main land. Don't worry. She doesn't suspect anything," he assured him.

"Stupid fool!" Candaz hissed through his teeth.

Anger propelled Zeth forward through the jungle. He seethed with it as he cut through the thick foliage with his sword. It was hot and sticky and the mosquitos were unrelenting in their attack. Even fantasy thoughts of Jesse did not assuage his discomfort today. *Stupid dragons! What a lousy place for a library.*

The entrance was hidden behind a heavy weave of vines. Candaz located it by running his hands over the rock face and whispering words indiscernible to Zeth. "Right here. This is it," he said and stepped back to let Zeth hack through the vines to clear the way. The door was sealed shut. It had obviously been many years since anyone had traversed through this entry. Candaz immediately began drawing a rune, which glowed bright blue upon completion. He and Zeth walked through the solid rock.

A massive room was immediately on the other side of the wall. Warm air assaulted their noses, strong with the musky scent of dragon. Light streamed in from the open volcano cone over their heads that served as ingress and egress to the dragons. The walls of the cavern were scrolled from top to bottom in an ancient language that Zeth was not familiar with. Candaz's eyes were already drinking in the text, looking for the information he sought. The walls were like black glass. Zeth ran his hands over the lettering and felt the sharp etching from the dragon talon that had engraved it into the heat seared wall. It was quite an impressive sight. He walked around the room letting his eyes take in the enormity of knowledge that was recorded there. His father was reading quietly to himself. A wide tunnel hidden back in the shadows caught Zeth's eye.

"Father, I'm going to take a look back there," he said, although Candaz did not respond, probably had not even heard him as absorbed as he was in studying the etchings. Zeth disappeared from the cavern.

The tunnel increased in diameter as it continued to slope down toward the center of the volcano. Heat increased constantly with every step Zeth took. He began to sweat and removed his outer coat and draped it over his arm. Down, down he went into the very heart of the dormant volcano. Light was visible up ahead glowing like an arched beacon at the end of a vacant conduit. The ground under his feet was solid, similar to the walls, but with bumps and crevices sporadically that he could feel through the bottom of his boots. He had to watch his footing carefully. The musky dragon scent was mixed with a strong sulfuric stench that grew more potent as he drew closer to the light. He didn't enter the room before him, but stopped and watched.

A white dragon, small by dragon standards, even small for an adolescent dragon, but beautiful in an array of iridescent colors was working in the midst of the room. He edged quietly closer. The room was extremely wide with a low-domed ceiling that glowed orange as it reflected the light from the stream of lava that surrounded it. A floor of the blackest sand Zeth had ever seen sparkled like crushed onyx. The sand had small mounds interspersed at various intervals. The white dragon was moving from mound to mound and reaching in and rotating an egg. A wisp flew quietly overhead giving advice to the white dragon as she went from egg to egg, mound to mound. Zeth recognized the dragon. It was his dragon; the one that escaped just as he was on the verge of discovering the secret to controlling the dragons. He constrained his first impulse to strike. After all, there was a wisp with the she-dragon and according to his father, wisps were unpredictable at best. He backed away, keeping his hand sliding along the wall as he went.

Half-way back down the tunnel, Zeth stopped and crouched down. On the floor he quickly drew a rune. Circling around the entire diameter of the tunnel, he drew rune after rune until a magical ring was formed. He whispered words to activate the spell. A glowing net of blue spanned the width and height of the tunnel, from wall to wall, floor to ceiling. It vibrated with energy. The barrier would be impenetrable by either side. The spell Zeth had produced would entomb the dragon and the wisp in the egg-laying grounds for all time. The baby dragons as well would only find death after hatching into this world. The only exit was sealed tight. It would also prevent any communication into or out of the tomb, mentally or otherwise. He felt pleased by his deed. That accomplished, he turned and walked back toward where his father remained oblivious to all else as he studied the walls.

His father's irritating voice met him as he entered the dragon library, "There is nothing here that will help us. This has been an utter waste of time. Let's go. I have a manuscript hidden back at Xandia, down in the catacombs that might contain the information we need. We will head there next. If only you weren't so foolish and impatient, we wouldn't be in this predicament. Foolish, stupid boy."

Terese had a warm fire going with three large fish skewered and cooking over the open flame when they arrived back at the beach. "Did you find what you were looking for?" she asked. "Oh, yes," Zeth responded as he produced a clump of leaves from a plant he had pillaged along the path. He would make a tea for Candaz to drink and hopefully the result would not be too unpleasant for the old man. He wasn't quite sure what type of plant it was but knew that it wasn't poisonous. "This should do the trick." He smiled warmly at Terese and she smiled back. Candaz sat quietly seething. Terese would think it was due to his pain. They would spend the night on the beach and leave first thing in the morning. Zeth again decided to delay killing Terese. She could sail, fish, build a great fire, cook, and was pleasant to look at. Besides, he liked her smile. Maybe he would let her live after all.

Lost Youth

Candaz watched his son flirt with the girl shamelessly and felt utter annoyance. He should kill her and be done with it. She was a distraction and could prove to be a detriment to their cause. Zeth had no experience with women. All she had to do was give him her sweet smile and the boy would do anything to get her attention. He could read the lust in his son's eyes as he gazed at the kendrite woman. She did have a certain appeal. But, she was young--too young for him. Maybe he could use her as a play thing. But no; they didn't have time for that. Killing her would be for the best. He would wait on Zeth, though. It would be another test of his strength of character. It would be another way to determine if the boy had what it takes to wield the power that Candaz would hand to him when the time was right.

The dragon's temple turned out to be a misuse of precious time. Historical records mostly were the dominate theme of the etchings. There was nothing about the mystery of the dragon's power. Their magic remained intangible to Candaz. The book hidden in the catacombs underneath Castle Xandia was one he had found ages ago in the library in New Chance. Besides the temple etchings, it was the earliest history recorded of the dragons and their exodus to Risen. Analyzing the ancient manuscript was always his intention, but he had never gotten around to it. In his youth he had other interests besides studying that he liked to pursue.

His eyes fell on the girl again. He could take her if he wanted to. She would be no match for him and it would teach Zeth a lesson. Maybe he should. He let the thought marinate his imagination for a while. It would be good to be young again. Youth was taken for granted when it was an everyday part of life. It was elusive like time.

Chapter 12

WOLFISH GRIN

Nicholas sniffed the footprint and knew immediately who it belonged to. The scent was very familiar to him. He had known it for years, really all of his life. It was Gabriel's. They were getting closer. The myriad of scents in the clearing were numerous, two different dogs, a male and a female, a banderg, three horses, and Jessica, lovely Jessica. Two older scents belonging to two different men were also strong. He looked back at Stephan and motioned for him to follow, "Rrowf."

"Gotcha, pooch." Stephan swung his horse around and followed Nicholas through the forest at a fast trot. They had been travelling all day and through the night and dusk was just starting to lighten the sky. Nick's stomach was complaining to him and he really wanted a long drink of water, making his long wolf tongue loll out of his mouth. They were catching up. The scents were fresh, less than a day old. He knew that realistically they should take a break soon, but for now he was going to stay on the trail. His cousin, Stephan, followed him easily on his horse, never complaining, always quick with a smile or a ration of wit.

He accelerated his pace, falling into the rhythm of his stride, letting his streamline body glide easily through the forest as he followed Gabriel's scent. The tension that permeated the forest was palpable. Corruption was in the air, reeking, putrefying the very essence of the wind. The reek was assaulting all Nicky's wolf senses, heightening his fight or flight reflex, alerting his instinct to flee with alarming insistence. Ignoring all the signals his body was giving him to do otherwise, he was running full force into the danger that threatened. His wolf instincts screamed at him over and over again to run away, but he did not comply. After all, he was not only a wolf with wolf instincts; but he was also a human with human intellect, emotions and purpose.

Crying wolf

Jesse's companions were packing up after a short break from the trail, stowing supplies they had used to make their meager breakfast and at least two pots of tog, when they heard the painful howling of wolves close by. All ears in the small camp went up, the horses bellowed and snorted anxiously while they pulled on their tethers frantically. Felcore immediately came to Jesse's side and began to growl as he looked into the woods to their left. Tica lay down and put her paws over her nose as if to hide from the world. The howling continued in a symphony of misery, beginning on their left and starting to fan out in all directions around them as the sun brightened the early morning sky.

Jesse looked at Gabriel and spoke urgently, "These wolves are tainted, corrupted with magic."

Gabriel was quickly synching up her pack. She secured it on her horse before answering her granddaughter, "You're right, Jess. Be ready."

The howls were all around them and closing in.

Kali was already mounted on her horse and had an arrow nocked in her bow. "Jesse, take my knife." She threw it to her deftly. Jesse snatched it out of the air and wished for something much bigger. "Kaltog," Kali called, "what weapons do you have on you?"

"My predator battle axe. I just sharpened it," he replied as he retrieved the heavy weapon from his saddle.

"Gabriel?" Kali asked.

"No. But, I have . . .," she began.

Felcore ran to the perimeter of the clearing and in less than a second was engaged in combat with a wolf-like creature. A wolf, however, it wasn't. Short horns grew out of the top of its skull, which had ridges, more like a ripgar than a wolf. It was a distortion, a corruption, something similar, but a disgusting deformity of a wolf. The growling, tearing, dreadful noise that came from the rolling, fighting circle of fur was horrendous as Felcore and the warwolf fought.

Before anyone could make a move, many other warwolves were upon them. A mass of muscle clad in fur launched itself at Jesse, throwing her to the ground. She reflexively brought up the knife in her hand and slashed the soft underbelly of the creature, spilling blood and gore all over herself. The warwolf lay twitching next to her, whining as it died. Clambering to her feet, she engaged the next warwolf that was upon her seconds after the first. Screaming in pain as it sunk its viscous teeth into her fore arm; Jesse stabbed with the knife at its face and then brought it down into the heart as she rolled with the creature on the ground. It fell to the side and breathed its last breath. Felcore launched himself at another animal as it attacked Jesse from behind, tearing at its flesh with extreme violence as he fought for his mistress's life. Jesse rolled and jumped back on her feet. She planted a tremendous kick to the animal's head and followed through with a knife across its throat.

There were warwolves everywhere. Kaltog was swinging his battle axe, arching up and over and under, slicing flesh and bone with biting efficiency. There were bodies and body parts everywhere at his feet as he fought his way toward Gabriel's side. The sorceress was using the freecurrent to fling the warwolves into the air and away from the group. Although the animals were disoriented and sometimes injured from sailing through the air, most were almost instantly back on their feet and surging back into the fray. Kali was having more success picking off their attackers one by one with her bow and arrow. Death was all around her. Tica kept the corrupted wolves from getting to her mistress by defending the perimeter around Kali's horse.

Felcore finished off another warwolf by clamping his mighty jaws into its tender throat, swiftly cutting off its life after a long struggle. Jesse's dog instantly returned to her flank. The two of them stood side by side as they were confronted with a snarling, spitting colossal of a beast. He stopped in front of them and waited, crouched and ready to attack. As it started to charge, it launched itself at them, all teeth and claws in a bombardment of solid bulk. A yelp bit off its life as an arrow penetrated through its head and it slid to their feet, it eyes staring up at them with a silent demand for justice.

"Jesse, behind you!" Kali yelled as she nocked another arrow in her bow.

Jesse spun around just in time to see a huge wolf in mid-leap. She brought her arm up over her head to protect herself and ducked quickly, avoiding the airborne wolf by inches as it flew over her head and immediately engaged the warwolf that was attacking her from the other side. Fur and flesh were flying in a turbulent ball of ferociousness.

She wondered why they were attacking each other for a moment and then noticed that the first wolf was *just* a wolf, not an abomination of one. It ripped out the throat of the warwolf, finishing him off, and turned quickly toward her. For a moment she thought he was going to attack. She made her knife ready and watched warily. The wolf paused to gaze into Jesse's eyes for only a moment with golden intensity and suddenly gave her a toothy, wolfish grin before turning to attack another creature.

Jesse didn't have time to evaluate what just happened. She continued fighting, getting into a rhythm as she used her martial arts training to strike with efficiency. The fluid motions of her legs, feet and hands came back to her with practiced ease. The small knife Kali had thrown her fit comfortably in her hand. The weapon was sharp and sliced through the warwolves' flesh easily. She fought alongside the big ruddy wolf and Felcore as part of a team, defending and protecting the other two as they defended and protected her.

Silence suddenly descended on the group as they caught their breaths and soaked in their surroundings. Each of them looked around for their next foe, but none came. The attack from the warwolves was over. Their pitiful deformed bodies lay everywhere around the clearing, sickening in their postures of death. Felcore trotted over and licked Jesse's injured arm. She winced. The wound was just beginning to throb painfully after the adrenaline rush subsided. Out of the corner of her eye she spotted another wolf and swung her knife in its direction as she turned. It was the wolf with the golden eyes and she brought her knife down again and watched as the animal instantly transformed into a man. Nicholas stood before her donning his charming crooked grin before he saw that she was injured. His smile turned into a frown.

"You're hurt," he said as he came toward her.

She absently brought her hand up to the wound and winced again. In one stride, Nick was by her side. With gentle hands, he examined the bite marks on her arm. "These need to be tended," he said. "Gabriel, over here!"

Felcore pushed his nose at Nick's hands, nudging him aside and again began to lick Jesse's arm. As the three of them observed the wound began to heal. "Wow!" Jesse said as she brushed her other hand over the newly healed flesh, looked up at them and smiled broadly with relief. "Wow," she said again. "Good boy." Felcore wagged his tail in happy appreciation.

There was another man on horseback that she had not seen before. He dismounted as she looked on and started toward them. The sword he carried was dripping with blood and he wiped it smoothly on the fur of a dead warwolf before quickly sheathing the weapon. His eyes spotted Jesse and a brief smile touched his lips. "Hello. You must be Jesse," he said and extended his hand. When Jesse reached out to shake it, he grasped hers and brought it swiftly up for a kiss. She could feel her cheeks blushing as she looked into his bright blue eyes that danced with good humor. "I'm Stephan," he said.

"Yes, I'm Jesse," she said.

Nicholas was instantly between them, disrupting their eye contact. "This is my cousin from Saberville," he said.

"Nice to meet you," Jesse said, as she looked around Nick at Stephan, who seemed quietly amused.

"Jesse," Gabriel pulled her away from the two men who immediately began harassing each other. "Was Felcore also given wisp magic? It seems he has the ability to heal," she said.

Jesse laughed, "I guess he's a dog that can heal." She laughed again at the play on words, feeling a hysterical edge to it that scared her more than a little.

Gabriel caught it too. "I think maybe you should take a little walk, Jesse. Get away from this mess and regroup. It's okay. I'll go with you," she said.

The two of them were soon joined by Kali and they walked a little way into the woods before they found a stream where they could clean up. Jesse's jeans and shirt were drenched in blood, as was her hair and face. She took off her clothes and washed them out as best as she could. She scrubbed her face and washed out her hair, wishing briefly that she had brought her favorite shampoo from home. Kali had retrieved her backpack and she changed into a clean pair of jeans and a new t-shirt after bathing in the cold water of the creek. It was refreshing and helped her to recuperate a calmer demeanor. As she brushed her hair out, the dogs joined them and frolicked in the creek washing out their own fur of the blood and gore that had coated them. Jesse examined both dogs for wounds and treated them by simply laying her hands of the lacerations or punctures and letting the healing power flow through her.

By the time they returned to the clearing, the men were well involved in incinerating the bodies of the warwolves in a funeral pyre they had built in the middle of the disarray. Kaltog, Nick and Stephan were covered in blood and sweat by the time the last of the warwolves was piled on top of the rest. It was well into evening before they were finished and retreated to the small creek to wash up.

Although their urgency was tantamount, they decided to find a place not too far down the trail to camp for part of the night. A few hours of sleep would do them all good after a very difficult day. After eating a meager portion of road rations and drinking plenty of water, they all settled down around a roaring fire. Gabriel and Jesse cuddled together under a blanket with Felcore close beside them. They both dozed as they held each other enveloped in warmth. Kali and Tica were sleeping soundly, also cuddled in blankets nearby. Kaltog snored loudly propped up against a nearby tree. Nicky and Stephan chatted quietly as they sat wrapped in their own bedrolls next to the fire before drifting off.

Jesse awoke with a sudden start. "*Tempest?*" she called mentally. She uncoiled herself from Gabriel's arms and stood up quietly. Felcore was at her side instantly. "*Tempest, where are you?*" she called again.

There was no answer, nothing but nothingness, an absence of connection that left her lacking, like a piece of her was suddenly missing. "*Tempest?*"

She jumped as somebody touched her elbow. "Is there something wrong, Jesse?" Looking up into clear blue eyes, Jesse discovered Stephan gazing down at her. His face was rough with the stubble of a new beard and he wore a bemused expression.

Swallowing an urge to let herself get lost in his eyes, she stepped back and diverted her gaze. "I'm afraid something is terribly wrong. I can't contact Tempest, my dragon friend. She seems to be lost to me. You don't think she could have been taken like the others, do you?" she asked.

He brought his hand up and pushed a strand of Jesse's hair behind her ear, letting his finger gently brush against her face as he did so. His touch made her shiver. "I don't know. But, it does seem unlikely," he said with a gentle voice.

Another man's voice cut quietly through the night, "What's going on?"

Jesse stepped away from Stephan and found Nicholas staring at them with an unreadable expression on his face. His gold eyes glowed in the moonlight and she felt a thrill deep inside her. She caught her breath. "I think something has happened to Tempest, Nicholas. I can't seem to communicate with her," she said. "How long has it been since you were able to talk with her?" he asked. Nicholas looked concerned as he took a step closer.

She thought for a moment, trying to remember and said, "The last time we spoke, she and Rew had entered the dragon egg-laying grounds and were counting the eggs. She told me that they counted twelve eggs in all, an even dozen. They were going to start turning them right away. That would have been early this morning, before sunrise. What if something bad has happened to her?" Jesse's voice was rising with her distress. "We've got to get going now. We can't wait until sunrise," she said.

"Yes," Nicholas agreed. "I think we've slept long enough. Stephan, get the horses ready. Gabriel, Kali, Kaltog, rise and shine."

Stephan gave Nick a wry smile and clapped him affectionately on the shoulder, "Yes, your highness."

Nicky reached out and took Jesse's hand in his own as he tried to reassure her. "We'll find her, Jesse." His gaze was penetrating as he said, "I promise."

"Okay. Thanks," she said as she withdrew her hand slowly.

After her heart was done racing and she had once again caught her breath, Jesse helped the others pack up camp and get ready to go. They were quickly mounted and moving through the forest, putting the horrors of the warwolves behind them.

The first moon was setting and the second moon was high in the sky, when they broke through the forest's edge. Luck had it that they exited exactly where they needed to be, south of Farreach and north of Colordale. They spurred their horses to a gallop and made great time with Nick flying scout overhead. The way was clear all the way to the outer cliffs. It was late morning when they first saw the ocean. The Island of Zedra was offshore to the west.

Chapter 13
NORTH TO XANDIA

Terese deposited Candaz and Zeth on the shoreline earlier that same morning. Although his father motioned for Zeth to execute their new friend, Zeth didn't think it necessary and was disinclined to kill her. He had actually grown quite fond of Terese. He knew that defying his father would require him to pay a price, but he was willing to do so. The decision to stay his hand made him feel awkwardly at peace.

"Thank you, Terese," Zeth said. "Father will be much better now that he can manage the pain. After we see his doctor in Saberville, we will head home and he will be able to rest. You have done us a great service and I am forever in your debt." Zeth took Terese's hand and bringing it up to his lips, kissed it softly. He gazed briefly into her unusual eyes and found an undeniable magnetism there. Not only that, but he felt a gentleness for her and a protectiveness, a desire to keep her safe. It was a foreign feeling and he didn't know how to process it.

She shyly pulled her eyes away from him and smiled. "You are welcome, Zeth. Safe travels," she said.

He turned over her hand which he still maintained possession of and pressed a gold coin into her palm. "For your trouble. Again thanks," he said.

Maintaining the pretense, he went to his father and helped the old man onto his horse to keep their farce intact. "Let's get going, father," Zeth said.

When Candaz was seated in his saddle he gave Zeth a scathing look. His eyes had daggers that could have killed his son where he stood. Zeth was not taken aback by his father's demeanor. He had seen worse.

The two men headed north. Saberville was about a three day ride and they planned on going around Farreach to avoid the great torg nation.

Fatherhood

The terrain was extremely rough along the rugged coastline and they had to walk their horses carefully or risk injury. One wrong step by a hoof would leave a lame horse that would be of no service to them at all. Candaz was livid with his son and very short tempered not only because Zeth had defied him, but because they had come all this way and had nothing to show for it. The dragons were gone without any sign or indication as to where they had been sent. As of yet they had not unveiled information that would help them to enslave the dragons when or even *if* the dragons could be found. The only positive thing that had occurred was that they had discovered the instruction manual to the gate and had it in their possession. It had yet to be determined what benefit would come from this asset, but surely it would prove useful. Gabriel had come through the gate and so had the girl. Candaz knew they had both come from the same place. They still had family there that could possibly be used to control the two women. There was an opportunity there. He wasn't sure how to take advantage of it yet, but he would find out.

As far as Candaz was concerned, he had one last chance to seize power from the usurper in charge of Saberville and to subsequently conquer the rulers of Brightening. The notorious King Theo, so full of himself, playing royal pain in the ass with his kendrite whore. Two races interbreeding was disgraceful! If he could find a way to take control of the dragons, he could use them to take over both lands and eventually to completely rule all of Risen. It was his last chance and he knew it to be so. His foolish son had sent the dragons away. To where? They still didn't know. It was up to him now to bring them back and enslave them for his own purposes. Should that fail, revenge would become his priority. Revenge against them all would be his highest ambition and his greatest pleasure. Gabriel would pay. Theo would pay. Serek would pay. All of them would feel his wrath.

"Zeth," Candaz spoke over the crashing of the ocean on the rocks below and the heavy breathing of the horses. "Take the next path that goes off to the right. It will take us south of Farreach and get us away from this accursed coastline. It is your fault we're in this situation. I never should have let you play at being sorcerer. You have no idea what you are doing. As always, you have failed me. You are a fool, boy." He let the words drip off his tongue without concern. His son had to learn how to be responsible or he would never be worth anything. The boy had no respect for the sacrifices that he had made over the years to provide him with an inheritance. He had lost so much for the boy.

His hand reached into the left pocket of his cloak and felt the familiar silky material that he kept there. Taking comfort in touching it, he let his hand linger there for only a moment before withdrawing it.

Once they reached Castle Xandia their situation would turn to their favor. He had a couple more tricks in his bag. Soon his time would come.

Under His Father's Thumb

When the path came into view, Zeth took it to the right and soon they were without the roaring of the ocean. It was a welcome break from the constant noise. They rode in silence for a while, but soon Candaz was voicing his displeasure with his son's recent choices. "I can't understand why you let that girl live. She was of no further use to us. There was just no point in it. You are getting weak. You are a fool, Zeth."

It enraged Zeth that Candaz thought of Terese with less regard than he would have for a fly. Why waste the life of such a pretty girl? He felt increasingly defensive toward her, wanting to protect her from him. *No point!?* There was no point in killing her! He didn't think it was foolish at all. His father was wrong.

Candaz was speaking his mind again, "This whole fiasco could have been avoided if you would have listened to me. You are such a fool. Now the dragons are further out of reach than when we began. If I can't put this whole thing right, I will never forget that it was you who put us here. This is my last chance. I won't have you ruin it for me. You leave it to me, Zeth. I don't want you to screw it up again. Fool!"

This might be his last chance, Zeth thought, *but it's not mine.* He said nothing.

"I'm sick of having to do everything. You are worthless, Zeth. I had such great hopes for you, and look at the way you have turned out. You are such a disappointment--a good-for-nothing disappointment," Candaz said.

"Sorry, father," Zeth responded through clenched teeth.

"You are sorry. That's exactly what you are, sorry. I am sick of you. Everything about you makes me ill. I wish you were never born," he seethed.

The day dragged on as Candaz continued to vent his displeasure and Zeth continued to take the abuse in silence. The boiling rage under the surface of Zeth's passive expression was becoming increasingly explosive. His father unknowingly, and foolishly, was adding fuel to the fire, pouring it on in buckets, savagely and unrestrainedly.

By the time they were ready to stop for the night and make camp, Zeth needed to find an outlet for his anger. He was ready to detonate and he couldn't let that happen. After building a fire, he went hunting. Rabbits were in abundant supply and he easily trapped four big specimens. He took his time preparing them to roast, skinning them alive and listening to them scream. The usual pleasure he took from the torture was not to be found. He felt somehow hollow, broken, and strangely sad.

The next day brought another day on the trail toward Saberville and continued abuse by Candaz. Zeth heard over and over again how it was his fault that his father had lost his kingdom. "If it weren't for you, Zeth, I would still be in charge of Saberville and I would still have my army. I gave up everything for you. Everything! I would have ruled all of Risen if it weren't for you. I could have had it all. I was just one step away from total domination. You are my bane child. My downfall. I despise you," he said.

Zeth listened to his father's rants with growing disorientation. In the past the anger he felt at being constantly berated was easily transferred, dealt with by inflicting pain on something or someone else. Of course, he was completely unaware that he did this; it was a spontaneous reaction, a reflex. As much as Zeth tried to dispel the feelings of hate he was beginning to feel for the old man, he couldn't shake it this time. All of the years of abuse, of listening to his father's voice demean him, humiliate him, hurt him was culminating into a mountain of feelings that he could no longer deflect.

Silence dominated Zeth's vocabulary that night as they finished off the rabbits from the night before. He listened to his father continue his tirade until well into the night when he finally fell into a fitful sleep. It was a long night of dreams and nightmares, coming in and out of sleep almost hourly. Jesse no longer was the object of his obsession. The nightmare that dominated the horrors of the night was about Terese. He was laughing as he dragged his knife across her throat and then he kissed her. She looked into his eyes and screamed in horror before dying. The image of her face before him haunted his thoughts throughout the rest of the day. His internal struggle was turning into an increasingly intense battle despite his outward calm.

The access to the catacombs was about a mile away from the populated area of Castle Xandia. It was a rocky and sparsely vegetated landscape with hills and mounds throughout the vast expanse of terrain. Barely noticeable, a small stone archway was tucked discretely into one of the many hills, camouflaged with rocks and straggly plants. The wooden door stood closed and locked. There was nobody around as the two men dismounted their horses and approached the entrance. Candaz quickly dispatched the lock and opened the door. A cold wet draft met their faces as they transcended the threshold into the catacombs.

Chapter 14

DRAGON TEARS

Time had no meaning anymore. All that mattered was the desperation that plagued Skymaster as he lay panting. He had dug into the surface under him until he could dig no more. There was no bottom, no end, nothing. It wasn't really substance after all. Nothing made sense. Physically, the dragon mage was spent. He had no idea how long it had been since he had taken in any food or water, but he knew that his condition was becoming increasingly hopeless. Weakness was taking over his once strong body. He wondered how the other dragons were doing. How could this have happened to them? The inability to do anything was driving him crazy, but action was getting him nowhere. Of course, he knew from his many years of living that his fate was not within his direct control. By acting or by making certain choices he could sway destiny in one direction or another, but ultimately fate belonged to a higher power. Silently, he cried out to the creator to help them.

Trapped

Tempest roared her disapproval into the air. The mighty sound echoed off the enclosed walls of the egg-laying cave in a cacophony of sound, hurting Rew's ears. The wisp quickly covered them and flew to Tempest's nose where he landed and looked the dragon square in the eyes. The swirling red reflected off from Rew's face, making him look like a little cartoon devil. If he had two of himself, one red and one white, they could sit on Tempest's shoulders and debate good and bad behaviors in the dragon's ears, maybe giving *her* a headache. Dragon and wisp communicated mentally, so no verbal words were spoken, but Rew did not hold back reprimanding the upset dragon. "*You cannot roar in this cavern, Tempest. I know you're upset, but such demonstrations give us nothing but a headache. No more roaring in this confined space. Please hush,*" Rew said.

"*I hate being locked up!*" Tempest pouted an extreme dragon pout.

They had tried to exit the cave that morning to hunt and get some breakfast when they found they were magically sealed inside. It was especially frustrating for Rew because it would be possible for him to break through the barrier with his wisp magic, but that was against the rules and he had already been reprimanded several times this year for breaking the rules. One more time and he would lose his position in watching over Risen and he loved taking care of the creatures here. The rules stated that he was not supposed to use his magic to interfere in the eventual outcome of situations that may or may not endanger an inhabitant of the world in which he served. *Stupid rules!* He would wait for now. Things were not quite desperate yet, although, he was getting very hungry. Maybe he could make a dragon omelet.

Tempest roared her disfavor once again, *"You cannot eat my babies!"*

"Please don't do that. Please don't roar again, Tempest! I wouldn't eat a dragon even if I was starving to death, which might be soon. But, you shouldn't be eavesdropping on my private thoughts," he said.

"I'm sorry. I'm hungry and thirsty. I'm worried about Jesse. I'm worried about the babies. I'm worried about all the other dragons. I'm sorry, Rew," Tempest said as she sucked in a deep breath, but before she could bellow it out in a roar, Rew put his hands over her dragon lips and pushed. The air came out in a lopsided raspberry.

"Please don't roar. Jesse will come for us," Rew said.

"When?" Tempest asked.

"I don't know, Tempest, but everything will be okay," he said. If Jesse didn't show up, Rew would have to take action, breaking the rules once again if he had to. Paying the consequences afterward would be the hard part. He loved Risen.

They had only been locked in the cave for less than a day. Although it was exceedingly hot and they had nothing to eat or drink, they were not yet in mortal danger. It would have been wise to have spent the night on the beach, but it was so warm and cozy in the cave. Both the dragon and the wisp had slept well, but when they had tried to leave this morning they discovered that someone had locked them inside.

They had turned the dragon eggs only once since they arrived there a day and a half ago. The twelve eggs were still alive, but after laying his hands on them, Rew felt that something was not quite right. He wasn't sure exactly what was wrong with the baby dragons who were quickly reaching maturity, but there was something off. According to Tempest, the eggs were supposed to be turned every three to four days. These eggs hadn't been turned since the disappearance of the dragons six days ago so maybe they were harmed in some way. He didn't know exactly what seemed off, but it was something. He hadn't shared his concerns with Tempest, choosing to protect her from worrying about that too.

"Why would somebody lock us in here? I don't like being locked up. It's like when that horrible human, Zeth, chained me up and tortured me. I can almost smell him. I want Jesse," Tempest was crying big tears that cascaded down her face and fell onto the blazing sand of the cave with a sizzle.

Rew patted her soothingly on the nose where he still sat. *"It will be okay, Tempest. They will come for us soon,"* he reassured her. He hoped he was right.

In A Clutch

Jesse watched as Nicholas glided down to them on the soft ocean breeze. His golden feathers rippled beautifully as he landed on a jutting rock before them and folded his wings. Magnificently, he transformed before them into the young man with unruly blond hair and bright gold eyes. He had a lean, but muscular form, and stood tall and proud as he smiled at Jesse and greeted Felcore as the dog demanded attention. Nick had an easy, approachable way about him.

"There is a woman on the shoreline, a kendrite woman. She has a small sailboat beached close by. It's possible that she may have seen those we seek," Nick said.

Gabriel spoke quietly, "Perhaps you and Jesse should go talk to her first, Nicholas. I believe it would be best. Personally, I think it would be awfully intimidating if we all approached her at once."

"That sounds like a good idea," Jesse agreed. "Come on, Nick."

The two of them walked over a small rise to the cliffs that overlooked the ocean. The dark-haired woman glanced up at them as they approached. Jesse waved and smiled, but the woman continued to watch them warily.

"Hello, my name is Jesse. This is Nicholas and that is Felcore," Jesse said. She laughed as Felcore approached Terese without reservation and demanded to be petted by pushing his face into her chest. Although the woman complied by scratching Felcore's ears, she kept her right hand on the knife in her belt.

Jesse continued, "We are looking for a couple of men who might have been this way recently. You wouldn't happen to have seen them?"

Eyes the color or light caramel watched them sharply. The woman looked down at Felcore before she answered, "Your business with these men, what is it?"

Nick responded, "They stole a book from us and we need to get it back. It is vitally important that we find them. Can you help us?"

She hesitated and upon reaching a decision spoke, "Two men I helped yesterday go to the island to get a plant for medicinal purposes. Great pain the older man was in. The younger, his son Zeth was trying to help him feel better. We spent the night on the island together and I felt no threat from either of them, although the older man Cal was cold and aloof, probably because of his pain. Charming and friendly was the man named Zeth. Liked him I did. They stole a book from you? Unlikely that seems."

"I'm afraid it's true," he verified. Nick didn't question the rest of her story, yet. "It's very important that we get the book back. Can you tell us where they went?"

"Early this morning we came back here and on their horses they left. They didn't say where they were going," she replied.

"You took them over to the island?" Jesse asked for confirmation.

"Yes," she nodded.

"Did they remove anything from the island, besides the plant?" Jesse asked.

"No. Just the plant they needed for the old man, Cal," she said.

Jesse and Nicholas looked at each other briefly before Jesse turned her gaze to the Island of Zedra in the distance. She wondered if Zeth and Candaz had found the information they were after. She said to Terese, "Our friends are going to be here soon. We also need to go to the island. Would you be willing to convey my grandmother and myself on your boat? We would be happy to pay you for your services."

Again the dark-haired woman hesitated as she thought before answering, "I will convey you and your grandmother. Terese is my name. Payment is not necessary."

"Thank you, Terese," Jesse said and turned to walk back, but the rest of the party was just cresting the hill. Kaltog on his mount could be seen first and then Gabriel and Kali leading their horses. Stephan brought up the rear astride his sleek black horse. Tica ran quickly down to them, greeted Terese briefly before the two dogs took off down to the beach to play.

Introductions were made. Terese offered to share her campfire with them. Kali, Stephan and Kaltog headed down to the shore to fish.

Gabriel was impatient and couldn't sit still. It wasn't long before she asked, "Do you think you could take us over to the island, Terese? We have plenty of time before dinner. We could be there and back before they catch anything to eat."

Terese stood up and stretched. She said, "Sure. Whenever you are ready, I am also."

The three women went down to the boat accompanied by Nicholas and Felcore. As they boarded the tiny craft, Nicholas transformed into a dolphin, melting from his human form into the smooth, sleek creature. Playfully, he jumped and swam back and forth, stopping to look at them and chatter in dolphin language. Jesse laughed, enjoying watching the joyous abandon that he seemed to have as a dolphin. She noticed out of the corner of her eye a peculiar expression on Terese's face. She wondered what it meant, but refrained from asking.

Nicholas, in human form, was waiting for them on the island when they arrived. He helped pull the boat up on the beach and they headed immediately into the jungle. The path that Candaz and Zeth had taken was evident and they followed the same route to the entry into the Temple of Neeg. Gabriel traced a rune and freecurrent energy blazed as they walked through the solid stone into the cavern.

The walls were smooth, like black glass all around the spacious round room that they entered. Gabriel made a small fire in the center of the area with freecurrent energy. It burned an eerie blue and green, reflecting dimly off the walls. The three younger people gazed around in awe at the Temple of Neeg. It wasn't the kind of library Jesse expected at all. The shiny walls were etched all over with the ancient language of the dragon mages, which over the years had been inscribed with their talons.

The room didn't echo but absorbed the sound as Jesse asked quietly, "Grandmother, what does it say?"

Gabriel walked along the wall and ran her hand over the surface. Without looking up she said, "Mostly it records the history of the dragons, births and deaths, that type of thing. But watch." Choosing a very specific spot, she drew a rune, which immediately began to glow blue. Dramatically, she spun in a circle and waved her hand at the walls surrounding them. Suddenly the words that were etched became enflamed with bright orange molten lava, but not only the etchings as they saw them when they first entered, but additional scripts as well. "When Candaz and Zeth were here, they would have read only what was inscribed for all to see. The added text gives us full knowledge as recorded by the mages over the years. It's like taking the phrase 'The child was born', but by adding the missing words, it says, 'The gifted child was loved and lived a happy life after his sister was born.' Do you see the difference?"

"Amazing this is," Terese's comment reflected what they all were thinking.

Jesse asked Gabriel the pertinent question, "Does it tell us what we need to know?"

Gabriel grabbed Jesse's hand and directed her to a portion of the text way up toward the ceiling. She said, "This section talks about the dragons' exodus here to Risen. They came through the gate from a galaxy called 'Arroyo' a long, long time ago. Arroyo was going to be destroyed by its sun that was about to go super nova. The dragons saved themselves at the last minute by coming through the gate. There were only five of them that survived to make a new life on Risen. I wonder if it's possible . . . "

Jesse was interrupted by a very insistent Felcore grabbing her by the arm and pulling her toward the back of the cavern. "Okay, boy. I'm coming," she said. He let go of her arm and guided the way to a tunnel that led off from the main cave. Felcore proceeded down it, but Jesse hesitated as she peered into the darkness.

"Nicholas," she called. "Could you come here for a second?"

Felcore was being very insistent that she follow him by the time Nick arrived from the other side of the cavern. They headed immediately down the tunnel after the dog. It wasn't long before they reached the spot where Zeth had put up the magical barrier. Jesse could feel it before she could see it.

"Look at this," she said to Nick, as she ran her fingers gingerly along the perimeter of the barrier. I'm not sure exactly what this is. She tentatively touched the energy current in front of her and quickly retracted her hand as it stung her fingers. Jesse didn't have the training that Gabriel did with the freecurrent energy, nor did she know runes or their use, but the wisps on Elysia had given her an internal ability to use the freecurrent, to recognize its properties and utilize it. Felcore and Nick watched as she placed her hands on the wall of the cave and absorbed the energy from the spell into her body and dispelled it harmlessly into the air surrounding them. The barrier disappeared.

Immediately Felcore headed down the tunnel toward the light that glowed like a beacon at the end. Jesse headed after her dog and Nicholas followed after her.

They entered a room that was amazingly hot. Black sand that sparkled brilliantly in the light of the lava that surrounded it covered a large expanse in the middle of a room. There were several mounds of black sand scattered throughout the area, big mounds, twelve in all. On the far side slept a beautiful white dragon with a snoring wisp sprawled out across the base of her nose.

"*Tempest,*" Jesse said quietly.

The dragon opened her swirling red eyes slowly and responded, "*Jesse? Am I dreaming?*"

"No. I'm here," she said. She started out across the sand to Tempest, her feet getting hotter with each step she took even through her moccasins. Felcore raced ahead of her and was greeted by a snort of the much bigger dragon, which awakened a startled Rew.

"*I haven't had anything to eat in a while, little gold wolf,*" Tempest said as she licked her dragon lips demonstratively.

"*Rrowff!*" Felcore leapt joyfully at the dragon, ignoring her threatening demeanor.

"*I'm so happy to see you, Tempest. What happened?*" Jesse asked.

"*Zeth trapped us in here, Jesse. He's mean,*" she said.

Nicholas greeted Rew with a grin, "Rew, old man, enjoying your day at the sauna?"

Rew flew up into the air with a big smile on his face. "I knew you would come and rescue us. I hope you brought some food. I'm starved. I've been hungry since we got here. You did bring food, didn't you?" he asked.

With a look of consternation on his face, Nick said, "Well, I'm afraid we don't have anything to eat with us. But, the good news is Kaltog, Kali and Stephan are busy fishing and I'm sure they'll have something ready by the time we get back."

Rew's face brightened even more, "Kaltog is here! Yes!"

The wisp flew to Jesse and gave her a big hug. He whispered in her ear, "Don't tell Tempest, but I think there's something wrong with the eggs." Jesse and Rew exchanged a long heavy look.

Jesse suggested, "*Tempest, why don't you go hunting? Get something to eat. You must be very hungry.*" She scratched the dragon's eye ridges and made her "coo" happily.

"*Okay. I'll be back soon,*" she responded. Tempest flew across to the far side of the cavern, sweeping them with a welcomed breeze from her wings. She folded them into her side and walked into the tunnel opening, waddling down it until she was out of sight. Jesse figured the much bigger dragons who came in here to lay their eggs must have to crouch down in order to fit through the tunnel.

"*Happy hunting, Tempest,*" Jesse called mentally after her.

Immediately she headed to the nearest mound with Rew and together they dug away the black sand and uncovered an egg. It was lying on its side and was big enough for a riding lawnmower to fit inside of it. The shell was the texture of porcelain with an iridescent shimmer to the shiny white surface, much like Tempest's scales. She knelt down next to it and pressed her hands gently to the surface, feeling the incredible energy emanating from it. Felcore came up next to her and pressed his nose to the surface of the egg at the same time Jesse leaned over and pressed her cheek against the warm smooth shell. The essence felt clean and alive. She moved her hands to several different spots and reached the same conclusion.

She commented, "Rew, I don't feel that there is a problem. Tell me why you think there's something wrong."

Rew hovered over the egg and touched it with his hands. "Hmm," he said. "It feels okay to me now. Whatever I felt before seems to be gone."

Nicholas nudged her gently and said, "Jesse, look." He pointed.

Felcore was running from mound to mound, uncovering the eggs one at a time, touching each one with his nose and then covering them back up. He worked with purpose, quickly and determinedly, with his doggy tongue lolling and his tail wagging happily as he went.

"I think he's healing the eggs," Jesse said to Nicholas and they both laughed in delight and amazement.

"That's extraordinary," Rew said.

"He healed me too. Is it wisp magic?" Jesse looked at Rew for the answer.

"I guess so. Imagine that," he said. Rew flew over to Felcore and gave him a great big hug. "You're a good boy. Yes you are." He scratched the dog's furry ears before the two of them started to play chase with each other.

Jesse walked over to an indentation in the sand. "Nick, look at this," she said.

He crouched down and examined the area, sifting through the sand with his fingers. "It looks like there was an egg here recently. That's odd," he said as he looked around at the other mounds. "Do you think someone moved it?"

"Maybe. There are twelve eggs and twelve mounds plus this one. Tempest says she didn't move any of them, just rolled them over. It seems strange," she said.

"That it is. Let's get out of here. I'm cooking," Nick said as he grabbed Jesse's hand and pulled her up. Spontaneously, he swept her up off from her feet and easily carried her across the hot sand to the other side of the cavern.

She tried *not* to enjoy it too much, but the scent of his skin and the feel of his strong arms around her were hard to ignore. "Thanks," she said shyly as he gently put her back on her feet. Turning quickly, she started walking.

He smiled his charming smile, which Jesse missed seeing, and followed after her down the tunnel.

Rew and Felcore beat them to the temple cavern entrance. "There you are," Gabriel said as they all entered together.

"What do you think, Grandmother?" Jesse approached Gabriel where she still stood examining the ancient etchings.

"I can't be sure without knowing what the actual spell was. We need more information. However, I do think we are done here," Gabriel said. She touched the wall, running her hand up and then down again and vanquished the fire in the etchings. All went dark except for the small freecurrent fire that burned blue and green in the center of the room. They left the same way that they had come in.

It was dark and they followed Felcore as he led the way back through the jungle to the beach. Nicholas transformed into his dolphin self, chattered happily at them in dolphin language as they launched the boat and headed back to the far shore.

A lively fire was blazing brightly and the rest of the group had obviously settled in for a comfortable night of camping. The atmosphere, despite their situation, seemed celebratory. They had a large selection of ocean fish cooking aromatically, wrapped tightly in leafy steam pockets sitting alongside the fire. Gabriel used freecurrent magic to produce a light ale that helped take the edge off from everyone's night. They lounged around the fire and spent the evening relaxing and getting to know one another better. Tempest slept a short distance away, enjoying her full stomach with a well-deserved nap.

Jesse was trying to help Stephan use her MP3 player. She pressed the buttons, selected one of her favorite rock songs, took the ear buds out of her own ears, showed Stephan how to place them in his own and waited for a response. The look on his face was priceless as he listened, somewhere between having toothpicks shoved under his fingernails and falling off a cliff. "I don't know, Jesse," he said diplomatically as he removed the buds from his ears. "I don't know if it's for me." He handed back the equipment. Nicholas wanted to try next. He wasn't too sure about the rock and roll either, but seemed less in torment than Stephan did listening to the rhythms. When Terese's turn came, she couldn't get enough. Jesse smiled along with her and gave her a thumbs-up. Terese copied her gesture haltingly and smiled.

Later in the evening Terese confided in Jesse that although she was a kendrite, she did not possess the ability to shape change. It had been a handicap for her growing up in Colordale without having the cultural iconic talent. Her parents had pushed her away, not necessarily intentionally, but they had none the less. She adapted, learning early how to fend for herself; to fish, to bow hunt, and to sail. She enjoyed her life, but although she didn't say so, Jesse could tell that she was lonely. With caution, Jesse told Terese that Zeth had not been completely honest with her about his father or their intentions. She didn't go into great detail about the lies that were told, but didn't want the deception to stay unaddressed either. Terese accepted Jesse's explanation with quiet reserve.

As the evening wore on, individuals wrapped in their sleeping blankets and drifted off to sleep. The cool ocean breeze was soft and fresh, the fire was warm and the camaraderie was congenial with friendships old and new. Rew was cuddled next to Gabriel and Felcore was cuddled next to Jesse as they slept snuggled together. Kaltog's snores kept a steady cadence in the rhythm of the night.

"The babies are coming. The babies are coming! Jesse, wake up!" Tempest trumpeted; waking everybody up in the middle of the night.

"What the . . .?!" Nicholas leapt out of his sleeping blankets with his sword in hand. He looked around searching for the threat that had awakened him from a deep sleep.

Stephan pulled his blanket up over his head and groaned. "Tell that bloody dragon to be quiet," he said.

Rew was up and pulling on Jesse's arm. "We've got to get back to the island. The eggs are hatching. Jesse, wake up. Hurry up!" he said.

She rolled over and looked up into Rew's anxious face. Felcore was running around nudging sleeping bundles into action. Pushing her blankets aside, Jesse climbed to her feet. Spotting Nicholas in his defensive stance, she giggled and said, "Nick, it's okay. Stand down. The dragons are hatching. We've got to get back to the island."

He lowered his sword and asked, "Can we watch?"

"Sure. Let's go," she said. Jesse mounted Tempest quickly and helped Felcore up in front of her. "Gabriel, are you coming?" "Yes, hold on. I'll come with you. Terese, can you bring all the others over on the boat?" she asked. "We'll meet you there in the egg-laying cavern." Gabriel swung smoothly up onto Tempest back behind Jesse.

"Okay, I'll have to make two trips, but it shouldn't take too long," she said. Terese immediately headed down to prepare to leave on the boat. She was going to bring Kali and Stephan over first and then come back for Kaltog.

Nicholas, Rew and Tempest took to the air without further conversation and flew over the ocean to the island. They came in through the cone of the volcano, landing inside the Temple of Neeg as the dragons did. Nicholas transformed back into human form while Gabriel, Jesse and Felcore dismounted Tempest. Gabriel made a small glowing freecurrent shape in the middle of the cavern that lighted the area with dim blue and green light. They all headed into the tunnel and made their way quickly to the other end. The heat of the egg-laying cavern hit them before they arrived into the expanse of the sand filled room. Gabriel turned to Jesse and said, "I'm going to go down to the beach and escort the others here. I'll be back soon."

Tempest went to the closest mound and pushed her nose against the egg that had a large crack running across the top of it. Felcore ran around in extreme excitement from mound to mound, egg to egg, inspecting each cracking egg individually.

Kali and Stephan came through the tunnel entrance where they took in the view before them. "Wow, they're bigger than I expected," Stephan said as he walked over to one of the mounds and inspected the large crack that was appearing to widen.

Kali and Tica had wandered over to the farthest egg and peered inside a fissure the size of her hand. A swirling red eye gazed out at her. "Look at this," she said to no one in particular.

Kaltog, Terese and Gabriel came in and began watching the slow action that was taking place in front of them. Each of them chose an individual egg to keep an eye on. All of them were spread out around the room watching the event take place.

Tempest started a deep down throaty hum as she went from egg to egg. The eggs themselves seemed to be humming and vibrating as the baby dragons slowly broke out of their shells. *"They're coming, Jesse. This is so exciting!"* Tempest said.

"Yes, it is," Jesse agreed. It was awesome. Rew was flying around the room completely involved in the excitement of the occasion.

The faces of Jesse's friends were bright with wonder and anticipation as they watched the baby dragons slowly break free from their nurturing cocoons. The first one to get his head all the way out of his shell was right in front of Stephan, who reached out to tentatively touch the nose of the little dragon. They were bonding Jesse realized instantly and she heard the baby's voice in her head as he spoke to Stephan. *"I am your Zlato. You are my Stephan."* The dragon suddenly stood up and shattered the rest of the egg. His wings were wet when he stretched them out and shook before folding them back to his sides. The scales on his body gleamed with a beautiful gold shimmer, like he had been dipped in liquid gold.

Next to break free was the dragon in front of Kali, who sat back as the she-dragon reached out her neck and pressed her nose to Kali's chest. Again Jesse heard the baby dragon's voice as she spoke to banderg girl. *"I am your Sweet Vang. You are my Kali."* She crooned as she destroyed the rest of her shell. She also was a magnificent gold.

Kaltog helped the little dragon in front of him by extending the crack that the baby had begun. This little gold dragon burst forth from his shell with a dramatic eruption. *"I am your Grand Oro. You are my Kaltog."* The torg reached out and scratched the dragon's eye ridges as he cooed happily.

The dragon egg in front of Nicholas was next to shatter his shell. Nick responded to him by touching him lovingly on the nose as the dragon pressed against him. *"I am your Golden Agape. You are my Nicholas."* Nick scratched the eye ridges on the youngster until the baby dragon responded with an audible "cooing" as he looked up at Jesse and gave her a warm smile that conveyed his feelings.

Six other dragons crashed loose within the next few minutes. They were all the same beautiful brilliant gold and Tempest greeted each one of them by touching noses. Four of them were girls and two of them were boys. They named themselves the same as the others, but did not bond with anyone there. Their names were Treasure, Nugget, Sovereign, Blaze, Pieces of Eight, and Krugerrand. Rew introduced himself to all of the newborns with exuberant joy. Jesse believed that the wisp was hoping for a bonding, but that didn't happen for him. She hoped he wasn't too disappointed when it did not occur. Neither she nor Gabriel bonded with a dragon, but of course, Jesse had Tempest and Gabriel had both B.F. and Skymaster always on call.

Two eggs remained. The rest of the dragons, freshly born were stretching their wings out and letting them dry in the heat of the cavern. Felcore was running around making fast friends with each one of them. Another dragon poked his head out and crooned loudly. Her name was Luster Dust.

The last of the dragons broke out into the chaos of his brothers and sisters, looked around and found Terese. He nuzzled against the kendrite woman immediately and said, "*I am your Gold Stone. You are my Terese.*"

"Oh," she said as she responded immediately to the golden dragon. "Hello, Gold Stone." Her face lit up magnificently.

Tempest was tending to the babies like a mother hen. Once all of their wings were dry, she had them follow her through the tunnel to the temple cavern and from there they tried their new wings by flying up and out of the volcano cone. "*Aren't they beautiful?*" Tempest purred to Jesse.

"*They are very beautiful, Tempest. Why are they all gold? Are all baby dragons gold?*" she asked. Jesse had never seen a gold dragon. Of course, she had never seen a dragon period until just recently. Skymaster and BF were silver. Although Jesse had never seen Breezerunner, she knew from reading Gabriel's diary that he was a silver blue color. Tempest, of course, was a beautiful iridescent white, like a prism when the light reflected on her just right.

"*They are one of a kind--well, twelve of a kind. It's Felcore's healing touch that instilled the golden hue,*" Tempest told her.

Jesse remembered Felcore running from egg to egg yesterday touching them with his nose. The dragons were gold because they were healed by a golden retriever. "*That's funny. Who is their sire?*" she asked.

"*Balls of Fire is their sire. Boomerang is their mother,*" Tempest replied.

Everybody headed to the beach. Tempest and the baby dragons went hunting as Terese conveyed the rest of the party back to the distant shore. It was late in the morning by the time they got back to camp and started packing up their gear to continue their search for Zeth and Candaz.

When the dragons returned from hunting, they seemed to have actually grown. *"What did you feed them, Tempest? They've doubled in size,"* Jesse asked.

"Just a couple of fish, well, a couple of hundred actually. Baby dragons grow very fast," her dragon told her. Tempest held herself very proudly.

"We were very hungry, Jesse," said Golden Agape.

"Yes, starving really, Jesse," said Krugerrand.

"The fishes were yummy," this was from Blaze.

"Can we go hunting again soon?" asked Gold Stone.

"Yes, can we? I think I'm hungry again," remarked Zlato.

"Soon, little ones, soon. First, we must carry our new family to where they wish to go," Tempest told her young companions.

They all mounted their various dragons. Tempest and Jesse led the way, a small line of dragons and riders in the sky, off to Farreach. Kaltog didn't ride Grand Oro, being that his size was a little too large for his newborn dragon. The two of them were about the same size at the moment. He rode his mount while leading the rest of the horses and was going to meet them at Farreach.

Chapter 15

ONCE UPON A TIME

Jessabelle flew down and landed gracefully on the hind quarters of Theo's horse. They had been traveling for two days and were nearly to Skyview. She transformed into a human and wrapped her arms around Theo's waist. She leaned over and whispered in his ear, "Clear the way is. Open stands the gate to Skyview." She pressed her lips to his neck and he brushed his cheek against her soft hair. It had been a long time since they had visited Skyview. Jessabelle missed Link and Berry, having not seen them since the last festival. They hadn't expected to see their friends again until the fall. Fibi was getting married in the fall and they had planned on attending, had indeed already sent their acceptance on the return card in the invitation. This visit was unexpected. Theo had decided to travel to Castle Xandia and they were just stopping over in Skyview for the night.

The southern gate to Skyview was ornately carved milkwood with scenes of bandergs in industrious occupations. An archway over the gate avowed, "Greetings weary travelers. Skyview will give you respite. Our home in the mountains is yours. Step through the threshold and be welcome one and all." Theo had known a time in recent history when the gate to Skyview was closed and locked. Travelers were indeed *not* welcome. Times had changed since Candaz's defeat thirty years ago. The races were once again embracing peace and tolerance. The restoration of the Table of Alliance had helped the relationships between the races to be mended. Free trade between the communities of Risen was making a come-back. The bandergs had only recently swung the gates to Skyview wide open in a demonstration of trust and openness.

They rode through the threshold and down the corridor until they entered a large common area. A huge fountain of stone graced the center of the room. It bubbled joyously with clear sparkling water. Down the center of the fountain was a scar in the stone, a clean line the color of dusty rose, evidence of when the fountain was torn apart by Candaz and subsequently healed by Gabriel. A banderg girl approached them and offered to take their horse. Theo dismounted and helped Jessabelle down by grabbing her around the waist, letting his hold around her linger as he pulled her closer for a moment. He smiled easily at the banderg girl who awaited his reins. "Please take him to the north gate stable for our departure tomorrow," Theo instructed her. He handed the girl some carrots along with a silver coin, "Make sure he gets brushed out and that he gets these treats. Thank you. Your service is much appreciated," he said.

"Come Jessabelle my love, let's go find Link," Theo said as he took his wife by the hand and led the way down multiple corridors. He knew Skyview quite well, having spent a good amount of time there after the Battle of Skyview.

"Know where you are going I assume, my king?" Jessabelle asked in a teasing voice. "I do not wish to find myself in a place alone, far removed from civilized society with a rogue such as yourself."

He responded playfully, "Ha. You would do well not to find yourself in such a situation, my queen." Theo squeezed Jessabelle's hand as he guided her around a corner. He spun her toward him and pressed her up against the wall. "A rogue such as myself might not mind his manners." The kiss that followed was one that showed the love and passion that still dwelt within each of their hearts after thirty years of wedded harmony and occasional disharmony. Marriage was work, but it had its benefits.

They heard the uncomfortable giggles of bandergs coming down the corridor and ended their embrace. Theo's green eyes drank in Jessabelle's golden ones with amorous hunger before breaking away from his wife. As the bandergs passed carrying baskets of food, they bowed their heads slightly, "Your highnesses."

"Ladies, good day to you," Theo said nodding his head at them. They giggled as they continued down the hall. Jessabelle yanked on Theo's hand and led the way to the kitchen.

A banderg kitchen is a kitchen that never rests. It was buzzing with activity and Jessabelle and Theo had to avoid many bandergs racing to do the bidding of their head chef. There was no time for courtesies and no one stopped or bowed or in any way acknowledged the royal couple in their presence. The two of them walked through the massive kitchen until they found the man in charge of it all. "Link!" Theo grasped his hand and shook it even though the banderg had not quite registered the appearance of his old friends. Link stood back and pulled on his beard a moment. He looked to one side and then the next and then back again.

"Theo? Jessabelle?" He stepped forward and gave them both warm hugs after their being there registered in his head. "What are you doing here?" he asked.

"We're on our way to Castle Xandia," Theo replied. He pointed to the stove. "Your pot's boiling over."

Link whipped around and turned the heat down on the stove. "Oh, dear. Mary, mind this will you?" he said to one of the chefs before returning his attention to them. "Xandia? Just visiting the relatives?"

"There is a problem, Link. The dragons are missing. Candaz is alive. Gabriel's son, Zeth also lives and apparently is up to no good," Theo told him.

"Oh my. That's terrible," Link replied as he started pulling on his long beard.

"We are traveling to Xandia to meet with Serek and Kris to make a plan. I can no longer stomach sitting around doing nothing but administrative work while B.F. and the others are missing," Theo said.

"And Gabriel?" Link asked.

"Track the pair does she and her granddaughter. Kali and Rew they are with. Nicky intends to join them as well. We have not heard from them," Jessabelle provided.

"All of the dragons are gone? Just gone?" Link asked.

"Without a trace," Theo said, his face reflecting his deep concern.

"I'm going with you," Link said simply.

"Link, we didn't come here to drag you away from your family. We're not even sure what the next course of action is," Theo said.

"I'm going with you," Link said again. "Just let me get things straightened out here. Mary, Toni, Jeri," he called. "Here's what I need done . . . " Link became very busy giving instructions to his staff. He completely forgot about Theo and Jessabelle. They excused themselves without being heard and went to seek out Berry and Fibi.

After a comfortable, enjoyable evening with old friends and a good night's sleep in the guest room, they met Link at the northern gate. He had been up earlier in the morning than they and had spent the morning giving directives to his chefs. "You ready?" Theo asked.

Link pulled on his beard in his typical worried fashion and mounted his pony before he said, "I think so. Let's go."

They headed out through the northern gate that had been destroyed by Candaz during the Battle of Skyview. A crew was at work restoring the ancient work of art that reflected in some aspects the intact southern gate. Originally the gate was made of milkwood which used to grow in Xandia, but milkwood was now extinct. Instead they were carving the door out of an ancient redwood they had imported from Farreach. The travelers stopped to exchange greetings and then found the trail that would take them north to Saberville.

A couple of days ride took them to the foothills that announced the boundary into Saberville. The landscape bore mild moguls with large rocks imbedded and sparse vegetation intertwined. Ocean breezes brought a strong scent of the salty sea that lay just over the terrain they traversed. Castle Xandia came into view in the distance. It sat upon a large rise just off the rocky coast. A large village had risen up around the castle grounds in the recent decades. The inhabitants subsisted mostly on a very healthy fishing trade. In the last decade the region had become well known for the fine wines they produced.

The approach to Castle Xandia was well maintained with colorful flowers in large pots and street lamps along the way. It was a warm beautiful night when they arrived. They left their horses in the stable and walked up to the main entrance of the castle. Traveling without an entourage enabled them to stay relatively unobtrusive. Unless somebody specifically recognized them as the King and Queen of Brightening, they could easily just be well dressed merchants or other such visitors at the castle. Bandergs were often seen in Saberville conducting business so the sight of Link posed nothing that would draw attention either. Theo knocked on the large double doors and waited.

The man who opened the door took a moment to recognize them and immediately ushered them in. "Please make yourself at home," he said before leaving the room. They were in a spacious living room with two large white couches positioned across from each other on a plush white rug. Deep blue and vibrant orange accents scattered throughout the room brought a nice splash of color. It certainly reflected Kristina's tastes more than Serek's.

"Theo!" Kristina ran into the room with a sparkling smile on her face and embraced her brother ecstatically. "Look at you. You're getting older." She ran her fingers along the gray hair at his temples.

Theo grabbed her hand and brought it away from his face. "You haven't aged a day, Kris. What are you? Seventeen? Certainly not a day over twenty," he said good-naturedly.

"I see you haven't lost your silver tongue, brother." She turned to Jessabelle, "It's so good to see you, Jessabelle. I have missed you. We have so much to talk about." The two sisters-in-law embraced warmly.

"Time to talk we'll have to find. Missed you too I have, Kris. It's been too long," she responded. Jessabelle and Kristina had become very close but seldom were able to see each other due to their busy schedules.

Kristina turned to Link and gave him a big hug. "Link. I haven't seen you in ages. How are Berry and Fibi?" she asked.

"They are well. Busy with wedding plans," he said.

"Of course," she said. "We are looking forward to the trip to Skyview for the wedding."

"Where's Serek?" Theo asked.

"He'll be back soon. He had to ride out to the vineyard," Kristina replied.

"And Stephan?" Theo asked.

Her light and airy visage slipped a little into concern as she answered, "Stephan went with Nicholas. Have you heard anything?"

"No nothing," Theo responded.

"Do you have any idea where they might be headed?" Kristina asked.

"Gabriel thought they would investigate the library at the Temple of Neeg," he told her what little he knew. Theo walked over to the window and gazed out as he talked. "This is so damn frustrating, not knowing what to do."

Jessabelle went to his side and touched his arm. He automatically put his arm around her. "I should fly to the south I believe, to the Island of Zedra. I will see something maybe," she suggested.

The door opened and in strode Serek. The burgundy and black he wore complimented his lean muscular form. A long black coat hung down over boots that topped his calves. His dark beard was neatly trimmed, but long hair hung in disarray down to his shoulders and had slight touches of gray. Dark blue eyes swept the room and a smile touched his lips as he greeted them. He embraced and kissed his wife last but not least. He walked over to a table laden with pitchers and glassware and opened a bottle and poured them all a glass. "This is excellent nectar the vineyard produced last year. I think you'll enjoy it," he said with pride.

Link's eyes lit up as he enjoyed the intricate flavors of the concoction. He raved, "This is wonderful, Serek; the best yet. Master Lankin continues to improve; putting him in charge of the overall management of the vineyard was a wise choice. I'm impressed with the quality of the product he's been putting out. Very impressed. Of course, the weather makes its own contribution to the quality of the grapes. Last year I know was exceptional."

Serek responded, "Yes, I've been more than satisfied with Master Lankin's expertise. Thank you for recommending him. He and his family seem to be settling into the community quite well. As far I as know they haven't had any trouble being bandergs in an otherwise human society.

We have recently made a deal with the torg nation at Farreach to supply the winery with oak barrels cut from the forests in their territory and made by their expert coopers. Our first shipment is due to arrive next month."

Theo finished his glass of nectar in a gulp and went to pour another. "The bandergs have been instrumental in many projects around Brightening as of late. It is good to see our different communities which were closed only ten or twenty years ago beginning to interact and open up. It is a start," he commented.

Theo continued, "Jessabelle's father, King Shane has always been quite adamant about keeping the kendrites isolated. Jessabelle has been working on trying to reverse that way of thinking in Colordale for many years with only limited success. The torgs and the kendrites together have been bridging the gap in trade between their two nations. Brightening has plans to complete a trade route with Colordale and Farreach, also. We've been working closely with Kaltog to facilitate this goal."

"We continue to make progress to further commerce between the nations. The vineyards for instance are becoming quite successful," Serek said.

"Serek and I have been tossing around the idea of resurrecting the community of New Chance. It is a prime area for grape production." Kristina tipped her glass back and forth and gazed at the color of the nectar as she held it up to the light while she said, "There also are apple orchards in that vicinity that could be brought back to production with some tending and a little tender loving care."

Serek smiled at his wife. "Yes, but that is for another day, Kris. Right now we have other problems to address. Theo, have you heard anything?" he asked. "Nick told us that Gabriel and her granddaughter are tracking Candaz and his son Zeth? Is that right?"

"We haven't heard anything. Communication is quite impossible without the dragons to relay messages for us. It's so frustrating not knowing anything. Jessabelle believes that it would be prudent for her to fly south and take a look around. Perhaps it would be wise," Theo commented.

Serek's voice became more impassioned, "We must not let Candaz get another foothold in this world. He breeds only fear and intolerance. It would be better not to be sitting here blind. Perhaps Jessabelle could find out what is going on."

Jessabelle stood up from the couch and placed her glass upon the table in front of her. "Go now I shall," she said. She went to Theo and wrapped her arms around him before giving him a quick kiss.

"Be careful," he said quietly to her before kissing her more thoroughly. "We will wait until you report back to act. Return as soon as you can, love."

Jessabelle transformed into a beautiful bald eagle before their eyes. Theo opened the window and let her fly free.

Chapter 16

FARREACH

The great torg nation of Farreach was located off the coastal cliffs and in a beautiful valley tucked into a bowl within those cliffs. Tempest soared down into the valley followed closely by twelve shiny gold dragons, five of which carried passengers. They landed in the common square where the memorial to Shareen was located. Torgs stopped to watch the spectacle as the dragons settled on the ground. Gabriel jumped off from Nugget and patted the dragon affectionately on the nose and said, "*Thank you, Nugget.*"

"*You're welcome, Mistress Gabriel,*" Nugget replied.

Stephan was the first to Tempest's side and he reached up to help Jesse down, stretching up and catching her around the waist as she jumped from the height of Tempest's back. She smiled at him as he slowly released his hold on her.

"Thanks. Did you enjoy the ride?" she asked.

"Yes. Very smooth. I've ridden on Breezerunner before, of course, but this was different; maybe because Zlato is much smaller than Breezerunner, maybe because we're bonded. I don't know, but, yes it was very smooth. You?" Stephan asked. He seemed to be trying too hard to impress her, which amused Jesse somewhat but at the same time disconcerted her. He was so cute and his blue eyes were so magnificent and he was charming and handsome *and a prince*. He had it all. She liked him well enough, it was just that . . . well . . .

Her eyes found themselves seeking out Nicholas, who was still sitting atop Golden Agape, scratching the dragon's eye ridges as he laughed with Kali about something. When he noticed her watching him, she quickly looked away, embarrassed. "Tempest is awesome in flight. We seem to fit together like a hand in glove. Thank you for asking, Stephan," she answered him with her cheeks blushing.

After they were all dismounted, Tempest took the baby dragons hunting again after many complaints about how empty their poor tummies were. The remaining party was greeted by old friends of Gabriel's. Lindi and Brandig both swept Gabriel right off her feet and hugged her tight in greeting. Rocnor, the king and Kaltog's father came thundering down the path and hugged Gabriel affectionately. It was decided by those in the vicinity of the square to have a celebration that evening to honor their guests. A tremor went through the torg village as word spread and excitement began to build that there was to be a party. By the time Kaltog rode in a little later in the day, preparations were well under way with food and drink being laid out on elaborate tables in the midst of the square. The torgs were evidently well practiced at throwing shindigs and were soon set up with little exertion.

The girls went with Lindi to bathe and get cleaned up. Jesse washed out her jeans and tee and hung them up to dry. The other pair of jeans she had with her had been drenched in blood by the warwolves, and although she had washed them out once already, they still needed a really good scrubbing with soap to get them good and clean. That left her with the small white summer dress that Jim's daughter Susie had given to her. It was comfortable and would be okay for tonight, but not for riding dragon back. She hoped her jeans would dry out in time. Gabriel and Kali had put on fresh clean clothes as well. They all brushed out their hair and felt much better after getting the dust of the road washed off. When they caught up to the men, it was obvious they had also spent some time washing up, and they looked refreshed and comfortable as they sipped on full mugs of ale where they sat in chairs around the fire.

A bonfire had been lit in the center of the square and paper lanterns hung in the trees, lighting the night with a beautiful array of colors. A band was playing on a small stage opposite where the food had been set up. Someone handed Jesse a mug of ale and she found a chair next to Kali and Terese and began sipping it very slowly. She didn't drink and did not want to become drunk, having learned already that to overindulge was just asking for trouble. But, if she took it slow and ate enough food, she knew she would be okay if she stuck to her limit, which was two. The atmosphere was casual and festive. Laughter and conversation came easy. Felcore walked over and sat at her feet and was soon sleeping quietly. Gabriel was in deep conversation with Kaltog and Rocnor where they sat at a table by themselves. Stephan and Nicholas were sitting across the fire from her laughing and joking with Rew. They seemed to be enjoying themselves.
Jesse asked Kali, "Do you have a boyfriend back home?"

Kali laughed and said, "No. I am too busy with work. How about you?"

"No. I guess I'm too busy with school and taking care of dad and Jacob," Jesse replied.

"Jacob is your brother, right? Gabriel talks about him," Kali said.

"Yeah. He's fourteen. He's okay for a brother." she answered. Jesse smiled as she thought of him. "I miss them both."

"I have three brothers," Kali said. "They are all older than me, married and have children. I am the auntie to eleven nieces and nephews."

"Wow. That's great. I'll bet Christmas is fun," Jesse commented.

Kali gave her a questioning look. At the same time the dragons trumpeted their return. They landed in the square and immediately looked for isolated corners to curl up in and go to sleep. Again, they seemed to have grown considerably after eating. At this rate, they would soon be as big as Tempest and would quickly outgrow her. *"Did you have a successful hunt, Tempest?"* Jesse asked.

"Oh, yes. We found a herd of black deer up in the mountains. Very tasty. I'm sleepy." Tempest yawned a big dragon yawn.

"Go to sleep, sweetie," Jesse said. *"Good night."*

"Good night," she said and was almost immediately snoring as were all of the babies.

Terese commented quietly, "Strange and exciting this fishing trip has turned out to be. Bonding with a dragon is not something I would have anticipated. This has become an adventure."

"I agree with you, Terese," Jesse sighed. "This has certainly become an adventure. I never expected to be here. Life certainly has a way of taking you for a ride."

Nicholas walked over and asked, "Jesse, would you like to go for a walk with me?"

She felt her heart speed up its pace. "Sure," she said as she reached out and took his proffered hand and stood up.

It was a beautiful night in Farreach. A warm breeze blew in from the ocean which could be heard crashing rhythmically on the shore in the distance, muted and relaxing in its cadence. The stars were shining brightly in the sky with the first moon high and the second moon low over the horizon. Colorful paper lanterns lined the walkway as they strolled slowly down the path. They were not completely alone. Other couples occasionally walked by absorbed in quiet conversation.

"The dragons seemed very satisfied and exceedingly happy having full bellies," Nicholas commented.

"Yes. I think that they would be purring in contentment if they could purr," Jesse replied as she walked casually next to him.

Nicholas stopped and turned with a question in his eyes, "What is 'purring'?"

Jesse laughed, "It's what cats do when they're happy. You know." She made a noise that was supposed to be a purr, but would have been hard to discern as such.

"Actually, I don't know what a 'cat' is," Nicholas said.

"You don't have cats on Risen?" Jesse asked.

"No, no cats." They continued walking in silence for a time before Nick said, "Stephan is really a nice guy. I think he likes you."

Jesse replied quietly, "Oh?" *This was unexpected.*

Nicholas continued, "I understand if you like him, too. He's very handsome I guess, for a guy anyway." He had stopped walking suddenly and was looking off in the distance, frowning.

"Nick, I . . . " she began.

He turned to gaze at her and she felt her spirit soar. There was something about him that took her self-control away; which made her somehow melt like warm butter...and yet brought her strength like she could face anything if he was by her side. Suddenly, she had an overwhelming need to touch him. She reached out her hand and brushed a lock of hair away from his eyes, shining gold eyes that imprisoned her heart. "It's you," she said.

They drew closer to each other. A strange but enjoyable shiver ran through her body. She could feel his soft breath as their lips met, warm and yielding . . .

The wind from a large set of wings interrupted the moment and when they looked up a large bald eagle stood majestically before them.

"Mom?" Nick said in surprise as Jessabelle turned into her human form.

"Nicky. Jesse." She acknowledged them with an appraising look on her face. "The others, where are they?"

"They're at the square. Why are you here?" Nicholas asked his mother.

"You know your father, Nicky. No longer could he sit still and wait. We travelled to Castle Xandia with Link, arriving there earlier this evening. I decided to fly south to see what I could see. Here you both are it seems," she said with bright eyes.

"Yes, here we are," Nick said as he looked at Jesse and gave her that irresistible grin that made her knees go weak.

Jesse tore her gaze away from Nicholas long enough to address Jessabelle, "We have a lot to tell you. We are heading to Castle Xandia tomorrow. Come on. We'll take you to Gabriel and she can fill you in on everything. Nick has some interesting news for you, too."

Jessabelle looked at her son with curiosity. "What is it, Nick?" she asked.

He beamed as he told her, "I bonded with a dragon. His name is Golden Agape and he is beautiful."

"Wonderful Nicky! The whole story I want to hear," she said.

They all started walking toward the square where music could be heard and the bonfire could be seen lighting up the clearing. Nick grabbed and held onto Jesse's hand as they walked together. She didn't mind at all and entwined her fingers with his.

Stephan stood up to greet Jessabelle properly, giving his aunt a friendly hug. He noticed Nicky and Jesse's hands clenched together and gave Nick a shrug of his shoulders and a raised eyebrow. His chances with her had been a long shot anyway and he knew it. Jesse wasn't someone who would be available for a fling. She was someone for a long term type of relationship, the type of girl he would someday marry. The depth of her character made her special. Although he thought with the right atmosphere he might be able to nurture their subtle attraction into something more; it was now out of his hands. The way Nick and Jesse looked at each other was filled with emotional fire. They had both fallen hard. He would bow out gracefully. Obviously, Nicky was her choice. He could live with that.

They all chose seats around the warm bonfire and filled Jessabelle in. Everybody excitedly talked about their experiences bonding with the baby dragons. Nick said, "You would not believe how fast they are growing, mother. Golden Agape has at least tripled in size since he hatched. They eat and sleep, eat and sleep."

"I can hear that they sleep well," Jessabelle laughed. The thirteen dragons could be heard snoring loudly in the little nooks they had chosen to curl up in. It was quite the chorus!

"What of Candaz?" Jessabelle asked.

Kali answered, "We believe he and Zeth are heading up to Castle Xandia. What their intentions are I don't know, but we will stop them."

Terese dropped her head, "I should not have helped them. I didn't know. Normal, even kind, seemed Zeth. Sorry I am."

Jesse reached over and put her hand on Terese's leg and said, "You didn't know. Zeth can be very charming. It's not your fault. You were simply doing a kindness to a stranger. Please don't feel bad that you did so."

Jessabelle added, "Regretted kindness should never be. You did not intend harm. Rest your heart, Terese. Tonight I will head back to Castle Xandia where we will await your arrival." Jessabelle got up and walked away from the group with Gabriel at her side. The two women hugged and Jessabelle transformed back into an eagle and launched herself into the sky. Gabriel watched her go before turning around and rejoining them.

"It's late. I'm going to get some sleep. We will be leaving first thing tomorrow," Gabriel told them all before retiring. They had been given a small cottage for the evening. Of course, small by torg standards was somewhat substantial. Kali and Terese went with her. Stephan was in deep conversation with Kaltog and another torg who apparently was the master cooper in charge of the barrel order for the winery in Saberville.

Jesse yawned, feeling suddenly very sleepy. She looked at Nicholas who was watching the fire and said to him, "I think I'm going to get some sleep, too."

"I'll walk you over," he said as he stood up and offered his hand to her. They walked slowly hand-in-hand over to the little cottage. She turned to him when they reached the door and without hesitation wrapped her arms around his neck, reached up and finished the kiss they had started earlier, sweetly and slowly. Nick's voice was husky as he said, "Goodnight, Jesse. I'm just going to check on Agape before I go to bed. . . .Jesse?"

"Yes?" she asked. She was lost in his beautiful eyes.

"I know maybe this is a little soon and I don't want to scare you away, but . . . I can't believe I'm going to say this. I think I'm in love with you," he said. Nick's cheeks flushed but he held her gaze.

She reached up and brushed his hair back with her fingertips. "I never thought I would feel this way about anybody, Nick. Maybe it's just chemistry. Love is something more. Let's just take this a day at a time and see what happens, but, I think I love you, too." Her desire for him was so strong she had to force her reserve.

They kissed again and then slowly let each other go. "Goodnight," she whispered to him.

"Goodnight, Jesse. Sweet dreams," he whispered back.

Falling

Skymaster awoke suddenly from a terrifying nightmare. He was falling from the sky and could not unfurl his wings to stop his deadly descent to the rocks below. A heavy groan escaped his parched throat and with much effort he shifted his mighty head to a new position where he lay. He felt so helpless. Mentally, he cried out to the creator for comfort, for aid, for relief. *"Help us!"*

Chapter 17
XANDIA DOWNUNDER

The catacombs of Saberville were carved ages ago in the soft volcanic rock underneath Castle Xandia. They extended out and down through the generations as the need arose for space. The main entrance was through a beautiful chapel and down a set of stairs tiled in an intricate mosaic pattern in the lower part of Castle Xandia. It was a wide staircase that narrowed gradually as it descended to the depths. A burial party would wrap their dead in linen cloth and carry the body into the catacombs with lit torches lining the way. The earliest graves were the first ones encountered on the way into the ancient tunnels. There were four layers of niches where the dead lay entombed behind stones and mud sealing them forever inside. Markers decorated the graves indicating who lay behind the closures in different forms such as a warrior's shield or a family crest. The tunnels branched off in all directions as they turned and twisted under Saberville. One could easily become lost in the endless maze.

The small forgotten entrance a mile or so away hidden in the hills of Saberville accessed a branch that had mainly been used for maintenance over the years; excavations often were transmitted through the tunnel and out into the surrounding landscape. It was kept closed and locked, denying easy admittance to any passersby. There were other such access tunnels in different sections of the catacombs; all of them as unobtrusive as the next. When burial caverns were excavated the excess soft volcanic rock would be hauled out. The remaining soil, when exposed to the air would become solid over time.

It seemed long ago, maybe days ago that Zeth had followed Candaz through the threshold and into the tunnel. It was dark despite the small light that the sorcerer had made with his fingers. A musty moist air smelling strongly organic embraced them. The tunnel declined gradually for about one hundred yards before leveling off. They took the first branch to the left and then the second to the right. For several hours they walked; either turning left, right or going straight until Zeth completely lost track of the path they had taken. Before long, every turn, every grave, every tunnel looked the same. Candaz strode through the tunnels with determination, but eventually began to grumble under his breath. Confusion was building in his body language as he hesitated before choosing directions and began turning his head from left to right before deciding on a course. They continued on all day, breaking only once to have some water and a bite of the jerky they had with them.

Zeth finally questioned his father, "Do you know where we are?"

"I'm lost. I'm sure I made the turns correctly. Maybe we came in from the wrong access point. They all look very much alike," he replied.

Claustrophobia was not a friend of Zeth's. Tight spaces were especially suffocating to him. Panic was threatening to overcome his rational thoughts. He tried to breathe calmly and deeply to overcome the fear that permeated his being. With a controlled voice, he asked, "Can you get us out of here?"

Candaz snapped, "I will get what I came here for! Getting out is not important. I will find the way. Don't question me, foolish boy."

Zeth persisted, giving in to his panic, "Can you get us out of here?"

"It doesn't matter if I can get us out of here. The only thing that matters is that I find the marker I seek!" he shouted.

"But, you don't know where we are, father!" Zeth shouted back.

Candaz took a deep breath, pinned Zeth with his dark pointed stare and said, "I will find what I am after or I will die trying."

The younger man gritted his teeth, biting back angry words, and turned away. The anxiety that assaulted him was familiar, unwelcomed, but familiar. *How could the old man have made such a vital mistake?* They could be lost in this accursed burial place for the rest of their lives, which might be very short if they couldn't get out of here. He never figured he would meet his end in a dark underground tomb, lost and starving to death. *How could the old man have gotten them lost in this maze?*

The two men continued walking without another word said between them. On and on they trudged in the cold darkness until they could go no more. Candaz sank down to the ground and rested his head in his hands. Zeth kept a sharp eye on his father as he leaned on the wall. He swallowed the questions that crowded his head and imploded unspoken in his mouth. Eventually he slid to the floor and waited, half dozing until Candaz stood back up. "Zeth," he said, demanding in that one simple utterance for his son to follow. He stood up and did as his father demanded.

Time had become an unknown parameter. Fatigue and hunger became a constant companion. Zeth had a feeling that madness would meet them soon around the next turn. They were mice in a maze, looking for the coveted but elusive piece of cheese.

As Zeth followed his father, he began to examine his own motivations. He had always obeyed his father and done his bidding as his father had trained him to do, without question. Most of his life had been spent studying and training for the future; a future in which he and his father would rule Risen together. It was his father's vision of the future that he chased. He had never really stopped to question what it was that *he* wanted for his own life. The darkness that overwhelmed him was oppressive and it made his future seem only bleak, suffused with anger and pain, forever to live under the shadow of a man who despised him. A heavy blanket of cruelty was his shroud.

Candaz picked up his pace as he turned into one of the many forks. "Come on, boy. Keep up," he hissed. The new branch they entered was older than many that they had passed through prior. Finally, they were on the right track. A couple of the burial sites they passed had crumbling seals. In the dim light, Zeth could just make out the skeletal remains within. As he peered inside for a closer look, vacant eye sockets stared out at him mockingly, daring him to find the courage to face his demons. He shouldered the heavy pack he carried and followed Candaz, turning down yet another branch of the old section of the catacombs.

Rubbing his fingers together, Candaz intensified the light and began looking closely at the tunnel walls, running his hands over markers as he walked slowly along. When he reached a specific family crest, he brushed off the dust and studied it for a long moment. He gave Zeth a meaningful glance. "This is it," he said. Turning back to the crest, he began to count; three caverns to the right, bottom crypt. He started removing the seal one rock at a time. The rocks had not been mortared in place. "Help me," he said to Zeth.

Tossing his heavy pack on the ground, Zeth knelt beside his father and began taking the rocks away from the barrier. It took them together a half an hour to break through to the other side. There was a leather bound book and a small crystal bottle. Candaz reached in and removed them both. Setting the book at their feet, he ran his fingers over the cover, wiping the dust from it. "This is it," he said. On the cover of the exquisite leather binding was the head of a dragon embossed and gilded in silver. "This is it," Candaz said again as he took hold of the small crystal bottle and uncorked it. "This is an elixir that will make me feel young once again. It is valuable beyond measure." He took a couple of sips before replacing the stopper and sticking it in his cloak.

Reunion

Theo looked up and watched the descending line of golden dragons led by the dazzling white Tempest glide effortlessly toward the courtyard. It was a beautiful sight, but the feelings it invoked in him were bittersweet because his heart ached for his missing dragon, B.F. "Jessabelle," he called, "they're here."

"Okay," she replied and came into the bedroom from the bathroom, brushing her long red hair. A white streak ran down one side where she had once been injured while in her eagle form resulting in a short term coma. She came up beside her husband and wrapped one arm around his waist and at the same time kissed him on the cheek. She looked down at the courtyard where the entire party was busy dismounting their dragons, taking down packs and scratching dragons affectionately on noses and eye ridges. She searched for her son amongst them. "Look, Nicky's dragon Golden Agape is right there," she pointed.

"He's amazing. They're all amazing," Theo replied. "Let's go greet them." He grabbed Jessabelle's hand and pulled her after him.

They were joined at the bottom of the stairs by Link, Kristina and Serek. "They're here!" Kristina cried with delight. Serek had a broad smile on his usually serious face reflecting his wife's enthusiasm. Link sat back and watched the hubbub with amused tolerance.

The door to the courtyard lay through the living room. All five of them were excited to see the travelers and meet the new dragons. Jessabelle released Theo's hand and ran to Nicholas and embraced him. Theo followed close behind, wrapping his son in a fatherly hug before greeting the rest of the party warmly. Stephan acknowledged his parents affectionately before introducing Terese and Jesse to them. Kaltog joined in on the reunion, lifting his old friends up in massive bear hugs, including Link who put up with the treatment good-naturedly. The dogs ran around to everyone in a very animated state of excitement, catching the heightened mood of the humans. Rew, like the dogs was exuberant as he embraced and kissed everyone in sight, including his recent companions with just as much fervor.

Down Under

Tempest broke into Jesse's thoughts as she conversed quietly with Kristina. "*The babies want to go hunting, Jesse. They're hungry. Do you mind if I take them north and find a couple of ripgars?*" she asked.

"Excuse me," Jesse said to Kristina. "My dragon Tempest wants to take the babies hunting. They seem to be hungry all the time." Jesse laughed before she responded to Tempest, "*Sure, sweetie. Take the babies. Happy hunting.*"

Jesse could hear all of the babies start to chatter excitedly about hunting for ripgars. It was a little bizarre having all of those voices in her head at the same time. "The dragons are very excited," she told Kristina.

"I think they are spectacular," she said. Kristina's eyes sparkled with wonder as she watched the dragons launch themselves into the sky once again.

Gabriel, immediately getting down to business, rallied the troops, breaking up the happy reunion. "We came here to do a job. Let's not waste any more time socializing. Serek, we need access to the catacombs."

"The catacombs? Why?" Serek asked.

"Yes, the catacombs. It's something Candaz said to me long ago. At the time, it meant nothing to me, just more of his bragging. He was always going on about something or another. One night he was ranting about how he wished he could get away from the responsibilities of governing. He talked about how easy it was to escape through the catacombs without being seen. He said he had done it before many times. Apparently he used the underground tunnels all the time. That must be how he and Zeth escaped that night. I think he intends to sneak back in through the tunnels to retrieve whatever it is that he has hidden away. My gut tells me I'm right," Gabriel said. "Now lead the way, Serek."

"Okay. This way," he said as he started toward the castle. To Jesse he said, "Who am I to argue with a sorceress's gut?"

There were thirteen of them in all plus two dogs. They followed Serek through the pristine living room, down the hall, into the throne room, which was presently more of an office than what one would think of as a "throne room" and out the back corridor. He unlocked another door with a massive ring of keys, which brought them to a staircase. The stairs were original to the castle, which had been rebuilt only thirty years earlier, with the entire construction project taking a little less than a decade. Most of Castle Xandia was new construction, but everything on the subterranean levels pre-dated the destruction of the castle by Candaz. They had been able to build on the existing foundation by removing the rubble of the previously destroyed castle.

They descended the stairs in single file and came out through another locked door into a large open hallway with tall ceilings and several doorways that led off in different directions. All of the doors were closed and when Jesse checked one found it locked. Using freecurrent magic with practiced ease, Gabriel kept the old lanterns along their path brightly lit as they went along. Serek led them to a large double set of arched wooden doors at the end of the extensive corridor. Again he used his keys to unlock it and led them directly through to the other side. Jesse was surprised to find a large chapel as Gabriel lit the lanterns one by one slowly revealing the underground room.

Serek took a moment to explain the historical significance of the chapel, "Funeral services have been held in this chapel for as long as Castle Xandia has been on this spot. From here there is easy access into the old part of the catacombs. Today, there is a chapel on the eastern end of Saberville that serves most of the community and has better access to the newer portion of the catacombs. This one is very seldom used, let alone visited anymore. However, the inhabitants of Castle Xandia, mainly the royal family are still interned in the older section where a whole room is set aside, my great-grandfather was the last, but services will still be held here when the need arises in the future--way,

way in the future." Serek laughed and gave Kristina a squeeze. She responded to his comment with a reproachful look.

They walked to the front of the chapel where a very wide staircase led down into the catacombs. Mosaic tiles on the stairs depicted a scene of ocean waves with sunshine blazing brilliantly through fluffy clouds at sunset. The clouds were a myriad of colors like orange, pink and purple. It was a beautiful work of art. "Great craftsmanship," Link commented, "Did a banderg do this?"

"It was a man who had trained under a banderg craftsman during the years just after New Chance's destruction. He did much of the work in the old castle. It's a shame so much of it was destroyed," Serek said.

Gabriel continued to light the way as they descended the stairs. She led the way followed closely by Serek and Theo, who kept their hands always ready on their swords. As the tunnel narrowed, it became too small for Kaltog, who decided to turn back and wait for them in the chapel. He grumbled something about humans and proportions as he turned back, clearly not happy about doing so. Link joined his old friend willingly, anxious to spend more time examining the mosaic on the stairs.

The air became moister and mustier as they continued down into the coolness of the tunnel. Kali, Rew and Terese were behind Nicholas and Jesse, who followed Jessabelle and Kristina. Stephan was directly behind Theo and Serek. The dogs brought up the rear. Nobody spoke. Soon they encountered the first of the crypts. It was sealed with an old shield displayed prominently. The shield itself portrayed a dragon's body and head in profile. There were two crypts over it and one under, but the other three had simple markers with single initials; a "T", a "G" and an "A". The graves were arranged at regular intervals along both sides of the walls of the tunnel, four at a time. Some were plain; others were marked with a shield or a family's crest. Serek took the first left and stopped at a closed door with a coat of arms and a large initial "L" embossed upon it. "This is the Landtamer family's vault," he told them quietly before continuing on. They made a couple more turns to the left, passing more crypts along the way.

Gabriel suddenly stopped and held up her hand. Jesse held her breath, waiting quietly as she reached for Nick's hand in the darkness. When she found it she gave the warm dry hand a squeeze and he responded by squeezing hers back. Gabriel indicated for them to wait. She and Theo went ahead and disappeared as they took a right at the next branch. The rest of them remained quietly on alert and waited tensely.

Encounter

Zeth heard a slight noise in the tunnel. He left his father crouched over the manuscript which he was completely absorbed in and cautiously went to investigate. As he turned the corner a bright blue light blinded him. He stopped immediately and backed against the wall. "Stop," a woman's voice commanded.

Quickly, Zeth turned and headed back to where his father was hunched over the book. "We've got to go," he said urgently. The fear that was assaulting him was monstrous. Whatever he was about to face scared him to death. Before he could grab his backpack, a woman and a man stepped into the tunnel with a bright light illuminating them. They stopped and stared.

The woman wore leather riding clothes which fit her trim figure smoothly. She had dark hair that was swept up in a bundle on her head and sharp coppery brown eyes. The man she was with was quite tall and had to stoop slightly to walk in the tunnel. His long blond hair was tied back away from his face.

He was richly dressed and had a sword drawn. Bright green eyes observed him warily.

Candaz stood up and turned to them immediately. "Well, well, well. Gabriel. It's been a long time. You haven't changed a bit. And your highness Theo Wingmaster," he made a slight bow at the waist, "the man who almost, and I must emphasize *almost*, killed me."

The breath left Zeth's lungs as he hung onto the wall behind him. His mother stood before him. Finally, she was right there with him. He couldn't move. He could barely stand on his feet as he stared at her. There was a mix of emotions that vied for supremacy and he couldn't make sense of what was what. This wasn't the way he had pictured meeting her in his imagination. The muscles in his body seemed to be frozen solid.

Gabriel strode forward and addressed Candaz without glancing at Zeth, "What did you do with the dragons? Where did you send them?"

"Why would I tell you?" he sneered.

Theo took a step forward and lifted his sword to Candaz's throat. "Because, if you don't, this will be the last thing you feel."

The old sorcerer began to laugh. It sounded maniacal to Zeth's ears. "You are so very full of yourself Theo Wingmaster, but it is all self-inflation. You could not protect your grandmother Shareen or your miserable people from me. You could not protect Gabriel from me. She was mine to have for as long as I wanted her. Once I facilitated a heart attack for her weakling husband she was absolutely mine. You are as ineffective a warrior as you are a king."

Gabriel's face was suddenly immersed in pain. "You killed my husband?" she asked.

"Yes, I killed him. I twisted his heart in my hand until it burst. Sight water can be used for more than just spying," he said. Candaz's own eyes were deadly.

She stood frozen in shock. Her mouth moved but no words were uttered.

"That's right sweetheart. Once your husband was dead you were free to marry me. You don't remember do you?" he asked. It was clear that he was enjoying himself.

"What?" Gabriel gasped. "Married?"

"You and me, sweetheart. Husband and wife. I wanted a legitimate heir to my throne," he said.

"You son of a bitch! You killed my husband! I'm going to kill you," Gabriel said as she pulled her dagger and lunged at him.

He ducked quickly out of her reach and away from Theo's blade.

The rest of their party made a poorly time entrance. Behind Gabriel emerged a whole group of people. They surrounded her in the small space and blocked her from getting to Candaz even though she struggled to get through them. Two young men followed by Jesse and her dog, a banderg and another dog, two women, a flying wisp, and last of all was Terese. Zeth was paralyzed by fear and indecision. His father was behind him. His mother and two of the women he wanted to be with were in front of him.

"Get out of my way," Gabriel screamed as she pushed to get through the throng.

Candaz's voice commanded, "Grab the books, Zeth. These people will not be leaving here alive. Imagine my luck, bringing down the royal families of both Brightening and Saberville and the Sorceress of Brightening with all of her little helpers all at the same time. They are giving us Risen on a silver platter." He began to laugh madly.

Zeth did not budge.

"Move it, boy!" Candaz shouted.

The degrading voice that had plagued him all of his life rang in his ears. *Foolish boy! Stupid boy! Worthless son!* He froze in place, both unable and unwilling to obey his father's latest demands. The pit in his stomach was threatening to engulf him. *Foolish, stupid, worthless!* The wall behind him held him up as he collapsed into it without moving an inch. He held onto the coolness that permeated the stone and seeped into his very bones. *Jesse, Terese, mother. No!* "No," he uttered through clenched teeth.

"Foolish boy, move it now!" his father screamed.

Gabriel's knife flashed in front of Candaz's face as she ran toward him. "You deserve to die," she shrieked.

Zeth's body started shaking uncontrollably and he slid down the wall and curled into a fetal position. Gabriel tripped over him and sprawled on the tunnel floor. Her knife flew from her hand and clattered across the stone.

The distraction gave Candaz his one and only chance of escape. He doused his light and they were plunged instantly into darkness. He grabbed the backpack, turned and ran.

A Second Chance

Nicholas let go of Jesse's hand, unsheathed his sword and went after Candaz. The mighty sword glowed bright blue in his hand as freecurrent energy electrified the blade. Stephan quickly followed after his cousin. In a split second they were both out of sight. The rest of them were once again plunged into darkness.

Theo swore and called after them, "Boys, come back," but they did not halt in their pursuit. Theo swore again and said, "Gabriel, can we get some light? Gabriel?" he said as he found her where she was getting up off the floor and grabbed her. "Gabriel?!"

Freecurrent blazed bright from her fingertips and she rolled the energy into an orb and placed it on the floor of the tunnel. "I'm going after him," she said.

"Gabriel, wait," Theo said. "We need you here."

When Serek started after him too, Theo held him back as well. "Let's get what we can out of him and then go after Candaz," he said and pointed at Zeth. Serek looked dubious at best as he strode toward the cowering man. He looked over at Theo and said, "See what he says. I'll be right back." He left to go in the direction that the boys had gone.

Rew flew before Theo's face. "I'm going too," he said pointing down the tunnel and was gone before the king could reply.

Terese came forward and knelt beside Zeth's shaking form. "Zeth," she said quietly, touching his cheek softly with her fingertips. He didn't respond, didn't even seem to see her at all.

"Let's get him back to the chapel," Theo said as he stepped forward.

"Wait," Gabriel put a hand on Theo's shoulder, and she stepped in front of him. Gently, she examined the man who was her son, touching his forehead and looking into his eyes. "Jesse, come here," she called.

Terese stepped aside and let Jesse kneel beside Zeth and Gabriel. Jesse saw that her grandmother had tears running freely down her face. Hesitantly, she reached out and touched Zeth's forehead. It was cold and clammy. She closed her eyes and focused, letting the freecurrent energy vibrate through her automatically, not willing it, just letting it flow. Against her skin the lightning bolt medallion seared hot, the gold heating magically as the freecurrent was absorbed into it. The disease that invaded her mind from the ugliness that enveloped Zeth's soul made her own soul cry out in horror. A rotting foulness poisoned him, gagging whatever might have once been good, making a deranged, merciless, violent rebellion within him. He had been hurt and he had inflicted pain. Layer upon layer of his being was infused with anger and bitterness. She was aghast at the degree of torture he had endured.

Slowly, with deliberate intent, she began pulling the fatal toxin from the man into herself and exuding it out into the stone of the tunnel. The flow of freecurrent power turned to piercing pain as Jesse absorbed the evil. An inferno tore through her body, starting at her fingertips, searing into her belly, through her limps and down to her toes. She took her time, examining every fiber of his being, removing the sickness and draining it forever into the rock that surrounded her. It was a long process, excruciatingly slow, but she persevered until the task was done. When Zeth finally began to stir, she shushed him, making sure she removed every bit of corruption that had been inflicted upon him. She was so focused, she didn't even notice when Felcore came up beside her and added his healing touch to the treatment. So much did she remove from him that he was left with extensive fresh tender material to be shaped and fashioned as he began to transform into what he wanted to be. The future would shape him into something of his own choosing. He would become his own man over time. It was done. Jesse sighed and sat back on her heels. She hugged Felcore to her.

A New Chance

When Zeth opened his eyes, he was confronted by Jesse's coppery brown eyes in front of him. She looked exhausted, but beautiful. He felt different. It was as if every bit of darkness inside him had been lifted. What a wonderful feeling! For the first time in his life, he was happy. Gabriel, his mother, knelt beside him and examined him critically. "Zeth, how do you feel?" she asked. The look in her eyes was something new to him and it made him feel beyond good. His spirit soared.

He smiled. "I feel different," he said.

When she smiled back, he felt his heart warm with the love he had for her. "Do you remember anything?" she asked.

"I remember everything that's ever happened to me, everything I've ever done. I can't make some things right again, I'm afraid. I'll do what I can to make amends, but some things cannot be undone. Three men in the forest were killed by father. I was there and I did nothing to stop him. There are other things, cruel things, like what I did to Tempest. The dragons are gone because of me. I'm so sorry." He began to weep with remorse.

Gabriel held him in her arms and let him cry. When he began to calm down, she asked, "Zeth, about the dragons, can you tell me about the spell you used? Tell me what you know about the dragons."

Zeth sat upright and wiped his eyes. "The book. Did he take the book?" he asked.

Terese walked forward and presented the leather-bound book to him. "This book?"

"Terese," Zeth breathed her name. "I'm so sorry I deceived you."

She handed him the book. "I forgive you," she said easily.

That was another feeling he was not used to--forgiveness. It was wonderful. Looking at Terese, another emotion became prevalent that he *had* felt before, but not quite like he was experiencing it now. She took his breath away. He knew it was love. *He was in love with Terese!* Grinning genuinely at her, he said simply, "Thank you." Her responding smile was radiant.

He handed the book to Gabriel. "Father thought the answer was in this book. I'll tell you everything I know. I will help in any way that I can," he said.

A man returned from down the tunnel and said, "They're gone. I missed them. Let's go back to the castle." Later Zeth learned that it was Serek Landtamer, the King of Saberville who made the suggestion, but they were yet to be introduced. He followed them back through the catacombs, up a beautiful set of tiled stairs and into a chapel. A torg and a banderg waited there and he was introduced to Kaltog, Link and the rest of the party. They continued up through the castle until they were settled into a sumptuous library. Serek called for lunch to be served and poured everyone present a wonderful glass of nectar. Zeth had tasted very good nectar before, but this was excellent.

As they ate sandwiches, Theo and Serek paced the room and Gabriel sat at a table studying the book with the dragon embossed on the cover. Zeth said, "The spell I used was supposed to summon the dragons to me. Instead it seemed to have the opposite effect. I saw the dragon mage coming at me out of a cloud, he was almost upon me and then he receded away and was gone."

Gabriel walked over with the book open in her hands. "It says here that the dragons came from a galaxy called 'Arroyo' when it became inevitable that their world was going to be destroyed by its sun that was about to go super nova. Five dragons were able to save themselves by coming through the gate to Risen. We also know this from the temple records. What I'm wondering is if it is possible that the dragons were sent back to Arroyo, or more accurately to where Arroyo used to be."

"The spell was to summon the dragon mage from his source or origin to the space designated. It was working and then all of the sudden reversed. What if the dragons were sent to their origin? What if they were returned to their motherland?" Zeth asked.

"Let's say it's possible," Jesse said, "that the dragons were sent back to their original home. "Where is Arroyo in the gate's rotation? We can't go there if we don't know what constellation to look for. Although if Arroyo was destroyed, there may or may not be a constellation there or it may be unrecognizable. It might not exist at all."

Kaltog grumbled, "If Rew was here, he might know."

Link agreed as he pulled on his beard, "Rew would know."

"The wisps might be able to help us, but their hands are tied as far as interfering directly. If I can get back to Elysia, I might be able to obtain the information we need about Arroyo." Jesse was up and walking now.

"How many dragons are missing?" Kali asked.

Jessabelle stood up and joined the march while she answered, "Fifteen missing in all."

Kristina also rose and began refilling nectar glasses, avoiding the pacers with graceful ease. "I wonder where the boys are," she said. She put the decanter back on the table and stood gazing out the window.

"I should have gone with them," Theo said. He and Serek just avoided colliding with each other as the intensity of their pacing increased. They gave each other humorless frowns.

"Me too," Serek agreed. "You shouldn't have delayed me, Theo. I should have followed the boys immediately. By the time I started after them it was too late. We are worthless waiting here."

"Let's go after them now," Theo said to his brother-in-law.

"I'm in. Let's go," Serek replied as he put down his glass and strode across the room.

"Gold Stone says that Golden Agape and Zlato say that their Nicholas and Stephan are chasing the bad man still," Terese offered.

"Candaz has the instruction manual to the gate. It was in the backpack," Zeth stated to no one in particular. "There is more you need to know. A dragon egg is being held at Wayfair Manor. It is surrounded by freecurrent energy to keep it alive. But, it cannot last in that condition indefinitely. Once it hatches, the dragon will be forced to serve Candaz. They are going to attempt to force a bonding with Candaz or if he isn't there when the hatching takes place with one of his remaining loyal men."

"No. That can't happen," Jesse said simply.

"That would be intolerable," Kristina added.

"Okay, I think I have a plan," Gabriel responded before she turned to Jesse. "Can you get back to Elysia, Jesse?"

"I think so," she answered.

Gabriel slammed the book shut. "I think that's our best option right now. I have a gut feeling about this. We'll go after the adult dragons first. We may not have much time. The egg will have to wait. Let's go."

Kali and Kaltog had been consulting with each other quietly where they sat together on the couch. Kali looked at them with a stern look on her face and said, "Kaltog and I will head to Wayfair Manor immediately to see what we can do about the dragon egg. We'll let you know through the dragons what we find out. I'm going to leave Tica here for now. She's had enough excitement lately and I think she might be pregnant."

"Okay. I think that would be prudent. Good luck. Let us know what you find," Gabriel said.

"I'll go with you," Link said.

"Yes. Good," Kaltog agreed.

"Be careful," Zeth said. "The men guarding the egg are heartless."

Jesse called instantly, "*Tempest?*"

"*Yes, Jesse? I am sleeping. Twelve babies are a lot of work,*" the white dragon responded groggily.

"*I need you here now. We are going north,*" Jesse told her.

"*Okay. I'll meet you in the courtyard in a moment,*" Tempest said.

"*Tempest, did you know that Candaz has a dragon egg at Wayfair Manor?*" she asked.

"*No. I did not know. We must help it, Jesse,*" she said.

"*We will. First things first,*" Jesse said.

"*Yes, if first things were last than they wouldn't be first,*" Tempest agreed.

To the others Jesse said, "I'll take Tempest to the cave immediately. If the wisps allow me to come to Elysia, I'll ask them about Arroyo and come right back here."

"No, Jesse. We'll meet you at the cave," Gabriel said.

"We'll head to the cave on horses," Serek said. To Theo he said, "We'll look for Stephan and Nicholas as we ride north."

"Yes. Let's get going," Theo agreed.

"We'll meet you at the cave," Jessabelle confirmed.

Kristina said that she wanted to go too. Jesse was impatient to get going and didn't want to wait for everyone to mobilize. The rest of them could figure for themselves out how they were going to get there. She was taking Tempest now. "I'll meet you there then," she said and left without further discussion.

"Right. Let's go," Gabriel said.

Chapter 18
THROUGH THE GATE

Tempest spread her wings and glided on the air currents high above the forest. Jesse hugged herself tight to the dragon's back, feeling the vibration of Tempest's breath through her chest and stomach. She was comforted by the warm musky scent the dragon radiated, a scent that had become as familiar to her as the dragon's voice in her head. Navigation to the cave was Tempest's responsibility and, of course, the dragon knew the cave well. It is where she had gone not so long ago to die. Felcore rode comfortably in a leather sack that was slung over Tempest's back, kind of like a side car to a motorcycle. It was Kali's ingenious design. She had developed it to ride with Tica while on dragon back. Jesse would have to get one made for Felcore, one that was custom-made for her beautiful she-dragon so her dog and dragon could fly together in complete compatibility.

Her thoughts drifted to Nicholas and she wondered where he was. Had they found Candaz? Was he safe? *"Tempest, where are Nick and Stephan?"*

"Let me check . . . Agape says that Nicholas and Stephan are tracking the bad man through the forest. He is heading north," she said.

Jesse spoke directly to Agape, *"Can you tell Nick that I'm going to the gate? Let him know that I might not be reachable for a while."* The last time Jesse was on Elysia, time on Earth stood still while she was there, or at least seemed to. It was very strange. She wondered if it would be the same. She was slightly apprehensive. What if for some reason she couldn't get back to Risen?

"Nicholas said he'll see you soon and to 'rock and roll', whatever that means," Agape said.

Jesse laughed.

"I like to hear you laugh," Tempest commented as she started to descend at an accelerated rate.

The forest came at Jesse fast and she hung on tight and enjoyed the ride. *Rock and roll,* she thought. They landed very close to the entrance of the cave. Jesse dismounted and helped Felcore out of the sling. He ran around sniffing this spot or that spot and lifting his leg to a few of those that met whatever his dog criteria were.

"Felcore, let's go," Jesse said, impatient to get started.

She walked to the entrance of the cave with Felcore and Tempest following close behind. Darkness prevailed except for star light coming from the lightning-bolt shaped opening at the rear and Tempest's shining red eyes. The gold medallion on her chest burned her skin as she approached. A constellation in the shape of a scorpion rotated into one shaped like a fish. She waited only a moment before light flashed strikingly bright, charging the air around her with freecurrent energy as it burned fast and hot. Felcore gave a sharp bark and pushed his head against Jesse's leg. She walked forward cautiously. Tempest was directly behind her. She could feel the dragon's breath on the back of her neck.

Wings like a hummingbird whirred past her ear. A wisp! She was on Elysia!

"Hello," she said.

Wes landed in front of her. "Jesse! You're here! You brought a dragon!" He gazed at Tempest with eyes wide in amazement.

"Wes, this is Tempest. *Tempest, this is Wes.*"

"A real live dragon! Rew told me about dragons. It is so big!" Wes flew up to the dragon's nose and examined Tempest up close, touching this and poking that.

"She," Jesse corrected.

"What?" he asked as he continued his examination.

"*She* is so big," she said.

"Yes, she is. Wow!" he said.

Tempest huffed forcefully at Wes as he put one of his hands in one of her nostrils. Startled by the sudden noise from the dragon, he retreated behind Jesse, looking at the Tempest over her shoulder.

Felcore barked.

"Are you hungry, Jesse?" Wes asked, while he kept an eye on Tempest. "It is almost dinner time."

"Wes, I need some information. This is really important. Have you ever heard of a galaxy named Arroyo?" Jesse asked.

"No, but it is almost dinner time. Maybe we could ask everybody at dinner," Wes said, looking hopefully at Jesse.

"I don't have time for that, Wes. I'm sorry. Do the wisps know anything about the disappearance of the dragons from Risen? Is there some way you can trace them if they travelled through the gate?" she asked.

"The dragons are missing?" Wes asked.

"Yes. Could they have travelled through the gate?" Jesse asked.

"I suppose it's possible. They originally travelled to Risen through the gate from a galaxy called . . . oh, it was from a galaxy called Arroyo. That was a very long time ago," he said.

She gave him a long look and asked again, "Is there any way to tell if they went through the gate recently?"

"There is a way, but it takes a reversal of time and space. How long ago did they come up missing?" he asked.

"About a week," she answered.

"It's a bit of a process. There might be a residual shadow from their passing," Wes responded. He walked to the back of the cave and placed his hand on the floor by the lightning gate. After a moment he turned to her and said, "There is definitely a shadow of their passing. They did go through the gate. I don't know where they went, though, only that they *did go*."

"Can you take me to the cathedral on Mount Galaxia?" she asked.

"Now?" he said incredulously. If a wisp could look pitiful, Wes certainly did. "But, it's almost dinner time. Perhaps we could go to get something to eat first, and then I'll take you to Mount Galaxia. Maybe we could go tomorrow after breakfast."

"I'm sorry, Wes, but I need to go now," she insisted.

"Oh, I wish I had sent Lodi to greet you. Although I really did want to see you and I *am* really excited to finally meet a dragon . . . but to miss dinner. Oh, I do hope I can get a snack later, or I'll starve to death. But, I am happy to see you, Jesse." Felcore barked. "And you too, Felcore."

"Wes, I really am in a hurry," Jesse said with a touch of contrition in her voice. She really did feel bad making Wes miss a meal, knowing how important eating was to her friend.

He reluctantly complied with her wishes. "Yes, to Mount Galaxia we go. Can we stop and get winter clothes? No, no, I guess not. Let's go," he said. Wes flew out of the cave, stopped, turned and waited for Jesse and her dog and the dragon.

They walked to the cave entrance and mounted Tempest. Jesse noticed the tree at the entrance remained ailing and continued to repel her. Tempest gave it wide berth.

Before they left she asked Tempest a question that she was curious about, "Tempest, can you communicate with Gabriel?"

The dragon turned her head this way and that. She turned completely around and repeated the process before she answered, "No."

Wes flew in the lead as they went to Mount Galaxia.

The snow covering the landscape on Mount Galaxia sparkled like diamonds in the moonlight as they landed in front of the cathedral. It was cold. Jesse could see her frozen breath as they walked to the main entrance. She thought that if they were there for too long, Tempest could easily create a dense fog in the valley with her hot breath. Without delay, Wes led them through the entrance and up the stairs, except for Tempest who waited outside. There was nobody around at this late hour. They had the place all to themselves.

The colored stones making up the mural glistened in the floor where they were arranged to depict the various galaxies of the gate. The distinct shape of a lightning bolt was the central image done in black and gold. In-laid diamonds made up the constellations along with the planets in various formations. They spread out from the lightning bolt in all directions as they plastered the floor.

The four of them examined the mural closely, looking for Arroyo in the multitude of galaxies depicted by the mural. A representation of the Big Dipper indicated Earth, the twenty-third galaxy. Risen, the third galaxy with the Condor was twenty over from Earth. How would they find Arroyo?

"Wes, any ideas?" Jesse asked.

"We can use the process of elimination," Wes started saying, "or . . . look." He pointed at Felcore.

The golden retriever walked directly to the five hundred twentieth galaxy, depicted by in-laid stone with a constellation in the shape of an eye. He barked once, sat directly upon it and wagged his tail.

Jesse walked over and scratched his ears. "Is this it, boy?" she asked.

"Rrowf!"

"Good boy," Jesse said.

She spent a long time examining the floor around Arroyo. Recognizing the exact point in which to go through the gate was vitally important to the undertaking at hand. She had to be able to recognize the sequence before the Eye and immediately after. Timing would be everything if their theory about the dragons being sent back to Arroyo was correct. Five minutes was a very short time for a journey into the unknown.

One of her concerns was that if Arroyo was in a void there might not be air to breathe. *"Tempest, if the dragons are on Arroyo, that no longer exists, how can they breathe? How can this be possible?"* she asked.

Tempest answered in a matter-of-fact tone, *"Dragons are magical creatures."*

"Right."

"Wes?" Jesse called.

"Yes?" he responded.

"Can I get a hold of the equipment they were using to go scuba diving at the lake? You know, when I was here last time."

"You want to go diving?" he asked.

"No, but I want to use the equipment to go to Arroyo." She had an idea about how to check out Arroyo without suffocating. "I can get you what you need. We just need to make a quick stop. Are you ready to go? I'm hungry," he said. Wes headed for the stairs. Jesse signaled to Tempest mentally and to Felcore visually with the wave of her hand.

After they were mounted on Tempest, they flew back to the cave with a short detour to a small village to get diving equipment for Jesse from one of Wes's friends. It took them just a few minutes to gather everything together that she might need.

They went quickly past the tree and into the dark cave beyond. The lightning bolt gate displayed constellations at a constant interval rotating approximately five minutes apart. As Jesse watched the Condor became visible. "There's Risen," she said hurriedly. "We have to go now."

"Wait," Wes said calmly.

"But, we can't miss it," she said anxiously.

"Wait, Jesse. It's okay. Let me show you something," Wes said.

As she watched the Condor passed by and was gone. "I missed it. Now I'll have to wait. I don't have time for this," she cried in a panic.

"Jesse," Wes said calmly.

"This is awful. I can't get back. What do I do?" she asked desperately. This was her worst fear, not being able to get back in time.

"Jesse, listen to me," Wes demanded.

She stopped her fretting and gave her attention to Wes.

"Watch," he said. Wes walked over to the lightning gate and placed his hand firmly on the edge of the chasm. The speed of the constellations' rotation sped up until they were racing by at an extremely accelerated rate. He removed his hand and the pace slowed down to its normal rhythm. Again, he placed his hand on the edge of the lightning bolt and it slowed to a stop before reversing its order. When he took his hand away again the rotation continued at its regular rate.

"Really!? Can I do that?" Jesse asked in amazement.

"You have wisp magic. In all aspects, besides physically, you are a wisp. We are guardians of the gate," Wes said, giving her a radiant smile.

"Thank you, Wes. Go get something to eat," she said and kissed him on the cheek while Tempest and Felcore said goodbye to Wes in their own ways, Felcore with an exuberant tongue licking and Tempest with a playful blast of air from her nostrils.

Jesse went to the back of the cave to the lightning bolt gate and reached out to touch it with her hand. She watched in awe as the constellations zoomed by. Amazingly, she was able to distinctly make out each and every one without much concentration. Waiting for the Condor, she removed her hand promptly and walked through to the other side with Tempest and Felcore close behind her.

Chapter 19

INTO THE VOID

With his nose to the ground, Nick plodded forward with an absence of sound, placing his paws with absolute stealth. Behind him Stephan stalked with his big human feet conjuring up a plethora of noise, at least to a wolf's ears. Nicholas gave him a look of exasperation, which was very comical on his wolfy face. "Rrrrr," he growled.

"Do you have a problem, fuzz face?" Stephan responded.

"Rrrrrowff!" Nick turned back around after telling off his cousin and continued tracking with his nose to the ground.

They were in the forest north of Castle Xandia following the elusive sorcerer Candaz. He had been steadily moving north since leaving the catacombs earlier that day. He was fast. Although Nick and Stephan were moving quickly, he was staying just ahead of them. The old man was slick and moved like a panther through the woods. Rew had gone on ahead and was keeping an even closer eye on Candaz from the air. He reported back from time to time, but they hadn't seen the wisp in a couple of hours.

"This is ridiculous. Why can't you become a horse? A horse would be useful," Stephan complained.

"Grrrr," Nicholas retorted.

"Okay, let's keep on the trail . . . *walking*," he said. Stephan had not yet worked out the best way to confront Candaz. Both he and Nicholas were proficient with a sword, but the old man was a sorcerer and he didn't want to be foolish enough to think that the old boy wouldn't try to use magic on them. When they caught up to him they needed to proceed with caution. He didn't want his cousin to be turned into a lizard; a horse, maybe, but not a lizard. The dragons might be able to help them, but he was reluctant to involve the babies in this escapade. They were just newborns after all, less than a week old.

"Rrowf," Nicholas stopped suddenly. He transformed before Stephan's eyes into his human form, his kendrite cousin. *Pretty awesome!* Stephan never got tired of seeing the mystical make-over.

"What is it Nick?" he asked.

"Shh. He's just up ahead," he whispered. "There's a small stream where he has stopped to get a drink and rest."

"How," Stephan started in a normal tone, but then lowered his voice to a whisper. "How do you know?"

Nicholas put his finger on his nose.

Skeptical, Stephan sniffed the air significantly and a scowl took his questioning look away.

"I think we should circle around him. We know he's heading north. Let's get to the other side of him and cut him off. Take him by surprise--an ambush," Nick suggested.

"And then what?" Stephan asked.

"We run him through," he said. Nick ran his fingers down his glowing blade. It sparked in response to his touch.

Stephan, for lack of a better plan, agreed.

Rew returned at that moment and concurred that an ambush might work. "I'll distract him from overhead. Be careful," he warned.

Arroyo

The wind whipped the words out of Gabriel's mouth, "Straight ahead. Follow me!" She was on Nugget flying north along with Terese and Zeth on Gold Stone. The remaining dragons were going to go with Agape and Zlato to find Nicholas and Stephan.

On the ground below Theo, Serek, and Kristina rode on horseback while Jessabelle flew nearby in her eagle form. They had left shortly after Jesse's departure and headed directly north through the forest. Evening was creeping up on them, making shadows longer and longer as it slipped into night.

"Do you really think the dragons could have been sent back to Arroyo?" Serek asked Theo as they rode.

"I guess it's as good an explanation as any. In any case, it's a place to start looking. The lack of progress in this situation is frustrating me beyond measure. Inaction is driving me crazy. It's been more than a week. I am deeply concerned for them all and of course I miss B.F. and his constant nagging," he said. Theo's horse shook the reins fiercely, jangling the harness as he instantly picked up on his rider's edginess.

The mount under Serek reacted to his stable mate, but his rider kept a firm hand on the reins. "Breezerunner has been an especially good friend to me. I will do everything in my power to find him," he was adamant with a rare show of emotion as he spoke. "Candaz had better hope I don't get to him first."

"We will find them all," Theo agreed with just as much conviction.

Kristina spurred her horse to a fast gallop, and surpassed her husband and brother. "Let's get moving," she said as she rode by. Overhead Jessabelle trilled as she flew a short distance ahead of them, adding in her two cents.

The two men exchanged a brief look before letting their horses pick up their pace and follow after their wives.

By the time night was well established in the dark forest, the party had gathered at the entrance to the cave. They had not found Candaz or Nick and Stephan and Rew. Jesse was still gone. The dragons were unable to contact Tempest either. Although Gabriel was frantic with the inability to act, they decided to build a campfire and wait it out.

"I hate waiting," Gabriel spouted. She did not settle around the fire like the others, but kept up a steady patrol. Constantly, she went into the cave to check for Jesse, observing the constellations rotating consistently in the gate at the back. "Jesse, where are you?" she whispered under her breath, turning once again and walking toward the fire just outside the entrance.

"Grandmother," Jesse said behind her.

"Jesse," Gabriel turned and ran to her granddaughter, embracing her joyously. "Thank God. I was afraid you were gone-- lost. Oh, thank God you are okay."

"No, I wasn't lost. Look, I'm fine. It's okay. I was on Elysia and I think I know how to get to Arroyo," she said.

The others came in and greeted Jesse anxiously. Felcore ran from person to person, demanding his own acknowledgements from each and every person in attendance. Tempest lay down and appeared to be napping the very minute she hit the floor.

Jesse addressed everybody gathered, "I know how to find Arroyo through the gate. My biggest concern is that there may not be air to breathe there and it may also be extremely cold. It very well could be more of a void than any place with substance. The wisps loaned me this breathing apparatus, which will allow me to go there and come back without suffocating and will protect my face from the cold. Extra clothing might save me from freezing to death. If the dragons are trapped on Arroyo, I plan on bringing them back. Evidence shows that they did go through the gate to somewhere. My gut is telling me that we're on the right track."

Theo strode boldly forward before declaring, "I will go."

"I think I should go," Zeth said. "It was my fault that the dragons disappeared. I should be the one taking the risk to get them back. Let me go, please."

"No, I can communicate with all of them. I should be the one to go and no one else," Gabriel said.

"Maybe this should be considered," Serek interrupted the argument that was erupting. "If Arroyo is now a void, a place that no longer exists, there would not be a cave or a gate on the other side. How do you plan on getting back?"

Everybody quit talking to consider this new revelation.

"I have an idea," Jesse began. "It's possible, I believe, to freeze the gate in place for a time. There will be no more argument about who is to go. It will be me who goes to Arroyo. But, what if I can't find my way back again? I don't know for sure. . .

"Jesse," Gabriel started to protest.

"Listen," she said, "Not only did the wisps instill me with their magic, but with the ability to control the gate. Tempest and I will go together. It makes the most sense."

"There is a possibility," Zeth was forming a plan, "that together Gabriel and I could develop a freecurrent rope of sorts to tether you to our side of the gate."

Gabriel looked pensive for a moment and then smiled, "Yes, I think that might work."

"I think it's worth a try," Jesse said.

She took out the breathing apparatus, examined and tested it. Although the group gathered had not packed for an extended stay away from home, they all wore layers of clothing and stripped off their warmest garments for Jesse to wear. She looked ready to go to the Arctic after she had donned all that was available to her and had the breathing apparatus in place.

Gabriel and Zeth were talking quietly together. As they prepared, Jesse spoke mentally to Golden Agape, "*Could you tell Nick that . . . well that . . . tell him that I'll see him soon.*"

The baby dragon's voice came back in Jesse's head. "*Nicholas says, 'Be careful, Jesse. Come back home to me.'*"

"Right," Jesse said aloud. "Okay, I think I'm ready to go. Zeth, Gabriel, are you ready?"

They stepped forward toward the gate, wrapped their arms around each other's waist, and Gabriel put her left hand in Zeth's right hand. A blue and green electrified light bloomed out of their hands and twisted together, extending until the end wrapped itself around Tempest's neck.

"Tempest?"

"*I'm ready. But, I really don't like this rope tied around my neck.*" Tempest swung her neck in agitation.

"*It's okay, sweetie. It's only temporary. Let's go,*" Jesse said and pulled herself up on Tempest's back. Felcore looked up at her and barked.

"Not this time buddy. Stay here," she said. It had been a long time since Jesse was without Felcore. It felt odd, but he could not come, not this time.

"Jesse, wait," Gabriel said. "Whatever happens, come back here safe. I don't want to lose you now that I've found you. Please be careful. I love you."

"Okay, grandmother. Don't worry. I love you, too. See you in a few," she said hastily and then positioned the breathing apparatus in place over her mouth. Tempest walked up to the edge of the gate and Jesse reached out and touched the lightning bolt with her hand. The constellations began to rotate at a much faster rate of speed. She waited and watched attentively for constellations that came before The Eye. The one before The Eye was The Arrow, before that was The Spider, before The Spider was The Hawk. She prepared herself and Tempest when she spotted The Hawk. *"You ready, Tempest?"*

"Tell me when," Tempest said.

Instinctively, she slowed down the rotation. The Spider turned into The Arrow. Next would be The Eye. She sat forward anxiously, anticipating the change. The next constellation to appear was The Bear. There was no Eye. *No Arroyo?* Slowly, Jesse reversed the rotation of the stars. She would have to try to go between The Bear and The Arrow. Confidence in this journey declined considerably. Her heart was pounding in her ears. The timing would have to be perfect. The moment was now. She froze the gate in place and urged Tempest through with her mind.

Black, cold, nothing.

"Tempest?"

"Jesse?" the dragon replied.

"You can hear me?" Jesse asked.

"Obviously," the sarcasm in Tempest's mental voice was welcomed to Jesse. At least they weren't dead.

"Right," she said.

Jesse could only hear Tempest and feel her body beneath her own. The only thing she could see was the freecurrent rope snaking out behind them and disappearing into nothingness.

"Tempest can you hear the other dragons?" she asked.

A moment of hesitation, then she responded, *"No."*

Jesse reached out with her mind, *"Skymaster? B.F.?"*

Faintly, she heard one single half-whispered word, *"Help."*

"Tempest did you hear that?" Jesse asked.

"Maybe. What did you hear?" she asked.

"I heard a whisper. Hush. Let's listen," Jesse said and then called out again, *"Skymaster?"*

"I'm here," it was a faint mental whisper.

"They are all here. I can feel them now," Tempest said.

"We'll come to you, Skymaster. Try to radiate your presence to me," Jesse said.

"I'm here," he said again, faintly but distinctly.

Jesse calmed herself. She reached out with the freecurrent energy, gathering everything she could to herself, from Tempest, from the dragons she now knew must be out there somewhere. The void offered nothing, no energy, just lifelessness, but the dragons had a magnificent life force and she focused on it, drawing it to her and sending it back out again--searching in the dark with her mind. Her gold medallion burned hot against her chest as it focused the energy that flowed fast and strong.

Suddenly she knew where they all were. She could see them in a way. Not *sight* in the conventional use of the word, but *see* them, know them, feel their existence, touch their essence. She guided Tempest to where Skymaster was until she could reach out and touch his face physically. Although she was right in front of the dragon mage, she was unable to *see* his bright swirling eyes in the darkness before her. They were blind in the eye, but their other senses filled in for them. Skymaster pushed his nose insistently but gently against her hand as he responded to her touch.

"Skymaster, can you follow us? Are you strong enough to fly?" she asked.

"*Get the others first,*" he said weakly.

"*Okay. I'll be back.*" she responded.

She flew Tempest over to where Breezerunner was. When she was close enough, she reached out and touched his nose. "*Breezerunner, can you follow us?*" she asked.

"*Yes, but I can't see you. How do I follow?*" he asked.

"*Hold on. I'm going to extend this rope around you,*" Jesse said. "*Tempest, touch wings with Breezerunner. I'm going to use the freecurrent to extend the rope to tie around Breezerunner. It should only take a moment. Hang on, sweetheart,*" she said.

"*Okay,*" Breezerunner responded.

Jesse climbed onto Breezerunner's back and worked swiftly despite the blinding darkness. Soon the freecurrent rope was encircling the necks of both dragons. *Let's hope this works,* she thought to herself.

"*Tempest, I'm going to have them pull us back through the gate. Keep the rope around you tight, but not too tight as they lead us back out. I'm going to stay on Breezerunner until we are back on Risen,*" she told Tempest.

"*Breezerunner, keep the rope between you and Tempest tight, but not too tight. Follow her out. Okay. Ready?*" she asked.

"*Oh, yes!*" Breezerunner said.

"*Ready, Tempest?*"

"*Ready,*" she said.

"*Okay, let's do this,*" Jesse said.

Jesse yanked on the rope twice. She felt two return yanks and then she let go of the rope and trusted in Tempest and the people on the other end to lead them out. As she relaxed on Breezerunner's back, she again hoped that this was going to work. She said a brief but fervent prayer asking for God's blessing on this rescue and left it completely in hands other than her own.

"*Are you okay, Tempest?*" Jesse asked.

"*Yes. I'm good, Jesse,*" she replied.

"*Hang in there, Breezerunner.*"

"*How far do we have to go?*" the big dragon asked.

"*We'll be there soon,*" Jesse assured him.

It seemed to take forever, but suddenly without warning they were through the gate and in the cave on Risen. Jesse said a quick "Thanks" to God before breathing a huge sigh of relief. Serek was the first to reach them and he laid his face and hands against Breezerunner's side and cried tears of relief. "Thank you, Jesse," he said as he helped her down off from the large dragon's back. "Thank Tempest for me," he said before giving her a huge hug.

"I will, but I have to go back now. We have fourteen more dragons to get before we are through. Let's do this!" she said.

Everyone was firing questions at her all at the same time.

Theo asked, "Is B.F. there? Is he okay?"

"Are the other dragons okay?" Zeth wanted to know.

After Gabriel hugged Jesse, she asked, "Is Skymaster okay? What's it like over there? Is there anything else we can do to help?"

Felcore ran to Jesse and greeted her excitedly. Pushing her dog away gently, she responded to everyone with one simple answer, "They are all there and alive. We're going to have to bring them home one at a time." Immediately she climbed back onto Tempest's back. "There's no more time to waste. I'm going back in now. Same plan. Let's go!"

Zeth and Gabriel redeveloped the rope as Jesse and Tempest quickly approached the gate. Donning the breathing apparatus, she wrapped her face in cloth to protect it from the cold before laying her hand on the crevice and caused the constellations to rotate into position and freeze. With more confidence this time, Tempest launched herself through the gate to the void where Arroyo had once been.

Jesse could easily focus the freecurrent energy on the dragons this time and found B.F. right away. She immediately guided Tempest down to the big silver dragon and landed directly in front of him.

"B.F., how are you feeling?" Jesse asked.

"I'm weak, tired, hungry and thirsty." He hesitated a moment before adding, *"and really bored."*

"Okay, let's get you out of here," she said as she climbed onto B.F.'s back and extended the end of the rope around his neck. After two tugs and two tugs in response, they were on their way back home. Soon they returned to Risen through the gate.

B.F. roared his greeting, the sound reverberating harshly off the walls of the cave. Theo came forward and hugged the nose of his huge buddy with great enthusiasm. *"B.F., I have missed you so much. Thank the Creator you are safe,"* he said.

"Even your scraggly looking face looks good to my eyes right now, Theo," B.F. said affectionately to his old friend.

Jesse wasted no time, but remounted Tempest and immediately returned to Arroyo to get the next dragon. They repeated the process twelve more times before returning one last time for Skymaster.

Rescue

The wait for Skymaster was excruciating. He was so hungry and thirsty; every second seemed like an eternity. But, still he knew Jesse and Tempest had come to rescue them all and would be back for him soon. All he needed to do was to hang on for just a little while longer. He could make it until she came back for him.

His thoughts turned to Tempest and he marveled at what she had done for them. She was responsible for saving them all today. He, *they all*, would be forever grateful to that little she-dragon. The legend of her rescuing the dragons would be etched into the wall at the Temple of Neeg on the Island of Zedra for all perpetuity. Her name would become one of legend.

Time to think had been plentiful of late and he had, without a doubt, found things he regretted in his life. He was a proud dragon and had served the races and his own dragon-kind to the best of his abilities through the years. But, he knew he had many failures as well as successes to his credit. It was inevitable in a life full of relationships that sometimes there would be remorse. With Tempest he had made a mistake by not appreciating or accepting her for who she was. He had been wrong and would ask her forgiveness and he knew she would absolve him. He was confident in this because they were dragons, after all, and dragons were honorable creatures above all else and forgiveness was in their nature.

Without warning, Skymaster felt Tempest come along beside him. *"Jesse, did you save them all?"* he asked immediately.

"They are all back on Risen. You are the last. We must hurry, though. My air is getting short," she said.

What does she mean? He wondered, but did not ask.

One More To Go

The indicator on Jesse's air breather was warning her that there was very little oxygen left in the tank. She was pushing her luck being there right now, but there was no way she would leave Skymaster behind. As she climbed onto his neck, she gave instructions to Tempest, *"As soon as I have the rope extended to Skymaster's neck, give it two tugs, and then let them lead you out. One more time, Tempest. We can do this, sweetie. One more time."* She was running out of oxygen faster than she had hoped. Her breath was coming in gasps as the tank stopped giving her its life-giving contents. Pushing down her growing panic, as quickly as she could manage she finished tethering Skymaster to Tempest just before losing the battle for consciousness.

Home Sweet Home

Zeth and Gabriel worked quickly together taking in the rope as it came toward them through the gate. They kept the magical rope taut, leading the dragon, Tempest, back to the gate from the void beyond. Tempest's nose was the first to poke through, followed closely by her shimmering white body. The onlookers backed away, making room for the dragon as she came swiftly toward them into the cave. Behind her tethered to the rope around her neck was a much larger dragon, silver scales glimmering in the dim light. Skymaster, even in his weakened condition, was a mighty sight to behold. Upon his back lay a lovely girl, lifeless and unmoving.

Gabriel came forward quickly with Jessabelle beside her. "Jesse?" she said.

"*Skymaster, what's wrong with her?*" she asked as she went quickly to his side. Theo and Jessabelle came up beside her.

"*She has no air. Help her,*" Skymaster said.

Theo helped Jessabelle climb onto Skymaster's back. She removed the air mask from Jesse's face and handed the limp girl down to her husband's outstretched arms. Theo gently lay her down on the floor of the cave where Gabriel was immediately by her side. Instantly she started breathing into Jesse's mouth. Kristina joined her and helped perform CPR by pushing on Jesse's chest. They coordinated into a rhythm, artificially making the girl breath in and out.

The minute Skymaster was free, he spotted Zeth and roared his outrage as he moved lightning quick and pinned the man to the ground with his front talons. The huge dragon mage's fangs were within inches of Zeth's face when Gabriel intervened, *"Skymaster, stop! He has repented. Give him a chance."*

"Why should I?" he growled.

"Because he is my son and I ask as your friend," she said mentally as she simultaneously tried to save her granddaughter.

He hesitated a long moment. *"Granted,"* Skymaster replied and he released the frightened man, *"because you are my friend, but I'll be watching him."* He quickly left the cave and joined the other dragons outside.

Felcore trotted over and immediately started licking Jesse's hand until she took a deep inward breath on her own. She started breathing again and Gabriel sat back and watched until her eyes fluttered open as she sat up. Felcore immediately pushed his head at her insisting on attention as she looked around. She smiled and hugged him close before reaching for Gabriel who hugged her back and cried tears of relief.

"They are all safe?" Jesse asked as she stood up and started stripping off the cumbersome wardrobe that had kept her warm in the void.

"Yes, they are all safe, thanks to you and Tempest. You did an awesome thing, Jesse," Gabriel replied.

"Tempest?" Jesse called.

"Yes, Jesse?" Tempest replied.

"Where are you?" she asked.

"Hunting again--this time with the adults," Tempest replied with pride.

"You are a wonderful, beautiful dragon, Tempest," Jesse told her.

"Of course," she concurred.

Chapter 20

ONE STEP AT A TIME

Quietly, cautiously they moved through the dark woods toward their target. The sword in Nicholas's hand glowed electric blue with freecurrent magic. It was leading them to the evil that lurked in their midst. Rew flew overhead somewhere, coming at the sorcerer from a different angle. They were going to waylay Candaz as he continued on his northern route. Crossing the stream up from where he was presently resting, Stephan and Nick left a wide margin between themselves and the sorcerer. It took them an hour to circle to the other side of the path they assumed Candaz would take. There they waited.

Rew appeared in front of them. "He's coming," he whispered and quickly flew off.

Stephan drew his sword. He signaled for Nicholas to follow him to an area that would be suitable for the planned ambush.

They both crouched down and waited without a sound. Candaz was quietly coming through the woods toward them. Each of them controlled their breathing as they waited. Footsteps, quiet as a single snowflake dropping on the snow covered ground approached. Muscles in the men were taut, ready to spring. He was almost there--a couple more steps.

"*Nicholas,*" Agape called to him.

"*Stephan,*" Zlato said.

Eight gold dragons were diving fast toward them from high in the night sky. They trumpeted their joy at finding their humans as they dove from the stars and began landing on the ground all around them. The baby dragons were now larger than Tempest so their arrival was as quiet as a herd of elephants trampling through a jungle.

"Oh. You've got to be kidding me," Stephan exclaimed in agitation as he stood up and witnessed the show.

Nicholas arose from his crouched position and looked up at the invading force. Rew came to land before all of the dragons made it to the ground. "He's gone," he said. "The dragons spooked him. He's heading east."

"No kidding! I guess we're back to following. Damn," he said. Stephan took a moment to scratch Zlato's nose as he greeted his happy dragon with a scowl on his face.

"We don't have time to waste. We almost had him," Nicholas said. He also greeted his dragon, but was quick to send them all quickly away again. "*Agape, I need you to take the other dragons back to Castle Xandia. We'll meet you back there later,*" he said.

"*Okay. We have brought you good news. The dragons are back. Tempest and Jesse rescued them all. She went through the gate and brought them all back from Arroyo. They are hunting ripgars right now. Can we go hunting too?*" Agape asked.

"Yes, but if you keep eating you're going to be as big as B.F. before too long," Nicholas warned.

"That is the way with dragons, Nicholas," Agape replied before he and the six other dragons took off into the sky and were soon gone from sight.

The two men watched them go with mixed feelings, before Nicholas said, "He can't be far. This way." He headed north into the forest toward the cave, followed directly by Stephan and Rew.

Wayfair Manor Revisited

Link, Kali and Kaltog began their descent over Blue Lake on their golden dragons after a long flight. Link rode behind Kali on Sweet Vang, but was not at all happy about riding on a dragon. They were tired but did not want to delay in order to rest. The water sparkled in the early morning sunshine and the dragons' golden scales reflected back like gold sequins on a flashy red carpet gown.

Kali and Link took the lead and they skimmed the shoreline until the roof of Wayfair Manor came into view. The mansion appeared to be abandoned by the dilapidated look of it. There were only two visible hints that indicated the presence of life- -one of the five chimneys had smoke wafting from it and a man slept in his chair by the front entrance. He did not awake or even stir when the shadows from the dragons floated like ghosts across his face.

They landed a short distance away in the very spot where Tempest had landed with Jesse a little more than week ago. With battle axe and bow in hand Kaltog and Kali made their way quietly down the path. Both of them were avid hunters and knew how to walk without making excessive sound. Link brought up the rear with his hand resting on the sheath that held his dagger.

He was trying his best to walk quietly like his friends but it was harder than it looked. Past the front entrance they went, around to the back of the house where the door to the kitchen remained unguarded.

Signaling to Kaltog and Link to standby and wait, Kali tried the door knob. It opened easily and she slowly swung to door inward until she could see inside. There was nobody present in the large space. She put her finger to her lips and silently motioned for them to follow her in. Kaltog had to duck under the threshold and continued to crouch once inside. Even though the ceilings in the mansion were high by human standards, they were low for the torg. Kali quickly checked the dining room and found it empty as well.

They made their way through the kitchen to the very back where a door led down to the cellar. It was unlocked. She opened it and hesitated. A radiant green glow emanated from the depths of the basement. As she stood there waiting and listening a strange feeling came over her. It was like a heavy blanket had fallen over her senses. Even though everything on the surface remained the same, the difference was profound inside her. She listened. The sounds within the large mansion were minimal. Right behind her she could hear Kaltog breathing and the subtle squeak of the floor as Link shifted his weight. Somewhere upstairs she could hear the distinct sound of snoring. In a nearby cupboard she heard the very quiet sound of chewing as a mouse enjoyed breakfast on some seldom used staple.

Kaltog's green eyes questioned hers silently as her gaze fell on his face. She shook her head, turned and continued down the stairs. The odd feeling remained as she descended the stairs, but she couldn't pinpoint the source of her discomfort. Link followed. Behind him the much larger torg bent over and squeezed down the narrow stairs as he followed.

The cavernous room they entered was much larger than she expected. There were crates stacked on the far wall and shackles in the center of the room securely anchored to the rock floor. The green light was coming from another separate room off to their left. She cautiously made her way over to the arched opening and peered inside.

A dragon egg was suspended in the middle of the small room with green freecurrent energy surrounding it. It glowed brightly and seemed to be humming. The massive egg dominated the space so significantly that there was hardly room for Kali to enter.

Kaltog was much too big to go into the small space. His eyes were alight with the reflected radiance as he gazed inside at the enormous egg.

"*Sweet Vang,*" Kali called. She got no response.

"*Sweet Vang, can you hear me?*" she asked. Again no response was forthcoming.

She turned to Kaltog. "Can you hear Grand Oro?" she whispered.

After a moment he replied, "No."

"We've been cut off from our dragons. I knew something felt wrong. Let's get out of here," she said.

"The freecurrent magic must be blocking communication," Link said.

"This place doesn't seem very well guarded. Maybe we should just take the mansion," Kaltog suggested.

"Yes. Maybe," Kali said, considering his proposal. "There is someone upstairs. I don't know how many someones. There is the sleepyhead at the front door. I think you're right, Kaltog. Let's do it."

The moment they turned to go they heard many footsteps coming down the stairs. How had she not heard them coming? The ceiling down in the cellar must be very thick. "Stop where you are," a man ordered. The men filled the first room. There were ten of them armed with swords and ready to use them. "Drop your weapons," the same man said.

Kali held her bow in her hand, but it was useless without an arrow. She noticed Kaltog's muscles spasm as he readied his battle axe. With the moment of hesitation behind her, she threw her bow down at the feet of the guards and immediately reached for her knife. She put her other hand on Kaltog's thigh to signal her intent. Beside her Link grasped his knife tightly.

Together they moved forward and attacked the first two men. Kaltog swung his lethal weapon with tremendous strength and killed one man instantly. Kali was at a huge disadvantage with her knife, but she kept the first man at bay while Kaltog hacked through his neck, severing it from his head. As he engaged the next man in line, Kali was overcome by a short man with a skilled sword hand. Link turned to attack, but stopped short. The guard grabbed her and held the blade to her throat as he kept a strong arm wrapped tightly around her torso. "Drop your weapons," he ordered.

"I'm sorry, Kali," Kaltog said as he threw the battle axe to the stone floor with a resounding clatter.

"This isn't over yet," Link said as he dropped his knife as well.

The three of them were chained up and left alone.

The two gold dragons began to wonder why they couldn't communicate with Kali and Kaltog. They both complained to Tempest that something was the matter with their bond mates. They two goldens waited anxiously by Blue Lake for their return, but their wait would drag on indefinitely.

Divide And Conquer

"Skymaster tells me that the spell Zeth used to summon him, which resulted in the exodus of the dragons from Risen remains dangerously viable. We need to return to the location where Zeth instigated the spell and negate the effects by neutralizing the properties immediately or the dragons will begin to weaken both mentally and physically until they are no more," Gabriel said.

They were outside of the cave discussing their next course of action. There was a difference of opinion as to what their top priority was.

"The dragon egg being held at Wayfair Manor needs to be rescued before it hatches," Zeth said.

"I agree that is important, but we cannot let Candaz escape through the gate," Theo said.

"The boys are following Candaz," Jessabelle said. "We need to make sure the dragons are safe."

"Tempest tells me that Kaltog and Kali are not communicating with their dragons. There is something going on there. I'm afraid the three of them could be in danger," Jesse informed them.

"Damn!" Serek swore. "We're going to have to get to Lakeside as soon as possible. If Link, Kaltog and Kali are in trouble, our priorities are clear."

"We're going to have to split up. We need someone who can work with freecurrent in both places. Gabriel and I can go south to negate the spell. The rest of you can go to Wayfair," Kristina proposed.

"I'll go to Wayfair Manor," Jesse said.

"Okay, Jesse. You are with us. Zeth is familiar with Wayfair Manor and can help us rescue the dragon egg. How good of a fighter are you, Terese?" Theo asked.

"Hold my own I can," she responded.

"Okay. Kris, I think you are right. Let's get going. It's a long flight to Lakeside," Theo said as he mounted B.F. "Zeth you are with me. Terese can ride with Serek on Breezerunner. Jessabelle, my love, are you ready to fly?"

"Let us fly fast," she said as she melted into an eagle.

Serek kissed his wife and then helped Terese up onto Breezerunner's back. They followed after B.F. and Tempest with Jessabelle in the lead.

Gabriel and Kristina got on Skymaster and immediately headed south.

A Wisp And A Prayer

Rew didn't have time to give a warning. Candaz was upon them in a split second without a sound. The sorcerer threw some type of magical net at Stephan, suspending his ability to move. Stephan struggled wildly against it. Although he was paralyzed, his face reflected the agony of the battle that waged in his muscles which were no longer under his command. Nicholas immediately drew his sword and engaged Candaz, who attacked with his own blade. The sword that Candaz had used in many battles and to take many lives was defiled with the corruption it retained; a residual of evil that was infused into the steal itself. The older man was experienced at sword fighting and although Nicholas was not battle-proven, he was a worthy and skilled opponent.

Candaz aggressively pushed his advantage as a ruthless and more seasoned fighter. He came at Nick hard and fast, swinging his sword expertly and moving in and out with astounding dexterity. The clanging of steel filled the woods around them, a ringing, clashing, biting of metallic collisions. Theo's sword in Nick's hands came alive with movement and light. The weapon was so well balanced that it literally danced in Nicholas's grip as he moved to parry blow after blow.

Rew flew into the fray, coming at Candaz's face and trying to distract him from Nick. He was able to make a nuisance of himself quite effectively. Stephan was fighting desperately to get loose as he watched his cousin wage war against the sorcerer. Back and forth they went. First one, then the other seemed to be winning. Nick was young and quick and the sword seemed an extension of his arm as he fought with skill that came from many hours of practice and expert instruction. Candaz was adept at the craft of warfare and he was ferocious and attacked without mercy. They were a good match. There was no telling who would prevail.

The clash of steel resounded in the darkness of the forest as the two men danced deftly in a deadly ballet. No words were spoken between the combatants. The sorcerer spun in a circle and when he came back around, his hand was up and a ball of fire rolled off of it as he flung the energy at Nicholas. The metal of Nick's sword absorbed the energy with a radiant blue flame as he brought it up defensively in front of his face.

As Rew came down for another strike, Candaz arched his sword at just the right time and sheared off one of the wisp's wings. Rew immediately plummeted to the ground at Candaz feet and lay there bleeding.

Nicholas pushed in toward Candaz, being suddenly aggressive with his attack as his rage festered after watching his friend suffer an injury. Candaz felt the bite of his blade more than once, but none of the blows were serious enough to be fatal to the old man. Stephan suddenly broke free from his magical bonds and ran immediately forward with his own sword drawn. Candaz turned and fled.

Stephan pursued him and was quickly gone from sight.

Nicholas watched him go with trepidation. He wanted to pursue also, but Rew was injured. Instead, he knelt down beside the wisp and said, "Rew? What can I do?" There was blood everywhere. A section of Rew's wing lay on the ground next to him. Nick put his hand alongside of Rew's face and said, "It will be all right." Although, at that moment, he wasn't sure that it would be all right at all.

Stephan returned and came up beside him. Taking off his jacket and then his shirt, he started gently wrapping Rew's injured wing in the fabric.

Rew sat up and looked at the portion of his wing that lay on the ground. His face turned ashen. "Tell Zlato to call Jesse. Tell her to meet us at the gate."

Stephan's face went blank for a moment as he communicated with Zlato to have Jesse meet them.

Nicholas slipped out of his own shirt and wrapped the severed portion of Rew's wing gently inside of it. He picked up Rew, cradling him, and they started walking briskly in the direction that Candaz had gone.

Healer

"Jesse?" it was Zlato's voice.

"Yes, Zlato, what is it you need?" Jesse answered mentally as she felt Felcore's nose push against her side.

"Nicholas needs you to come now. Rew is hurt," he said.

She responded immediately. "Where are they?" she asked.

"I'll guide you," Zlato said.

"I'll meet you in the courtyard at Castle Xandia," Jesse told him.

"B.F., tell Theo Rew's been injured and I need to return to Castle Xandia," Jesse said.

"Okay Jesse. Take good care of Rew," B.F. answered. Theo waved to her as Tempest turned and headed in the opposite direction.

"Meet Zlato in the courtyard," Jesse told Tempest.

"Okay, Jesse," Tempest replied.

"We are going to follow Zlato to meet with Nicky and Stephan," Jesse told her.

"Okay," Tempest responded.

It took them awhile to get back to Castle Xandia and meet up with Zlato. Jesse felt sick; anxiety for Rew was tying a knot in her stomach. The baby dragon met them in the air and they headed north together. It wasn't too long before they began to descend. She scanned the ground under them but could not catch a glimpse of her friends.

"They're just up ahead," Zlato told her.

"How's Rew?" Jesse asked.

"Not good. We'll be there soon," he said.

A small clearing in the trees lay before them and the dragons set down gently there. Jesse dismounted Tempest and spun around as Nicholas came out of the cover of the trees carrying Rew.

"Jesse, Rew's been badly injured. Can you help him?" he asked as he laid Rew at Jesse's feet where the wisp groaned and opened his eyes.

"Hi, Jesse," he said. "I heard you have become a dragon saver." He laughed until the pain stopped him. "You know, a 'dragon saver' instead of a 'dragon slayer'." Laughing again turned quickly into small gasps.

"Hush now," Jesse said touching his face and looking into his eyes. His agony was evident. She looked up at Nick and saw Rew's pain mirrored in his own eyes. Stephan brought the severed part of his wing and lay it down beside them. Felcore sat just to the side of them, watching.

"I don't know if I can do this?" Jesse said quietly.

"Jesse, you have got to try," Nicholas pleaded as he reached out and put his hand on her shoulder. "Please try."

"Of course I'll try. I'm just not sure that I can," she said.

"*Tempest, do you have the ability to make Rew sleep?*" she asked, hoping the dragon could bring some relief to him.

"*If he'll let me, I'll make him sleep,*" Tempest replied. In a moment Rew closed his eyes and was fast asleep.

Jesse gently unbound his wing from Stephan's blood-soaked shirt. The rest of his wing she extricated from Nicholas's shirt. Although the ethereal nature of the wing made it nearly impossible to put back together, Jesse meticulously lay the two cut pieces together matching the edges as closely as she could. It was like putting two pieces of intricate lace that had been torn in two back together. When she had them just where she wanted them, she lay her hand on Rew's forehead and let the freecurrent energy flow freely through her body and into his. The healing was reflexive, involuntary. The gold medallion against her chest burned with freecurrent fire. The results were not to Jesse's satisfaction. Blood had ceased to flow from the cut in the wing, but the two halves were not fusing together. She tried again with the same results.

She looked up at Nicholas and Stephan, "I've got to get him to Elysia."

"*We are just south of the cave, Jesse,*" Tempest reported.

"*How far?*" she asked.

"*Not very far, probably fifteen minutes in flight,*" Tempest told her.

To Stephan and Nicholas Jesse said, "I'm going to take him on Tempest up to the lightning gate."

"Felcore," she called as she got up. He hadn't moved from where he sat watching her, but Jesse hadn't noticed the dog until just now. Without hesitation he went to Tempest's side and waited to be helped up.

"Do you want us to go with you?" Stephan asked as he wiped a hand across his furrowed brow.

She walked over to Tempest's side before answering, "You can go with me as far as the gate, but I don't think the wisps will let you onto Elysia." She hesitated and then turned to them and asked, "What should we do about Candaz?"

Nicholas was contemplating his sword, which was still on fire with freecurrent energy. "We'll pick up his trail again without too much trouble. Let's get going," he said.

Jesse mounted Tempest. Nicholas helped Felcore up and then carefully picked up Rew and handed him up to Jesse. He climbed up behind her and then took Rew into his own arms. Leaning in close to her, he kissed her neck and said quietly, "I'm ready, Jesse."

She turned her head and kissed him softly on the lips while she said mentally, "*Tempest, let's go.*"

They launched into the air, followed immediately by Stephan on Zlato. The treetops below were just under Tempest's belly as they cruised along. Rew was resting quietly in Nick's arms. Jesse did not know if the wisps could help him. She certainly hoped so. What would he do if he couldn't fly? She didn't even want to consider the possibility.

Candaz had certainly caused a lot of misery over the years. Now he had injured this glorious creature. She had felt every wretched thing he had ever done to Zeth during his healing by her. He had raped her grandmother and murdered her grandfather. Those three executed men in the forest would never see their families again. Who knew how many more lives he had impacted? This had to end.

Their descent began almost as soon as they leveled off. Tempest landed directly in front of the cave and walked inside before letting her passengers dismount. Stephan and Zlato were just entering the cave when Nick handed Rew's sleeping form down to Jesse. He jumped down after, landing gracefully. She paused only a moment to look up into his face. He looked weary and worried. She wanted to reach up and brush a lock hair out of his face, but her arms were full. Instead, she leaned up and kissed him. "I'll be back soon, Nick," she said.

"I'll see you soon, Jesse. Stephan and I are going to get back on Candaz's trail. Let me know through Zlato or Agape when you get back. We'll be waiting to hear from you," he said as he bent over and kissed her again. "I love you, Jess," he said quietly, making her smile.

"Be careful, Nick. I love you too," she responded, making him smile in return.

Stephan placed the severed part of Rew's wing on his body as he lay in Jesse's arms. "Take good care of him, Jesse," he said. She replied, "I promise."

"Wait here, Tempest. I won't be long," she told the dragon.

"I'll be here when you get back," Tempest replied as she settled herself on the floor of the cave for a nap. Before Jesse was able to walk to the back of the cave, the dragon was snoring softly.

Jesse put her hand upon the lightning bolt gate, feeling at that exact moment the gold medallion on her chest burn with heat. Freecurrent energy electrified the air. With one last look at Nick, Jesse walked through to Elysia.

It was dark and silent in the cave. She walked forward one step at a time to the entrance with Felcore by her side and Rew in her arms. For a half a second she feared that she had gone to the wrong galaxy, but only for a half a second.

"Jesse, is that you?" she heard Wes's voice and relaxed a little.

"Wes, I need your help," she called.

She heard the vibration of his wings and then he was instantly there. "What happened?" he asked and he looked down at Rew's slumbering face.

"He's been injured. His wing has been severed. I have stopped the bleeding, but was unable to reattach the rest of the wing. Can you help him?" Jesse asked.

Wes took a moment to examine Rew's injury. He winced visibly as he replaced the wrapping over the wound. "We'll take him to Lodi. She'll know what to do."

They walked out of the cave together, past the ailing tree, and down the path to the village, which was a short distance away. An adorable little cottage with an abundance of colorful flowers was Wes's destination. The small wooden door was arched at the top and had a wreath of pink and yellow blossoms circling a small window. As they approached Lodi opened the door and gave them serious consideration. "Bring him in," she said immediately.

The kitchen table was clean and the ideal place to lay Rew down. He was still sleeping quietly. Lodi pulled back the wrappings of Stephan's and Nicholas's blood soaked shirts and carefully examined the wounded wing. She looked up at Jesse and smiled sweetly. "It will be all right. Don't look so scared. Everything will be okay," she said.

Walking over to a kitchen drawer, Lodi took out a large knife and began honing the edge on a sharpening stone. She went over to the table and Jesse watched in horror as she sliced cleanly off Rew's remaining wings. Lodi looked up at Jesse and again reassured her, "It will be okay, Jesse, I promise." She called Wes over. The two of them smiled, kissed, held each other's hands and focused their eyes on Rew. As Jesse watched, fresh new wings began to sprout from Rew's back where his old ones had been removed. They grew out of his back moist and wrinkled until they reached the right size. Lodi placed a kiss on his forehead and went to clean her knife in the kitchen sink. As he began to slowly wake up, he sat up and extended his new wings until they were dry moments later.

"Thank you," he said as he lifted into the air and fluttered around in sheer delight. "Do you want to come meet my family, Jesse?"

"I really need to get back, Rew," she replied with a smile.

"I know. It's just next door, though. Come on," he said and he motioned with his hand for her to follow.

She followed him to the door and Wes and Lodi followed after, along with Felcore. Just next door was a similar cottage, only bigger to accommodate all of Rew's children. After an extremely exuberant greeting by his wife, Dolli, Rew introduced Jesse and Felcore to his mate and his many children, seven sons and ten daughters, only a dozen of which were home at the time. Their names were given to Jesse, but she could only remember a couple of them--Gabi, Bela and Kalto. They all came and went so fast, greeting their father happily, that she wouldn't be able to identify any one of them anyway, except for the fact that they resembled Rew. Jesse enjoyed watching him relax and enjoy his family. He seemed so happy it made her happy to share in this domestic moment with him. "Rew, I've got to go. Dolli, it is so nice to meet you and your family," she said.

Rew escorted her to the door and said, "I'm going to stick around here for a while. Nick and Stephan can take care of Candaz. I'll see you soon." He gave her a big hug and patted Felcore on the head. "Bye boy."

"Good-bye," Jesse said. Wes and Lodi walked with her and Felcore back to the cave. They hugged her goodbye and waved as she put her hand on the gate and waited for The Condor to appear.

Chapter 21

BEAUTY IN GRACE

Skymaster was a fast flyer, but it took a couple of days for the three of them to reach the clearing in the forest where Zeth had summoned the dragon mage and sent all the dragons into the void.

Gabriel could feel the power radiating from the area before they drew close. "*Do you feel that Skymaster?*" she asked.

"*Oh yes. It is very strong. Even though the fire that cooked the spell has grown cold, the ingredients have melded together to take on a life of their own,*" he said.

"*Any ideas on how we can counter it?*" Gabriel asked.

"*I cannot use dragon fire. That would develop it into something even more powerful. You cannot use freecurrent on it because the energy will be absorbed and again it will enhance the spell,*" Skymaster said.

"Holy cow. Look at that!" Gabriel said out loud.

"Good creator. What is that?" Kristina said.

A whirlwind twisted in the air starting from its source where the fire pit used to prepare the spell rested in the middle of the clearing up into the sky. It cycled around and around, stripping leaves off from trees and sucking debris into itself as it continued to grow into a monster tornado.

"*Land me as close to it as you can, Skymaster,*" Gabriel said.

"*What are you going to do?*" he asked as he made a sharp bank and dove toward the whirlwind.

"*I don't know yet,*" she replied as he landed.

The wind whipped both women's hair into wicked hairdos and dirt flew painfully into their eyes. Kristina shouted in order to be heard, "What are you going to do?"

"Hang on, Kris. Stay with Skymaster," Gabriel said as she climbed down from the dragon's back.

"Gabriel, wait!" Kristina shouted, but she wasn't heard.

Gabriel had to crawl on the ground to keep from being pulled into the vortex. The wind roared in her ears and she had to close her eyes tight, but she fought her way to the cold fire pit. She lay prostrate on the ground and stretched her hands out to lay them on the ashes. Slowly she began absorbing the energy into her body. She screamed in agony as the power permeated her flesh. It took what seemed like forever to Gabriel but in actuality only took minutes. The vortex diminished in size, being sucked away by Gabriel until it was no more. She did not move.

Kristina climbed down from Skymaster's back and ran to her. "Gabriel," she said and rolled her over so she was face up. "Gabriel," she said again and touched her cheeks. Gabriel wasn't breathing. "Gabriel!" Kristina shouted as she swung her hand back and slapped her across the face.

The sorceress sucked air into her lungs in a heavy gasp.

"Can you sit up?" Kristina asked. She assisted her by wrapping an arm around her back.

"I'm okay," Gabriel said. Her body seemed to be vibrating from the energy she had absorbed. When she tried to stand up, her legs wouldn't hold her. "Help me up," she said to Kristina.

"*It is not abolished yet,*" Skymaster said.

"*No. I just removed the energy from it. What do you suggest?*" Gabriel asked.

"*I have an idea. I will dilute it,*" he said.

"*How?*" she asked.

"*You might want to stand back,*" he said as he strolled forward and lifted his leg.

"Kris, let's step back--far back," she said.

Kristina helped her as they moved to the edge of the clearing and let Skymaster empty his bladder in the middle of the fire pit. His urine steamed as it hit the cold ashes and the spell was instantly rendered powerless.

A Path Once Visited

Zeth watched as Jessabelle landed in a tree close to where he used to fish. She waited for the dragons to land before joining them on the ground and transforming into her human form. Theo greeted his wife with a gentle kiss. Terese's eyes flashed through her eyelashes as she looked at Zeth from where she stood. When he glanced in her direction she smiled.

He felt strange being at Wayfair Manor again. He had changed so much and would never be the same again. His old life was gone.

He stood on the shore where he used to torture fish and looked out over the lake. A warm hand grasped his and held it softly. "Are you okay?" Terese asked.

"Yeah. I just did some things that I am not proud of. I understand that my mind wasn't right. But, I still feel remorseful," Zeth said. He squeezed her hand and turned to her with a wan smile on his face.

"It will take time, Zeth. Give yourself time," she said as she squeezed his hand and then let it go.

"Zeth," Serek said. "This way?" He pointed down the path.

"Yes. I'll lead the way," he said.

"Zeth," Serek said, stopping him.

He turned and said, "Yes?"

"Take this," Serek pulled his sword from his sheath and handed it to Zeth. It was a sign of trust that was communicated at the same time silently as they equaled each other's gaze.

"Thanks," Zeth said and turned back to the path. He had walked this same path so many times in his life. He was free from that person. He was free from his father. Grasping Serek's sword tighter in his hand he slowly approached the guard at the front entrance. The man was busy cleaning underneath his fingernails with his knife. He was called Klaus and he was loyal to Candaz. Klaus was cruel and took pleasure in abusing women as he was known to brag about often. Zeth was unseen as he approached and quickly pressed the tip of the sword against the man's throat.

"Zeth?" he said.

"Shhh. Are the prisoners in the cellar?" Zeth asked.

"Yes. There are three of them; a big fellow and a small man and woman. How did you know?" he asked.

"I have my ways. Where are the keys?" he asked.

"They're hanging on the hook in the kitchen. Are you going to torture them . . . or something else? Are you going to kill them?" Klaus asked.

"Something like that," Zeth said.

"Can I watch," he asked.

Zeth resisted the urge to strike him. "Stay here. Don't move from this spot," he ordered.

"Who are *they?*" he asked, indicating Zeth's immediate comrades as he eyed them suspiciously. "Your father doesn't like strangers," he said.

"They are my friends. Don't concern yourself. Do as I say," Zeth said.

"I'm afraid it does concern me. None of you move," Klaus said as he reached for his sword.

"I said it's none of your concern," Zeth said and ran him through. He collapsed into his chair dead. His eyes rested on the dead man for a long moment before he turned away. "Follow me," he said to his companions.

They headed to the back of the house where the kitchen door was and cautiously opened it. Zeth motioned to Serek who was right behind him that there were two men inside. Putting his back against the door, he paused, took a deep breath and pushed it open.

The surprised men put down their meals hastily. "Zeth, is your father home? Who are these people?" one man asked as he reached for his weapon.

"We're going to take the prisoners and the dragon egg off your hands," Zeth told him.

"Not without your father's authority," the second man said.

"My authority is right here," Zeth answered, raising his sword.

The two men assessed Zeth and the strangers before drawing their own swords. "We will not let you pass," the first man said.

Theo pushed his way into the room with his weapon in hand. "You have my friends. Get out of my way."

The sound of steel crashing rang through the kitchen as Theo and Zeth engaged the two men in battle. Theo was quick and fluid with a sword and dominated the first man easily. He was dead before he hit the floor. Zeth wasn't quite as practiced, but he held his own without giving ground until the man used a fancy twist move on him and he lost his grip. The sword flew from his hand. Zeth struck him with freecurrent energy which stunned the man long enough for Zeth to recover his weapon. Theo stepped in and stopped the man's heart with a fast stab through the chest.

From another part of the house came the thumping of running feet. Serek, Jessabelle and Terese headed into the dining room and met several other men who had heard a noise coming from the kitchen.

"Come on Zeth," Theo said, motioning with his hand for him to follow. They entered the dining room after their companions who were fighting five guards. Jessabelle had two daggers; one in each hand and she spun and ducked and darted, slicing with lethal precision. Terese had a different fighting style, using kicks and punches to overcome her opponent before finishing him off with her knife. Serek used his daggers to fend off their swords. When he saw Zeth and Theo enter, he flung one dagger that penetrated the chest of one man, spun quickly on his heel and flung his other dagger killing another. Theo was at his side immediately and finished off the last guard without pause.

Serek retrieved his daggers, wiping the blood on one guard's shirt before patting Theo on the back. "Good timing, brother," he said with a smile.

"Let's check upstairs to see if that is all of them," Zeth said as he started up the staircase, taking them two at a time. Serek and Theo followed right behind him. They came back a few moments later. "I think that's all of them. The upstairs is clear. Let's get down to the cellar."

As Zeth walked to the kitchen he was bombarded by a mix of emotions. He felt bad for the men they had just killed. They were just doing their jobs. Theo and Serek seemed to take the killing all in stride. He guessed that it was just a part of their job too. Maybe he wasn't cut out to be a warrior. Being in his old house was strange too. It didn't feel like home. In fact, the memories that these walls contained were not good ones and he just as soon put that all behind him. Another emotion that he felt that was unexpected was a sense of belonging, of fellowship. He felt accepted and even liked by his new companions. It felt amazing.

Zeth opened the door to the basement and started down. The stairs into the cellar were lit only by the illumination of free-current energy surrounding the egg. A green glow gave eerie shading to everything it touched. As he stepped off from the last step, Link, Kali and Kaltog looked up from where they lay on the cold stone floor. Kali gave warning, "Watch out!"

A guard swung his sword and sliced through Zeth's arm. He turned to the man, raising his own sword in defense. The blades sparked as they impacted each other. There was no talking. The guard aggressively attacked while Zeth did his best to defend himself. He worked the sword up and down parrying blows as they came. Finesse or even skill would not describe the choppy and panicked handling of the weapon in Zeth's hand, but he was managing to avoid further injury.

"Why are you doing this?" the man asked between breaths.

"Father is on the wrong side. If you yield to me and release these prisoners, I'll let you go freely," Zeth said.

"I am loyal to Candaz. He is the future of Risen. His reign will come again," the man said.

"Not if I can help it," Zeth replied. He attacked this time and soon won the advantage.

"Surrender," Zeth said.

"No, traitor," the man spit out.

"Then you will die," Zeth pressed forward and drove his blade into the man's stomach, withdrew it quickly and then finished him by slashing his throat. He stood back and stared at the man where he had fallen.

Terese came up beside him and grasped his arm. "Injured you are," she said.

"I'll be all right," Zeth said as he turned to her and let her wrap her arms around his waist. He buried his face in her hair.

"Well done, Zeth," Kaltog commended him as Jessabelle worked on unlocking his shackles after removing Kali's.

"Thanks, Zeth," Kali said as she reached up and planted a warm kiss on his cheek.

"You did what you had to," Link said as he rubbed his wrists where the shackles had been.

"I guess it was necessary," he said.

"You bet," Theo said behind him and smacked him firmly on the back.

The humming coming from the egg was increasing in intensity.

"What the hell?" Serek said as he strode toward the back room.

"That's odd," Kali said. "It's been consistent until now."

They all walked to the back of the cellar and peered through the door. Within the protective freecurrent orb that surrounded the egg, a crack was forming in the fine porcelain surface. It ran from the bottom and spread out toward the top, where the shell moved in and out as the creature within tried to get out.

The group who watched in fascination parted to let Zeth through. He entered the small room with a look of marvel and fear etched across his face. Extending his arms, he stretched his hands out until they touched the freecurrent with the tips of his fingers. Green electricity arched through the room, sizzling the air and making Zeth's hair stand on end. The freecurrent wrapped around his body and the egg forming a bridge between them. A primeval scream left Zeth's lips as he collected all of the energy into himself. He collapsed on the floor.

Terese and Serek came up beside him. "Zeth, are you okay?" Terese asked.

"I'm fine. Help me up," he said.

Serek easily lifted the other man to his feet.

"Look at your wound," Terese said.

Where the sword had cut a long gash in Zeth's arm was a scar where the wound had been cauterized by the freecurrent.

"A badge of honor," Serek said.

The egg cracked wide open and out peeked a little dragon nose. They watched as the baby dragon shattered the rest of its delicate shell and awkwardly tested its legs with first one step and then two. She extended her wet wings as far as she could in the small space and shook like a dog. Her scales were shimmering green, the color of faceted emeralds. With a quick glance around, her swirling red eyes fell on Zeth and she said inside his head, "*You are my Zeth. I am your Grace.*"

"*You are my Grace?*" Zeth asked in amazement.

"*You are my Zeth,*" she said as she began to coo.

Zeth went to her and scratched her beautiful nose. "This is Grace," he said to his companions. "She has bonded with me." Zeth was overcome with emotion. To have a dragon bond with him was the ultimate gift of forgiveness after everything he had done. He wept as his heart embraced the love that flooded through him.

Chapter 22

PURSUIT

Candaz paused to rest behind a large tree. He took a small sip of the elixir to refresh himself. The drug it contained was giving him the strength to outdistance the young bucks who pursued him. It also alleviated the pain that had plagued him for years. He felt like a new man. The little crystal bottle was one of only a small number that he had in his possession. The other ones remained locked away in his laboratory. It had been many years since he had visited his old refuge. He used to frequently visit the small lab back when he ruled Saberville. That was before Gabriel and before Zeth.

What they would do to Zeth he did not know. They might kill him. They might make him their prisoner. Whatever it was, he was sure it wouldn't be pleasant for the boy. There wasn't anything he could do about it. If he tried to rescue him, he would just end up dead himself. It was the boy's own fault. He had refused to move when Candaz had told him to. The boy was weak and foolish. Perhaps it was good to be rid of him. Even at seventy, he could produce another heir. It was a shame to have to start training all over again, though. He had invested thirty years in the boy. He was far from perfect but he did have some potential. Maybe he could find a way to get him back.

The pack he carried with him had the instruction manual to the gate in it. He opened it up and paged through it, running his fingers along the pages of strange writings. There were numbers and symbols and if he could discern the pattern . . . Yes, there was a definite pattern. If he could use the manual to get back to the land where Gabriel was from, he could find her family and maybe if he brought one of them back he could make a trade for the boy. The girl Jesse had a brother. He had seen pictures of him in Gabriel's home. The child resembled his sister some-what. Candaz was sure Gabriel would be willing to trade one for the other. Maybe he could get Zeth back after all. If Zeth was dead, he could still use the child to manipulate Gabriel. Many years ago he had sent one of his minions to follow Theo through the gate to Earth. If he remembered correctly the constellation was called the Big Dipper. It looked like a ladle with a crooked handle. He flipped through the pages. Yes. There is was. He would go to Earth.

Maybe he would produce another heir as well. Just in case Zeth didn't become the man he wanted him to be; just in case he needed to find another path to his dynasty. He would have to consider who would make a good mother to his new heir. This time she would be someone he could control. The girl Terese came to mind. She was a kendrite though and he abhorred cross breeding. But, perhaps in this one instance it would be justified to give him a powerful heir. Letting his mind consider Terese as the possible mother of his new heir brought him some satisfaction. He would consider it as a viable possibility.

For now the dragons were gone and he did not know how to get them back. Golden dragons filled the skies from the egg laying grounds where they had recently hatched. A possibility remained that he could find a way to control them and use them for his own gain. He would not give up on that dream quite yet. He also had the egg. That prize had potential. When he returned to Risen from Earth he would continue that quest. He would find a way to harness their power or he would find a way to kill them all.

Candaz was not done yet. Power or revenge would be his for the taking. He would not be denied his destiny.

Getaway

Stephan and Nick had left the baby dragons curled up next to each other sleeping and snoring in a beautiful synchronization of noise. The sword in Nicholas's hand blazed from tip to hilt with blue freecurrent energy, indicating the presence of corruption and guiding them ever closer to it. That "it" would be Candaz, no doubt. He was close.

Nicholas and Stephan had hunted together numerous times growing up both in the lands around Brightening and in Saberville. They knew well each other's strengths and weaknesses. Stephan let Nicky track, he would take the point position when it came to attacking. They walked quietly, almost noiselessly through the forest just south of the cave. A black shadow crossed Nick's vision, which he caught out of the corner of his eye. He motioned to Stephan with his hand to investigate in the direction he pointed.

Stephan nodded once and prowled slowly in that direction. Nicholas followed just behind his older cousin, being sure to keep a lookout behind them at the same time, just in case. As they followed the dark silhouette in front of them, he realized that Candaz had circled around and was heading for the cave. Nick knew that they had to hurry. They couldn't let Candaz take the book off from Risen. They couldn't let him leave through the gate. He grabbed Stephan's arm and held him off as he took the lead, increasing their pace; seeing the need for expedience superseding the need for stealth.

Nicholas ascended a small rise and caught a good glimpse of Candaz's cloak billowing out behind him as he ran a short distance in front of them. Off to his left he heard a low growl. Before he could react a ripgar was bearing down on him fast. He swung his sword in a wide arch, grazing the animal's chest. It quickly turned around and confronted him head on. Long spiked teeth, dripping with saliva, threatened to tear him apart. Stephan sprang in front of Nick and plunged his sword into the ripgar's massive head. It roared in pain and outrage and immediately attacked the man who had inflicted the extraordinary pain. Stephan danced out of the way and Nicholas sank his sword in and out of the side of the charging animal. It stumbled, but quickly regained its feet and came at them again. With a mighty leap into the air, the monster knocked Nicholas on his back. He immediately jumped up and spun around to face the monster again. The ripgar ran at him and pummeled him to the ground. It was within inches of completing its attack when out of the sky came a golden flash. The gilded dragon, Zlato, sunk his mighty talons into the ripgar and left with it screaming in his clutches as he flew high into the sky.

"Are you okay, Nick?" Stephan asked as he came over to him and helped his cousin to stand up.

"Yeah, I'm good," he wiped some blood off his mouth with the back of his hand. "Let's get going. Candaz is getting away." They started moving through the forest rapidly. Stephan and Nicholas were soon at the entrance of the cave. Advancing without hesitation, they entered. Candaz was at the back by the lightning gate. It was rotating at a regular interval. He held a large book in his hand. The old sorcerer hesitated, watching, waiting.

"Stop!" Nicholas demanded.

Candaz turned for just a second to rake them with his gaze before turning back to the gate. The next constellation to be visible through it had a ladle-shaped star pattern.

"Candaz, stop! Don't take another step," Stephan ordered as he advanced swiftly with his sword lifted.

The sorcerer laughed without turning back around, stepped through the threshold and was gone.

Stephan and Nicholas looked at each other.

"Well, I guess we go?" Stephan probed.

"Let's do this," Nick said at the last minute. He and Stephan ran forward without further hesitation and disappeared through the gate.

Home

Tempest watched the whole scene from where she lay "sleeping" in the corner of the cave. She blinked her swirling red eyes as a short time later Jesse entered the cave from the lightning gate with Felcore right behind her. *"Jesse,"* Tempest said calmly.

"Hi, sweetie," Jesse responded. She walked over to the dragon and started scratching her eye ridges which all dragons love.

"How is the wisp?" Tempest asked.

"He is completely okay," she said. *"Nick and Stephan?"*

"*Gone,*" Tempest said.

"*What do you mean, gone?*" Jesse asked.

"*They followed the bad man through the gate,*" Tempest replied with little interest. Felcore pranced over to her and licked her nose affectionately. The dragon gave the dog a look of almost bearable tolerance before she sneezed.

"*How long ago?*" Jesse insisted, getting extremely concerned.

"*What do I know of time? I am a dragon,*" she replied.

A huff of complete exasperation escaped Jesse's lips. "*It's important that I know. Do you think that maybe you could hazard a guess?*" she asked.

"*I could guess, I guess. It was some time after you left and a little time before you came back; some time in between those two events. Zlato was here sleeping and then he was gone. It was after he had left to kill the ripgar that was attacking Stephan and Nicholas,*" she said.

"*They were being attacked by a ripgar?*" Jesse asked. She was getting more agitated with every passing moment.

"*Yes. Zlato went to take care of it, though,*" Tempest said and then yawned with a wide gaping fang-filled mouth.

"*Tempest, you are exasperating me,*" Jesse told her.

"*Well, forgive me for not knowing everything. Would it help if I told you that the constellation that was visible when they left was the big ladle?*" Tempest huffed, blowing dust into the air.

"*The big ladle? Do you mean the Big Dipper?*" Jesse asked.

"*Whatever,*" Tempest proclaimed with attitude. Jesse could swear she saw an eye roll, which would be a swirling eye roll, hard to pull off.

"Okay. Oh no!" Jesse said aloud. Felcore barked excitedly. "It looks like we're going back home, boy."

She quickly evaluated her situation. She hadn't been gone long enough for her to have fallen off the radar of the authorities in the U.S. Felcore would still be in danger because he had killed Mat, even though it was self-defense. It didn't even occur to her not to go. She was going to go. Leaving Nick and Stephan alone to hunt down and destroy Candaz in twenty-first century America was not going to happen--not on her watch. "*Skymaster?*"

"*Jesse?*" he answered.

"*Let grandmother and the others know, Nick and Stephan and I are going through the gate to Earth to continue tracking Candaz. Yes, he's escaped through the gate to the U.S. We'll be in touch when we return, hopefully with that scoundrel dead or in tow. Please, tell Gabriel that I love her,*" she said.

"*I will convey your message, child. I have forgiven Zeth, but Candaz has much to answer for. Be careful, Jesse,*" Skymaster responded.

"*Tempest, I have to go. You go back to Castle Xandia and wait for me there,*" Jesse told her.

"*No. I am going with you,*" Tempest protested.

Jesse laughed and said, "*You cannot go.*"

"*Yes. I am going with you, Jesse,*" she said stubbornly.

"*No. It's not possible,*" Jesse responded.

"*I'm going,*" Tempest said.

"*There are no dragons where I come from. I'm sorry, sweetie,*" Jesse said.

"*Change me,*" Tempest suggested.

"*What?*"

"*Change me. Make me a golden wolf. You have those, right?*" she asked. Tempest stood up next to Felcore and looked down at him.

"*Make you a dog? Really? How?*" Jesse asked in return.

"*Use the freecurrent magic. Know in your head what you want to do and do it. Simple,*" Tempest said, making it sound palpable.

"Okay," Jesse said out loud as she thought about what Tempest had just said. If she could do this, she could disguise Felcore, keeping him safe, and somehow bring Tempest with her, too. Was it really possible? *"I'll try,"* she said to Tempest. *"But, I'm going to try it on Felcore first."*

"You are going to make the wolf a dog?" Tempest asked in confusion.

"No." She thought for a moment and giggled. *"I'm going to make a dog a cat. Now hush so I can focus."*

Jesse called Felcore to her and knelt down in front of him. She put her hand on his head and looked into his golden eyes. The freecurrent energy rushed through her, igniting the medallion that hung around her neck, tingling through her fingers that rested on Felcore's soft fur. The image of a cat came into her mind, a yellow tabby with gold eyes. She closed her own eyes for a moment and when she opened them back up Felcore was a cat. "Mrrarr," Felcore, the cat said. He looked confused, stood up and walked around in a circle looking for his tail, which was there but different, flattened his ears, wiggled his whiskers and finally sneezed.

"Wow," Jesse said, as Felcore brushed his face against her hand and began to purr.

"Okay, your turn," she said to Tempest.

"I am ready," the dragon said casually.

Walking to the dragon's head, Jesse placed her hands on Tempest's nose and looked into her swirling red eyes. With freecurrent energy flowing through her, she imagined a little white dog, something of a combination between a West Highland Terrier and a Yorkie. She closed her eyes and when she opened them beheld a dog standing in front of her. The little dog shook herself from nose to tail.

"Tempest?" Jesse asked hesitantly.

"*Obviously. Who else would I be?*" she asked. Tempest and Felcore began sniffing and examining each other curiously.

"*You're so cute!*" Jesse said. The little dog had swirling red eyes, dragon eyes.

"Mrrarr," Felcore said.

"RRowf," Tempest replied.

"Weird," Jesse contributed.

Jesse along with her two little friends walked together to the gate. She pressed her hand against the edge of the lightning bolt, rotating the constellations until The Big Dipper came into view. With an anxious intake of breath, Jesse walked back through to the other side.

THE END

**Look for Book III of the
Freecurrent Series "Dynasty"**